P9-DDN-885

Southern Sewing Circle Mysteries

Taken In

"What first hooked me on the Southern Sewing Circle Mysteries . . . and what keeps me coming back for more, is Casey's characters and the ties that bind them."
—*Smitten by Books*

"I was completely *Taken In* by this story and I know you will be, too!" —*Escape with Dollycas*

"I love the setting and the coziness of the town. I've loved getting to know each and every one of the characters— feeling right at home among them. And I've loved the murderous predicaments they've all found themselves in. But the camaraderie between the ladies is what makes the story so much fun!" —*Marie's Cozy Corner*

Remnants of Murder

"Eccentric characters, small-town quirks, and southern charm . . . This book is a winner." —*MyShelf.com*

"A well-written, character-driven, and definitely cozy mystery." —*Fresh Fiction*

continued . . .

Let It Sew

"Elizabeth Lynn Casey has created wonderful, caring characters and placed them in a beautiful place . . . Whether it be a book fair or a crafting session, you will be inspired."

—*Escape with Dollycas*

"A definite page-turner . . . Casey always keeps me guessing . . . Warmth, good ole southern comfort, with a dose of small-town, friendly chatter gossip."

—*Cozy Mystery Book Review*

"The best book yet in this wonderfully crafted series."

—*Dru's Book Musings*

Reap What You Sew

"The Southern Sewing Circle Mysteries are full of down-home fun and charm and a group of ladies readers will look forward to visiting with again and again." —*The Mystery Reader*

"Tori is fun, sassy, smart, and crafty in more ways than one. I loved her wit, humor, and the small-town-girl feel I got from her . . . I like feeling the connection to the characters, like they are old friends coming into my home for the night to sew and solve mysteries together." —*Two Lips Reviews*

Dangerous Alterations

"I always look forward to seeing what disaster of the criminal vein befalls Tori and the sewing circle. And why not? This series has its own brand of charm, intrigue, and unique characters." —*Once Upon a Romance*

"Elizabeth Lynn Casey keeps her readers entertained with *Dangerous Alterations* through her wonderful storytelling skills that feature light humor, gentle romance, and always an intriguing, suspenseful mystery to be solved. What more could you ask for in a cozy mystery?"   —*Fresh Fiction*

Deadly Notions

"I always enjoy visiting Tori and her friends in Sweet Briar. They are their own band of sisters who squabble and pick at each other yet will drop most anything to lend a hand."
—*Once Upon a Romance*

"A perfect addition to the Southern Sewing Circle series. With strong personalities vibrating off each page, the twists and turns of the story line, and the exceptionally exciting ending, this one will please them all!"   —*The Romance Readers Connection*

Pinned for Murder

"[Mixes] a suspenseful story with a dash of down-home flavor . . . Visiting with the charmingly eccentric folks of Sweet Briar is like taking a trip back home."   —*Fresh Fiction*

"A relaxing and pleasurable read. Ms. Casey has sewn together a finely crafted cozy mystery series."
—*Once Upon a Romance*

continued . . .

"An excellent read for crafters and mystery lovers alike. Elizabeth Casey has a knack for threading together great story lines, likable characters, and surprises in every page. The women in the Southern Sewing Circle are friends we all wish we had. This book was terrific from beginning to end."
—*The Romance Readers Connection*

Death Threads

"A light, fun mystery with southern charm and an energetic heroine."
—*The Mystery Reader*

Sew Deadly

"Filled with fun, folksy characters and southern charm."
—Maggie Sefton, national bestselling author

"Sweet and charming . . . The bewitching women of the Southern Sewing Circle will win your heart in this debut mystery."
—Monica Ferris, *USA Today* bestselling author

"A smooth, entertaining read, especially for those who like their stories light, and the mystery is clever. Settle down with some tea and a nice piece of red velvet cake and enjoy yourself."
—*RT Book Reviews*

Berkley Prime Crime titles by Elizabeth Lynn Casey

Wedding Duress

Elizabeth Lynn Casey

FOUNTAINDALE PUBLIC LIBRARY

300 West Briarcliff Road
Bolingbrook, IL 60440-2894
(630) 759-2102

BERKLEY PRIME CRIME, NEW YORK

THE BERKLEY PUBLISHING GROUP
Published by the Penguin Group
Penguin Group (USA) LLC
375 Hudson Street, New York, New York 10014

USA • Canada • UK • Ireland • Australia • New Zealand • India • South Africa • China

penguin.com

A Penguin Random House Company

WEDDING DURESS

A Berkley Prime Crime Book / published by arrangement with the author

Copyright © 2015 by Penguin Group (USA) LLC.
Penguin supports copyright. Copyright fuels creativity, encourages diverse voices,
promotes free speech, and creates a vibrant culture. Thank you for buying an authorized
edition of this book and for complying with copyright laws by not reproducing, scanning,
or distributing any part of it in any form without permission. You are supporting writers
and allowing Penguin to continue to publish books for every reader.

Berkley Prime Crime Books are published by The Berkley Publishing Group.
BERKLEY® PRIME CRIME and the PRIME CRIME logo are trademarks of
Penguin Group (USA) LLC.

For information, address: The Berkley Publishing Group,
a division of Penguin Group (USA) LLC,
375 Hudson Street, New York, New York 10014.

ISBN: 978-0-425-25786-9

PUBLISHING HISTORY
Berkley Prime Crime mass-market edition / April 2015

PRINTED IN THE UNITED STATES OF AMERICA

10 9 8 7 6 5 4 3 2 1

Cover illustration by Mary Ann Lasher.
Cover design by Judith Lagerman.
Interior text design by Laura K. Corless.

This is a work of fiction. Names, characters, places, and incidents either are the product
of the author's imagination or are used fictitiously, and any resemblance to actual persons,
living or dead, business establishments, events, or locales is entirely coincidental.

If you purchased this book without a cover, you should be aware that this book is
stolen property. It was reported as "unsold and destroyed" to the publisher, and neither
the author nor the publisher has received any payment for this "stripped book."

For you, my readers . . .
Thank you.

Acknowledgments

While there are still many more adventures ahead for Tori and the rest of the sewing circle, I would like to take this opportunity to thank the people who have allowed these wonderful characters to become part of my world.

Thank you, Emily Rapoport. It has been my honor to bring the Southern Sewing Circle ladies to life. They've made me laugh many times over the past several years and for that I am eternally grateful.

A thank-you is in order, as well, for my editor, Michelle Vega, who has embraced this series. Knowing they make you laugh in all the right places has been great fun! I can't wait to see where we go next!

And last but not least, a huge thank-you goes to my agent, Jessica Faust. Having you in my corner has made this whole journey even more special.

Chapter 1

One by one, Tori Sinclair watched each of her friends emerge from the bank of dressing rooms in a burst of autumn color, their chosen hues and styles stealing her breath as they stepped onto the semicircular platform and turned in her direction.

"You look absolutely"—she stopped, swallowed, and started again, her voice choked with emotion—"*stunning.*"

Leona Elkin's flawlessly manicured hand fluttered to her chest just before she spun around to face the trifold mirror on the opposite side of the platform. "As we all know, there's not a single color out there I *can't* showcase, but that said, I have to agree with you, dear, Smoldering Blaze may well be one of my best."

"Said no one ever," Rose Winters groused from her spot in the center of the group. Sweeping a trembling hand to her left, the eighty-something matriarch of the

Sweet Briar Ladies Society Sewing Circle met and held Tori's gaze. "If you want me to take mine and Dixie's in at the waist so they're a bit more fitted like everyone else's, I can do that, Victoria."

"No. No. They're perfect. *You're* perfect. *Everyone* is perfect. I couldn't be more pleased than I am."

"Mine wasn't supposed to be fitted neither, but the start of a new school year always means more cookie-eatin' for my grandbabies and me." Leona's fraternal twin, Margaret Louise Davis, peeked down at her even plumper than normal Warm Cinnamon–hued self, shrugging as she did. "Don't really matter none, I s'pose, on account of it bein' your weddin' 'n all. Anyone with a workin' lightbulb in their noggin won't be lookin' at anyone 'cept you, Victoria."

Slowly, Leona turned back, her lashes half-mast across her hazel eyes. "That may be true of Milo, but he won't be the only man there . . ."

"Oh, put a sock in it, will you, Leona?" Rose stamped her thick-soled dress flats on the carpeted riser and scowled. "When Victoria said *stunning*, she was talking to all of us, not just you. And last I checked, there weren't any dimwitted male thirty-year-olds on the guest list for you to play temporary sugar momma to, so all eyes *will* be on Victoria . . . as they should be."

Lips twitched up and down the line as Leona's mouth gaped, then closed, then gaped again.

Tori began a mental count to ten, reaching seven before Leona's retort finally came.

"There is nothing *stunning* about an Old Goat in a Harvest Wheat"—Leona took in Rose from head to toe—"*housecoat* shuffling her way down the aisle at a speed akin to dripping molasses."

Then, before anyone could react, Leona snapped her finger in the direction of the cameraman positioned just over Tori's left shoulder. "You're getting a good, long, close-up angle of this one for the show, right, Skip?"

"*This one?*" Georgina Hayes, clad in Dusky Sunset, echoed from her place at the opposite end of the line. "Do you mean *Rose*?"

The faintest hint of a smile appeared on Leona's seemingly ageless face in conjunction with the answering nod she sought from her cameraman. "Skip knows what I mean, don't you, gorgeous?"

The handsome twenty-year-old added a wink to his second nod and then ducked behind the Cable TV camera perched atop his shoulder.

Nina Morgan, Tori's friend and fellow employee, blinked once, twice. "I—I . . . I'm not sure what to say right now."

"I can think of a few things," Rose muttered as she took Debbie Calhoun's ready hand and stepped down off the platform, stopping briefly to address Tori directly. "If you want to go with eight bridesmaids instead of nine, I understand."

Reaching out, Tori took hold of Rose's hand and squeezed it gently. "It would be unfair of me to remove Leona from the bridal party after she's already paid for the dress."

A flash of amusement, magnified by Rose's bifocals, temporarily eased the hurt Tori hated to see on anyone, let alone one of her dearest friends. "I wasn't talking about Leona, Victoria."

"I was," she whispered back. "Now come on, Rose, you know how Leona is. Shake it off, okay? You earned my distinction of *stunning* just as much as everyone else."

"Maybe in my earlier days, when I wasn't wincing with every move I made." Rose closed her eyes for a moment, only to open them as she turned toward her dressing room. "I'll take this off now and hang it up."

When the elderly woman was out of earshot, Dixie Dunn waddled across the platform in Muted Pumpkin to stand in front of Leona, hands on hips. "Must you always be so *nasty*? So—"

"*Hateful?*" Georgina added. Then, holding her hand upward, Sweet Briar's long-standing mayor began ticking off more options. "*Mean? Thoroughly unlikable? Despicable?*"

Leona sliced her hand horizontally in front of her neck to indicate Skip should stop filming and put away his equipment. Once she was sure he was otherwise occupied, she turned angry eyes in the mayor's direction. "*I'm* hateful, Georgina? *I'm* mean?"

As heads began to nod across the platform, Leona took several long moments to include each and every member of the assembled bridal party in her death glare. "What about *Rose*? Did you *hear* the disparaging things she said to me just now? The way she implied men are only interested in me for my *money*?"

Georgina laughed. "And your point?"

Again, Leona's mouth gaped.

Again, Tori began to count, this time making it to nine before being cut off by Beatrice Tharrington.

"Did I tell all of you my ace news?"

All eyes turned toward the soft-spoken, twenty-two-year-old British nanny, dressed in Quiet Barley, and waited.

Beatrice took a deep breath and then let it out, her

greenish-colored eyes round with a kind of wonder and excitement that was rare for the otherwise shy girl. "My governess is coming, here—to Sweet Briar! To work for Jim and Julie Brady. I made the suggestion after they fired that rather cheeky Cynthia Marland and had no one to look after their three children. I suggested Miss Gracie as the perfect replacement and she's actually coming! In fact, she's due to arrive first thing in the morning. Isn't that luvvly-jubbly?"

Margaret Louise's eyebrows rose upward. "Luvvly-jubbly?"

Beatrice's pale skin reddened just before her gaze dropped to her feet. "It means . . . lovely," Beatrice whispered.

"I think it's a wonderful expression," Melissa Davis said from her spot on the edge of the platform. Then, turning to her mother-in-law, she added, "Sounds like something *you* might say, Margaret Louise."

"Well, then, I reckon I might be addin' it to my repertoire after today." Margaret Louise winked at Beatrice. "Assumin' you don't mind sharin' it with a loudmouth like me, of course."

Debbie stepped forward in a burst of Soft Russet and touched a gentle hand to the young girl's back. "When you said *governess* just now, did that mean this woman took care of *you* as a child, Beatrice?"

"Oh yes! Miss Gracie made my childhood *magical*," Beatrice replied. "And now, because she'll be with the Bradys, I'll see her at the park and school events just about every day. It will be divine!"

"Certainly helps explain why you've been grinnin' like a possum eatin' a sweet tater ever since you walked through those doors." Margaret Louise pointed toward the bridal shop's front door. "I reckon it'll be like havin' your momma here, won't it?"

Beatrice didn't need to utter a word. Her face-splitting smile said it all.

"Would you like to bring her to the wedding as your guest? It might be a great way for her to meet people," Tori offered. "In fact, at last check, every single teacher at Sweet Briar Elementary School will be at the reception, along with most, if not all, of the office staff. Miss Gracie can meet the children's teachers and principal, and they can get to know her a bit, as well."

"I shall ask her as soon as I see her." Beatrice ran her hand down the front of her satiny dress and then rose up on the balls of her one-inch silver heels for a little twirl. "I feel like royalty in this dress, Victoria. Thank you so much for including me."

For a moment, she was afraid Leona was going to widen her battlefield to include Beatrice, but whatever smart-aleck thought lifted the woman's eyebrow halfway to her hairline remained unspoken, setting off a domino of relieved sighs around the room in the process.

Tori wished she could attribute Leona's sudden self-restraint to some sort of spiritual awakening but she had a sneaking suspicion it was more likely due to the click of Rose's dressing room door and the chance to get one last jab in where her true nemesis was concerned.

Leona, of course, didn't disappoint. Lifting her body-hugging dress halfway up her calves to reveal her own four-inch version of the agreed-upon silver-colored shoe, the woman *tsk*ed audibly beneath her breath. "I'm so glad

I don't have to wear flats with a satin gown. It's just so— so *nursing home*, don't you think?"

"Hush, Twin!" Margaret Louise scolded amid a chorus of gasps from the rest of the bridal party.

"What?" Leona batted her false lashes with feigned innocence. "Did I say something wrong?"

"You opened your mouth, didn't you?" Rose hissed as she shuffled across the room to Tori with her bridesmaid dress draped across her arthritic arm. When she reached her destination, the matriarch lowered her voice so only Tori could hear. "I tried to carry the shoe box out here, too, but I'm afraid I dropped it one too many times."

"I'll get your shoes and your dress to you tomorrow evening when I come to your house for *my* final fitting." Tori liberated the dress from Rose's arm and draped it, instead, across the back of her chair before turning to take her friend's frail hands inside her own. "Thank you for coming today, Rose. You looked lovely."

"I wouldn't miss your special day for anything in the world, Victoria." Tugging her left hand free, Rose cupped the side of Tori's face. "Milo Wentworth is a lucky, lucky man."

"And I am a lucky, lucky girl to be able to spend the rest of my life with a man like Milo *and* the truest, most wonderfully loving friends a girl could ever hope for." Tori captured Rose's hand inside her own and held it against her skin more closely. "I love you, Rose."

A single tear escaped from beneath Rose's bifocals. "I won't let this thing with Leona threaten your day, Victoria. You have my word."

With the underside of her thumb, Tori wiped all

residual wetness from the elderly woman's cheek while doing her best to smile through the answering tears she, herself, refused to shed. "Thank you, Rose, that means a lot. But really, I can't imagine *anything* threatening my wedding day."

Chapter 2

Sometimes, when she was staring up at the ceiling waiting for sleep to win out over her latest crazy day, Tori would imagine her fiancé's face.

His burnished brown hair, cut short on the sides . . .

His tall, lean frame that towered eight inches above her own five foot five . . .

His brown eyes with the little amber flecks that lit up the moment he saw her . . .

His dimples that melted her knees every time he smiled at her . . .

By the time she completed her inventory, she would invariably be so content and so at peace, she'd drift off to sleep if for no other reason than to make another day with him come sooner.

"I wish there was a way we could freeze this place so

it never changes," she said, tightening her hold on his hand. "It's everything I always wanted for my life."

Milo glanced down as they continued walking, their destination still a mystery to Tori. "You mean Sweet Briar?"

"No. I mean the way it is right now—between us. It's so good, you know?" She met the handsome third grade teacher's curious gaze and responded with a happy shrug. "Since I got back from New York with the crew, things have been—"

"Don't say it." Milo's laugh started deep inside his chest before receiving backup support from his lips and dimples. "You'll jinx us."

She turned with him as they reached the corner and stopped outside the gated area to Sweet Briar's newest park, the limited number of squeals from the recently completed maze of play forts catching her by surprise as much as the destination itself. "You're an elementary school teacher! Are you sure you want to be here?"

"With you? Absolutely. Unless you pick a fight with someone . . ."

"It doesn't look like there's anyone to fight with," she quipped.

"That's because most of them are either still eating dinner or getting ready for an early bedtime, I imagine." Milo lifted the latch and pushed open the metal gate, his opposing hand guiding her through its opening via the small of her back. "I've been wanting to push you on the new swings ever since they finished this place."

Tori spun around and wrapped her arms around his neck, the happiness she felt at that moment overpowering. "This is what I'm talking about. This place where all we have to really think about is how we want to spend the next day together . . . and how the bridal party is going to look on our wedding day . . . and how, exactly, to best word the joy you bring me in my vows. It's the way it should be *all* the time."

"And we'll do our best to make it so." He kissed her gently and then disengaged her arms from his neck so he could take her hand once again and resume their trek across the playground to the swings. "So, tell me, how did the fitting go this morning? Did Leona's TV crew manage to stay out of the way so you could do what you needed to do?"

"There was really only one camera guy and he was so unobtrusive I actually forgot he was there most of the time."

"And the different dress colors? Did they come together the way you wanted?"

"Oh, Milo, they were gorgeous," she answered. "It was as if I had the most brilliant autumn leaves standing in front of me."

"I'm glad. But you have to know it's *you* I can't wait to see." Milo raked a hand through his hair, releasing a half moan–half grunt as he did. "I just want to stand next to you, in front of all of our family and friends, and finally start the rest of our lives together."

"And two weeks from today, we'll do just that." She heard the breathless quality of her voice but could do little to stop it. Their wedding couldn't come soon enough in her book. "I'm doing my final fitting at Rose's tomorrow evening. After that, all that's really left are a few final touches here and there."

"Do you want me to pick up both rings at Brady's?" he asked. "Because I can if that makes it easier."

"Oh no, getting our rings is part of the fun."

They picked their way around a small grove of trees and a smattering of empty picnic benches to reach the clearing and the endless play equipment it hosted. "My mom said your folks are coming in from South Africa the night before the ceremony? Is that right?"

"I think so. That's where their last postcard was from anyway." She felt the grass give way to a soft, rubbery material beneath her shoes as she closed in on the swings and the romantic image Milo had stoked inside her thoughts the moment he shared his intentions for their evening. "And Charles is coming in from New York earlier that same day. From what I've been able to gather, there's quite the pull going on between Margaret Louise and Leona as to who will be hosting him while he's here."

"I finally get to meet the infamous Charles . . ." He laughed.

"Yes, yes you do. And boy, are you in for a treat." She claimed the first of five swings and positioned her grip around the chain-link ropes tasked with supporting her as she glided through the air. Slowly, push by push, she pumped her legs, the cool autumn air refreshing against her cheeks. "Oooh, it's been a long time since I've been on a swing like this."

"And?" he prodded.

"It's fun!"

"Good. Count on it becoming a regular occurrence, my soon-to-be wife."

"I shall—"

"Victoria? Milo? Is that you?"

She stopped pumping her legs and looked to her side to find Beatrice and her charge, Luke, pointing and waving from halfway across the playground. Lifting the tips of her fingers ever so slightly, she did her best to return the wave while Milo grabbed hold of the chain and brought her to a full stop.

"We didn't mean for you to stop," Beatrice said, her petite hand atop Luke's shoulder. "We were just surprised to see you here, is all."

Luke hopped from foot to foot, his smile nearly reaching his ears. "I've never seen a big person on the swings before."

"Even us big people like to play and have fun, don't we, Milo?" At Milo's agreement, Tori gestured in the direction from which Beatrice and Luke had just come. "So what were you two playing on?"

"We just got here, didn't we, Miss Bea?" Without waiting for a response, Luke continued on, his excitement evident in every crack and crevice of his six-year-old being. "But we're gonna play in the new fort."

Milo smiled down at the boy, nodding as he did. "That sounds like fun, Luke."

"It is! Sometimes we pretend it's a castle, but today, it's gonna be a boat, isn't it, Miss Bea?"

Beatrice straightened, threw her shoulders back, and released her gentle hold on Luke's back long enough to give the little boy a proper salute. "Aye, aye, Captain!"

The youngster's answering laugh disappeared in favor of a soft but strangled sound followed by a distinct "uh-oh."

Beatrice pulled her hand from Luke's shoulder and moved it to the base of his chin, guiding his gaze until it met back up with hers. "Luke? What's wrong? Is your tummy acting up again?"

Slowly, the boy extended his right index finger to guide their collective attention from his face to that of a lone figure standing just inside the tree line, staring in their direction. "It's her again, Miss Bea. And she's got that mad face just like before."

Tori looked from the woman she didn't recognize, back to Beatrice and Luke, the change in the boy's demeanor impossible to miss. "Who is that, Beatrice?"

An unfamiliar cloud passed across Beatrice's face just before she repositioned her grip on Luke, pulling him closer. "Perhaps we should play captain-of-the-ship back at the house, Luke, what do you say?"

For a moment Tori was virtually certain the six-year-old was going to protest, but when he looked toward the far side of the park again, his nod of agreement came easily. "Okay, Miss Bea."

Reaching out, she grabbed hold of Beatrice's arm. "Wait. I don't understand. Why are you going back home to play when you just got here?"

"It's simply too nice of an evening to have a row."

Again, Tori looked toward the woman on the far side of Luke's treasured fort before reengaging eye contact with her friend. "Beatrice, I've known you for almost two and a half years now, and I've never known you to fight with anyone."

"And I shant with Cynthia, either. But I don't have to utter a word to get her started."

"Cynthia? Who is Cynthia?"

"Cynthia Marland. The Bradys' former nanny."

"And . . ."

"And she's unhappy with her firing." Beatrice leaned

close to Tori and Milo, dropping her voice to a whisper. "But she deserved to be fired. She was a horrible, *horrible* nanny to those poor children. All she cared about was the shiny objects Mr. and Mrs. Brady gave her to use— the car, the fancy phone, and the like."

"Reenie almost died!" Luke supplied.

Beatrice lifted a finger to her lips and shook her head. "Luke, we must not spread gossip. It's not nice. Besides, Reenie is fine now and my special Miss Gracie is going to take good care of her and her sisters just like I promised you. Remember?"

If Luke answered, she didn't hear, because she was too busy trying to process everything Beatrice had said. "Is Reenie one of the Brady kids?"

Milo nodded. "Reenie's older sister, Kellie, is in my class. From what I heard in the faculty lounge after school, Reenie has a seizure disorder that requires medication. Only the medication was never sent in with the child on the first day of kindergarten. Three days into the first week, she had a seizure. Not having the proper medication at the right time nearly killed her."

"And this Cynthia was part of that?" Tori asked.

"Ultimately it's the parents' responsibility, of course, but as the person hired to look after the needs of the children while the parents are working, yes, Cynthia certainly shoulders a large chunk of the blame, as well."

"Wow."

Beatrice leaned still closer. "And that was just the *final* incident, Victoria. There were others along the way that should have had her out the door long before now."

"Why didn't they?" she asked.

"That, I cannot explain any more than I can the hiring of half the nannies in this town. Some of them—like Amanda and Stacy—are just bloody awful."

A quick peek at the trees showed Cynthia hadn't budged. To Beatrice, Tori said, "Okay, but why is this Cynthia person upset with *you*?"

"The same reason Amanda and Stacy are upset with me, too." Beatrice closed her eyes momentarily, swallowing as she did. "Because it was my phone call to Mrs. Brady that prevented Cynthia from getting the second chance she was talking about on the playground last week. And it has some of the other families starting to rethink things, too."

"Your phone call?" she repeated. "I don't understand."

"When I heard Cynthia talking about a second chance, I was worried about the children. If this woman could be so careless once, she could be careless again. I wanted Mrs. Brady to know that the Nanny Go Round Agency wasn't the only choice." Beatrice looked down at Luke and smiled. "So I told her about Miss Gracie, didn't I, sweetie?"

"Miss Bea?" Luke's shoulders drooped in reaction to a conversation that had already gone on far too long for a captain in search of his ship. "Can we go home and play boat now? Please?"

"Of course, Luke. And then, it's straight on to bed. We want to be waiting at the airport when Miss Gracie arrives, don't we?" Beatrice smiled shyly at Milo and quickly brought him up to speed on the news she'd shared with Tori at the bridal shop. "Miss Gracie was *my* governess as a child and she's absolutely wonderful."

"I get to hold a sign with Miss Gracie's name on it at

the airport tomorrow morning," Luke added, beaming. "I used my bestest writing and I didn't make the *R* go all backwards like I usually do!"

"Good work, Luke." Milo collected a high five from Luke and then slipped his arm around Tori's waist and gave it a gentle squeeze. "Let's let them get back to their evening, okay?"

Tori reached out, rested a quick hand on Beatrice's lower arm, and smiled. "I'm glad you're going to have some family here now, Beatrice."

"*More* family," the nanny corrected as she zipped Luke's lightweight jacket a smidge higher in preparation for their walk back home. "Luke and his parents are my family here in the States, as are all of you in the sewing circle. Miss Gracie being here will be like adding a mum."

Chapter 3

Slowly, Tori fingered the hand-sewn lace and tiny seed pearls that adorned the fitted top, her gaze jumping ahead to the satin bottom that rained to the floor of Rose's sewing room in a classic A-line style.

"Oh, Rose," she whispered. "It's . . . it's like something out of a fairytale."

"A fairytale that's 'bout to happen for real in thirteen days, Victoria." Margaret Louise stepped back to afford a better frontal view of Tori and then nudged Rose with a gentle elbow. "Why, I reckon that's the purtiest dress I've ever seen."

Rose grabbed hold of a two-tier step stool she'd positioned off to the side and used it to help lower herself to the ground and the hem of Tori's wedding dress. Once there, the elderly woman pulled a pin from between her lips and tucked it into one tiny section. "Other than this—which will take but a moment to fix—I think it fits perfectly." Rose peered up at Tori. "How does it feel?"

Again, Tori looked down at the detail work and then at her reflection in the full-length mirror. "Rose, it couldn't feel more perfect."

"You done good, Rose," Margaret Louise said in agreement. "Real good."

Brushing a quick hand across her eyes, Rose merely nodded before struggling back to her knees and, eventually, her feet. "Is it everything you envisioned for your special day, Victoria?"

She turned from the mirror to take Rose's hands inside her own, the trembling she found there more than a little alarming. "Rose? Are you okay? You're shaking."

"I just want you to be happy with the dress."

"Happy doesn't even come close to describing how I feel in this gown, Rose. I mean, look at me, I'm . . ." She stopped, swallowed, and tried again, her predisposition toward modesty losing out over her current Rose-created reality. "I'm . . . *beautiful*," she finished in an emotion-infused whisper. "Absolutely beautiful."

Rose's lower lip disappeared behind her bridge only to reappear in time with a slow, but definitive smile. "I couldn't say it better myself." Then, pulling her hand from Tori's, Rose waved it toward the hallway. "Go into my room and take it off. I'll put an extra stitch or two in that spot at the hemline and you can take it home with you."

She spun back toward the mirror for one last look. "I'll take it off, but I'd like to leave it here so you can help me into it on my wedding day."

Rose looked down at her trembling hands and made a face. "I'm not sure how much help I'll be with the buttons."

"We'll take it one button at a time." Tori gathered the bottom half of her dress in her hands and made her way down the hall, stopping as she reached the door to Rose's room. "Margaret Louise? Could you find the right channel on the TV so we can watch Leona's show before we have to call it a night?"

"You betcha."

By the time Tori returned to the main part of Rose's tiny home, her friends were seated on the sofa in front of the television with a bowl of freshly popped popcorn. The familiar jingle of Leona's new Cable TV show faded into the background as Leona's prerecorded voice took over with its familiar welcome.

"Have you always wanted to dress like a princess? Have you always wondered how you can turn heads by merely choosing the right outfit at the right time? If so, you've come to the right place. Over the next twenty minutes, I'll teach you to dress with style by inviting you into *Leona's Closet*."

The music picked up for a beat or two then faded as the station went to commercial.

"I still can't believe your sister has a TV show," Tori said as she rounded the backside of the couch and claimed the vacant spot between her two friends. "It still seems so . . . so . . ." She cast about for the best way to describe her feelings but was beaten to the punch by Rose.

"Ridiculous?"

"Now, I didn't say that," Tori protested around the laugh she couldn't quite muffle.

"Well, I sure did."

The trio of commercials highlighting local establishments in and around Sweet Briar ended and brought Leona front and center once again. Only this time, instead of just her voice, the camera panned in on Margaret Louise's twin sister and the red velvet chair that had become her televised throne.

"Hello, everyone, and welcome to my show, *Leona's Closet*. For those of you who have been here before, I can see—thanks to the many pictures and e-mails I've been receiving these past few weeks—that many of you are taking my advice to heart.

"We still have a lot of work to do, of course, but we'll get there if it's the last thing I do."

Leona clasped her flawlessly manicured hands atop her lap and smiled at the camera, taking a moment or two to add a few seductive blinks of her eyes. "This week I'm taking you all on a field trip . . . to a fitting I attended for an upcoming wedding in Sweet Briar."

Tori leaned forward on her cushion, plucked a few pieces of popcorn from the waiting bowl, and watched as Leona-on-the-chair morphed into Leona-in-her-Smoldering-Blaze-bridesmaid-dress-at-the-bridal-shop. "We've all been to weddings and seen the catastrophe that is synonymous with bridesmaid attire, but as you can see in this shot, there can be a few noteworthy exceptions."

Step by step, Leona took her audience through every nuance of her dress and the way it came together to further enhance her natural beauty. Then, as the bridal shop picture faded to reveal Leona holding court on her chair once again, they were taken through various body shapes and the styles each one demanded.

"Let's take a look at a few of my fellow bridesmaids to see what I'm talking about."

This time, when they went to a shot from the bridal shop, Leona remained on half the screen.

"For those of you who frequent Debbie's Bakery in downtown Sweet Briar, you know that Debbie Calhoun is surprisingly slender and petite. Her dark blonde hair and pale blue eyes would normally not be a candidate for wearing Russet. But because of Debbie's skin color and infectious smile, she pulls it off well.

"And then there's my sister, Margaret Louise Davis, who manages to make Warm Cinnamon inviting in her own way."

Tori glanced to her right and smiled. "Well, look at you, Margaret Louise. Not only did you score a mention on Leona's show . . . she's actually saying something nice."

"Well, I'll be . . ."

One by one, Leona took her audience through the bridal party and the various dress styles and colors each wore. While she didn't gush about anyone the way she'd gushed about herself, Leona managed to find a detail or two about each dress that complemented the body type it adorned.

Dixie . . .

Melissa . . .

Georgina . . .

Beatrice . . .

Nina . . .

As Nina's image disappeared from the right side of the screen, Leona took over, her eyes bright with anticipation. "Which brings us to the final bridesmaid and the final segment of our show—*Who Dresses You Anyway?*"

Tori felt her jaw slack as the enormity behind Leona's words took root.

"All over this country," Leona continued in her scripted lead-up, "people are dressing in ways that embarrass not only *them* but also those of us who are forced to look at them across the office, across the restaurant, across the street, across our very own living room . . . and, sadly, at weddings, too."

"Don't do it, Twin," Margaret Louise admonished from behind the plump hand she'd slapped against her mouth. "Don't you dare do it . . ."

"There are, of course, the young women who feel the need to leave nothing to their date's imagination when they go out to dinner." Leona tilted her head to indicate a snapshot of a woman's body clad in short shorts and a tube top that covered little more than the essentials. "To these women, I say, tease them with *hints*. Make them wonder. Make them imagine. Make them yearn. It staves off boredom.

"Then, lest we forget, there are the women who dress like men. To them, I simply ask, *why?*"

Tori and Margaret Louise released a sigh in tandem, only to have Leona's next description hitching their breath once again. "And finally, there are the women who simply don't get the concept of a mirror. Or if they do, they don't care."

Leona and her chair disappeared from the screen in favor of a full shot of Rose in her Harvest Wheat bridesmaid dress and sensible silver flats.

She tried to make sense of what she was seeing, tried to rationalize it away as some sort of bad dream, but when her focus invariably shifted in Rose's direction, Tori knew it was all too real.

"As God is my witness, when I get my hands on my sister's neck, I'm gonna—"

The return of Leona's voice pulled their collective focus back to the television and the impeccably dressed woman commanding its screen once again. "To women like this, I have but one simple piece of advice: Do the world a favor and invest in a mirror.

"For everyone else, I'll be back next week with even more do's and don'ts from *Leona's Closet*."

Chapter 4

Tori relinquished the plate of white chocolate brownies to Georgina's trusted housekeeper, Betty, and followed the mayor down one hallway and across the next. The constant chatter that usually guided her feet toward the correct room on any given Monday night was noticeably absent.

"We are meeting tonight, aren't we?" she asked, hiking her sewing bag higher on her shoulder.

Georgina's answer came via a nod and a direction-gesturing finger that led her to the sunroom and the five very quiet members of the Sweet Briar Ladies Society Sewing Circle it was tasked with hosting for the evening. Stopping in the doorway, Tori took in the room and the unfamiliar semicircular seating arrangement it offered.

"You can sit anywhere you want except there." Georgina's finger shifted direction to indicate a lone chair positioned at the mouth of the semicircle, its only real view the faces of the women who barely looked up in acknowledgment of Tori's arrival. "That one is being saved."

Debbie looked up from the piece of pale blue material stretched across her lap and nodded toward the vacant spot to her left. "There's room right here between Melissa and me if you'd like."

Crossing the room with tentative steps, Tori accepted the bakery owner's invitation and settled herself into place, conducting a mental inventory of the room's occupants as she did.

Margaret Louise . . .

Dixie . . .

Melissa . . .

Debbie . . .

Beatrice . . .

"Where's Rose?" she asked. "And—"

The melodic peal of the doorbell and the gnashing of teeth to her left and right cut her off mid-question.

"The rat has arrived," Dixie said from between clenched teeth.

Margaret Louise's head and shoulders shifted against the back edge of the couch she shared with Dixie, her normally boisterous voice void of anything resembling humor or lightness. "Okay, everyone, it's time to paint your butt white and run with the antelope."

"We're ready," Debbie and Melissa said in unison while Beatrice's chin dropped closer to her chest.

Georgina gave one final look around the room and then crossed to her own chair beside Margaret Louise. "I think I'll just let Betty show her in rather than exert the effort it would take to greet and escort her myself."

Confused, Tori leaned into whisper territory with Debbie. "What's going on? Who's here?"

"Tell me you really don't need me to answer that . . ."

"I—wait. Leona is actually *coming*?" she clarified more loudly than she'd intended.

"Why wouldn't she?" Melissa interjected. "Aunt Leona never thinks she does *anything* wrong."

"I reckon she's 'bout to think differently real soon." Margaret Louise pushed her sewing project off her lap and replaced it with two tight fists. "Why, I've always known my twin was prickly, and maybe even a bit mean at times, but *this*? Why, she's as crooked as a hound dog's hind leg and twice as dirty."

Melissa nodded along with the rest of the women in the room then pointed at her mother-in-law. "What she said."

"It's high time Leona got an earful or two about the way she treats people," Debbie said, scooting forward on the couch. "It's just not right."

Slowly, Beatrice's chin parted with her chest to reveal a tentative yet hopeful smile. "Guess what, Victoria?"

She slid her gaze in the direction of her young friend. "What?"

"Reenie, Kellie, and Sophie are delighted with Miss Gracie."

"Reenie, Kellie, and . . ." The words trailed from her mouth as the staccato sound of Leona's heels in the hallway kicked off a mashing of lips and grinding of teeth across the room.

"The Brady children," Beatrice said by way of whispered explanation before returning to the scout patches she'd chosen as her sewing project for the evening.

Georgina grabbed a pair of dress slacks from the table

to her left and positioned the hem of one leg across her lap. "No one look at her, no one acknowledge her," the mayor hissed from between clenched teeth. "When she squirms, we let her have it with both guns blazing."

In true domino style, one head after the other tilted downward to focus on whatever project was being tackled by each person—Luke's scout uniform, Georgina's dress slacks, Dixie's pillow, Debbie's latest apron, Tori's candy pouches for the wedding guests, denim overalls for Melissa's youngest, and something delicate and blue just getting started in Margaret Louise's capable hands.

"Good evening, everyone," Leona said as she breezed into the room with a Chanel handbag on one arm and a bow-laden bunny under the other. "I'm sorry I'm late but it simply couldn't be helped. Paris had her fitting for her extra special bow for Victoria's wedding and the fabric the girl had used was completely and utterly beneath my standards.

"I mean, truly, could you imagine my precious Paris wearing cotton for an event that clearly demands the finest silk?"

The only sound Tori detected in the room came from her own throat as she swallowed and then stole a peek in Leona's direction.

Sure enough, she was rewarded for her attention with a glare that was subsequently shared with the top of each and every head in the room.

When the panoramic death glare was complete, Leona addressed her nose-twitching sidekick. "This is why I've spent so many hours discussing the finer points of manners with you, my precious angel. They make a person stand out in a world that's growing ruder by the second."

Margaret Louise laid her needle atop the pale blue fabric and, pinning her sister with a stare, addressed her son's wife with her words. "It's a shame how many folks think the do as I say, not as I do mentality works, ain't it, Melissa?"

"It sure is," Melissa said as she, too, found a holding place for her needle. "Especially when it almost never works."

"Kids learn more from observation than they do words." Debbie smoothed her hands across the apron taking shape across her thighs and then sighed. "So if a parent is nasty, the offspring tend to be nasty as well."

"Poor Paris," Georgina clucked. "If only someone had warned her off outside of Ella-May Vetter's house all those years ago."

Leona's mouth gaped, then closed, then gaped again.

"Maybe it's time to return Paris to the wild, where she'll have a fighting chance to live out her days as a decent bunny," Dixie said before dropping her pillow cover into her tote bag.

"You take that back, you old—"

Georgina rose to her feet, stopping Leona's angered response with a splayed palm. "Don't you dare stand in my home and insult Dixie."

Stunned, Leona stepped back. "Excuse me?"

"You heard me."

Leona's eyes widened on Georgina. "You're going to reprimand *me* for insults?" Without waiting for a reply, Leona pointed at each and every sewing circle member in the room, except Beatrice. "Have you *heard* the way I've been treated since I arrived? The lack of greeting followed by the blatant disrespect toward me as Paris's mother?"

"No. I heard it. Heard each and every word. But that was all true . . . and justified." Georgina placed her hands at her hips and continued her stare down with Margaret Louise's taken-aback twin sister. "You yourself said you spend your days teaching Paris about manners yet display none of your own."

"*I—I* have no manners?" Leona sputtered before pointing a finger at each and every woman in the room and then setting Paris on the floor and matching Georgina's stance. "How many thank-you notes have you gotten from any of the people in this room following a sewing circle meeting you've hosted? Wait. I'll answer that for you. *None*."

"We ain't talkin' 'bout those kinds of manners, Twin."

Leona transferred her stare to Margaret Louise. "What other kind of manners are there?"

"The kind that have you bein' nice." Margaret Louise's focus slipped to her feet as her normal lighthearted tone became one of hushed disgust. "The way Mama and Daddy always taught us to be."

"What on earth are you babbling about, Margaret Louise?"

"We saw your show last night," Debbie said, joining in the exchange from her spot beside Tori.

Leona's scowl morphed into a pleased smile and a noteworthy blink. "It was even better than the first few, wasn't it?" Flipping her free hand over and curling her fingers inward, Leona examined her latest manicure for any sign of chipping. When she saw no evidence of any flaws, she stroked the top of Paris's head. "Stan, at the station, told me they've been getting calls all day from viewers who want more—more style hints, more color hints, more—"

One by one, they went around the semicircle completing Leona's sentence with "meanness," "nastiness," and a few other appropriate fill-ins. Some, like Georgina and Dixie, seemed to take pleasure in as many synonyms as they could possibly come up with before Margaret Louise brought an end to it all with one simple question.

"How *could* you, Twin?"

"How could I what?" Leona asked, perplexed.

"How could you hurt Rose the way you did?"

"Hurt Rose?" Leona echoed. "How did *I* hurt Rose?"

Georgina opened her mouth to respond, but instead walked away.

Tori searched Leona's face for any indication her friend was kidding, but there was none, the absence of such evidence only serving to replace her own anger with an all-encompassing sadness.

For Leona.

"Leona, I feel sorry for you, I really do."

She heard the immediate gasps from Dixie and Georgina, and the delayed ones from Melissa and Debbie, but she opted not to let either derail her from the rest of what needed to be said. "Anyone looking at you from the outside knows you are a beautiful, stylish woman. Those of us who have had the opportunity to see beyond the surface know your inner beauty can be even more breathtaking when you let down that guard you have against the world. Yet despite those blessings, you still have this insatiable need to elevate yourself at the expense of others."

When Leona said nothing, Tori continued, the memory of Rose's face the previous night guiding the appropriate words through her lips. "When I moved here two-plus years ago, I was still in a tremendous amount of pain from my great-grandmother's passing. Getting to know all of you helped the healing begin by giving me a core group of friends whom I could both laugh and cry with. But Rose? She showed me the tenderness and quiet under-standing that I always equated with my great-grandmother. And I know I'm not the only one she does that for."

"You couldn't be more right, Victoria," Debbie said quietly.

Beatrice, who'd remained silent until that moment, looked up long enough to blink away a tear of her own. "She was my Miss Gracie right up until Miss Gracie arrived here yesterday morning."

Tori nodded. "I know you two spar a lot. And I know she starts it every bit as much as you do, Leona. But I've also seen her look at you with the same love and tender-ness she shows the rest of us . . . and you can't deny that."

Margaret Louise held up her hand to indicate it was her turn at bat. "Any love and tenderness Rose has shown you, Twin, has been misplaced. In fact, thinkin' 'bout the way you've been included in this group 'cause of me makes me sick to my stomach."

Leona's left brow rose nearly to her hairline. "Oh?"

"This is a sewin' circle, Twin."

"And your point?"

"You don't sew."

"I bring color to an otherwise dull group simply by being here."

"That may have been true on occasion, Twin. But more often than not, you've brought pain . . . to people I care 'bout."

Leona's eyes narrowed to near slits. "Are you saying you don't want me in this sewing circle anymore?"

Margaret Louise's chin rose into the air. "For starters, yes."

Tori touched the grandmother of eight's arm with a gentle, yet firm grip. "Margaret Louise, don't . . ."

"Why, Victoria? Leona can't blame the cow for the milk goin' sour. *She* did this . . . not me."

A steady vibrating sound somewhere off to their right brought Beatrice to her feet with a hushed apology and a much-needed break in the tension. "I'm sorry . . . I didn't realize I'd left my phone on."

Then, reaching into the tote bag Luke had decorated for her the previous Christmas, Beatrice retrieved the still-vibrating device from its depths, flipped it open, and held it to her ear. "Is everything okay with Luke, Mrs. Johnson?"

Tori stole a glance in Leona's direction as the rest of the room waited for Beatrice to complete her call, the blatant sadness on the sixtysomething's face poorly hidden behind exasperated anger.

"I'm at Mayor Hayes's home for my sewing circle meeting . . . Yes, my friends are here with me now . . ."

Tori tried to take advantage of the unexpected temporary cease-fire between Leona and everyone else to come up with a way to make things right, but it was hard. She was every bit as angry at Leona as the rest of them.

Leona had hurt Rose, publicly humiliating their elderly friend in front of a town Rose had called home since birth. Sure, Leona could be forced to apologize to Rose for her cruelty, but the damage was already done.

"No, Mrs. Brady hasn't rung me up . . ."

And judging by Rose's face the previous night, the hurt Leona's actions had birthed went far deeper than any simple "I'm sorry" could ever erase.

A flash of movement snapped Tori's attention back to Beatrice and the chair the nanny was in the process of reclaiming. "Okay, Mrs. Johnson, I'm sitting just as you asked . . ."

Tori exchanged a curious glance with her friends only to look back in time to see the nanny's face contort in confusion.

"Miss Gracie? Yes, yes, of course I've spoken with Miss Gracie . . . Luke and I spent time with her and the Brady children at the park this afternoon. We all met there after school to play. We pushed the kids on the swings, played a few rousing rounds of Simon Says and Follow the Leader, and then made a lavish birthday cake out of sand to celebrate the arrival of the teddy bears Miss Gracie brought for Reenie, Kelley, Sophie, and even Luke. Yes, we had a wonderful day.

"Yes, of course it is a day I will always remember with Miss Gracie . . ."

With nary a look exchanged between them, six resolute bodies stepped forward in silent solidarity just as the muffled voice on the other end of the line grew even more muffled.

"*Dead?*" Beatrice shrieked as she shot upward onto her feet once again. "What do you mean, Miss Gracie is—"

Dixie's horrified gasp echoed around the circle just before Beatrice's phone hit the ground and five sets of arms lurched forward to keep their young friend from doing the same.

Chapter 5

It was nearly eleven o'clock when Tori walked into her room, dropped her cell phone on her nightstand, and flopped onto her bed, exhausted. Yet even as she let her eyelids drift closed for one glorious moment, she knew sleep would elude her for hours to come.

Beatrice's heartbroken wail at the tragic news of Miss Gracie's passing had known no end as Tori held her close, assured Mrs. Johnson she would see their nanny home, and even stayed beside the young woman's bed until sleep temporarily silenced the pain.

She'd shed countless tears herself as she returned call after call from the Johnsons' driveway before finally heading home, each sewing sister's voice mail–delivered concern for Beatrice only serving to highlight Leona's silence.

"*Why*, Leona?" she whispered as she stared up at the

ceiling. "*Why* do you insist on showing this awful side to everyone around you?"

Grabbing her phone off the nightstand, she clicked on her message center and noted the zero next to her voice mail box.

Maybe Leona was still smarting from her sister's words . . .

Maybe Margaret Louise, Georgina, and the rest of the crew had been too hard on her . . .

Maybe—

Tori sat up tall and scooted herself backward until she was flush against the headboard.

No. What Leona did to Rose was wrong—horribly, awfully wrong, and she deserved to be called out on her behavior. Leona's lack of concern for Beatrice was a separate issue entirely, and one that bared a second and, perhaps more thorough, chastising at the very least.

But that was for another day. When she had more energy and staying power . . .

Looking down at her phone once again, she scrolled through her contacts until the smile she desperately needed found its way across her mouth. Pressing the call button, she held the device to her ear and hoped against hope her soon-to-be husband was still awake.

Her wish came true on the second ring.

"Hey there, beautiful, how was your meeting?"

She pulled her knees to her chest and wrapped her free arm around them, releasing a long-held sigh as she did. "We never really got to have one."

"Oh?"

"Miss Gracie is dead."

A momentary pause in her ear gave way to a more

alert-sounding Milo. "Miss Gracie? Why does that name sound familiar?"

"Because you heard it the other evening. When we were at the park together." Tori rested her chin atop her knees and tried to block out yet another mental encore of Beatrice's cry. "Miss Gracie was Beatrice's governess when she was a little girl in England, remember?"

"The one who was coming here to be the Bradys' new nanny?" Milo clarified.

"Yes. Miss Gracie arrived yesterday morning as planned. Beatrice and Luke met her at the airport, drove her here, and got her settled at the Bradys'."

"What happened?"

"From what Chief Dallas was able to tell us, it appears as if she lost her footing at the top of the basement stairs and tumbled all the way to the bottom, hitting her head multiple times in the process." Tori closed her eyes as she recalled turning down the Bradys' road with a sniffling Beatrice in the passenger seat. The pulsating emergency lights up and down the Bradys' driveway had intensified Beatrice's cries on sight. "Beatrice insisted we stop there as soon as she heard, but fortunately, Miss Gracie's body had already been removed. I think it would have destroyed Beatrice to see her that way."

A long, low whistle permeated her ear just before Milo's deep voice. "You're probably right. Wow. I'm so sorry to hear this, so sorry Beatrice has to go through this. Is there anything I can do for her?"

"Hmmm . . . that does seem like the normal response when someone you care about suffers a loss like this, isn't it?" She released her legs, stretched them across the top of her bed, and wiggled her toes back and forth, the motion doing little to alleviate the knot of tension she felt building inside her body. "Everyone called and left a message on my phone at some point while Beatrice and I were at the Bradys'. Dixie, Georgina, Melissa, Debbie, and Margaret Louise—they all called. Even *Rose*, who wasn't at Georgina's when we first heard about Miss Gracie, called to see how Beatrice was doing and whether there was anything anyone could do, you know?"

"Okay . . ."

"Everyone except Leona, that is." She cocked her head against the edge of the headboard and stared, unseeingly, at the ceiling once again, the irritation she'd felt prior to calling Milo beginning to resurface at an alarming rate. "She not only stayed silent when the call came in, she also failed to check and see how Beatrice was after we left."

"Leona has never been good with sympathy. You know that, Tori. She probably just didn't know what to say amid the initial shock, and then, after you took Beatrice home, maybe she thought it was best to give you space to focus on Beatrice rather than a potentially bothersome phone call."

She swung her feet over the edge of the bed and worked to keep the irritation in her voice under control. "No. That's not it at all. Leona was pouting because her sister and a few of the other ladies called her out on the way she humiliated Rose on that precious Cable TV show of hers last night."

"Oh, no. Tell me she didn't."

"I wish I could," she answered simply.

"Why didn't you tell me this when we talked last night?"

"Because I was far too angry to speak about it coherently."

"I guess that's understandable." He took a deep, audible breath and then released it slowly. "So everyone came down on her pretty hard for it this evening?"

"You could say that. In fact, I've never seen Margaret Louise that angry before and, I suspect, neither had Leona. She actually seemed to think we should all just laugh it away as if she did nothing wrong. But we couldn't. She hurt Rose deeply . . ."

A second, longer pause finally gave way to Milo's yawn-peppered words. "I'm . . . sorry, Baby. Excuse the . . . yawning. I've had a really long day, and you've obviously had a long night, so why don't we call it quits for now and get some sleep? We can talk more about this tomorrow, okay?"

A siren somewhere in the distance held her agreement at bay for several seconds and sent an inexplicable shiver down her spine. "Do you hear that?" she asked.

"Hear what?"

"Another police car."

"Yeah, actually, I do. Hang on . . ." Seconds later, Milo returned to the line with another yawn-dotted report. "It wasn't a cop car. It was an ambulance, heading out for a call based on the direction it was going. Now get some sleep, okay? I need you in tip-top shape when we get married in twelve days."

"Twelve days," she echoed in a whisper. "Can you believe it?"

"I can, and I can't wait."

She savored the genuine joy that elbowed its way past all residual anger at Leona and inhaled deeply. "Neither can I. I love you, Milo."

"I love you, too, Tori."

"Sweet dreams, I'll talk to you—" Their standard good night died on her lips as her gaze fell on the answering machine and its blinking red light atop her dresser on the other side of the room.

"T-Tor-i?" he yawned. "Is everything okay?"

She waved a dismissive hand in the air and then realized her mistake. "Everything is fine, Milo. I just realized I have a message on my house phone. I'll check that when we're off and then get some sleep. I promise."

"Good. Sleep well, my love."

When she heard the line disconnect, she stood, walked across her bedroom, and pressed the play button.

"Good evening, dear, it's me. I thought about calling your cell to check on how Beatrice is doing, but I didn't want to take the chance it would come in at a bad time. So I'm calling this line instead. Give me a ring regardless of how late you get home and let me know how she's doing, all right? I'm worried."

"Worried," she repeated aloud as the message ended and the tape rewound. "Well, I suppose that's a start."

Retracing her steps back to her nightstand, she grabbed hold of her phone once again and dialed Leona's number, any and all mental preparation she did for the call a waste as six rings came and went, unanswered.

"So much for wanting to know," she mumbled.

Chapter 6

Tori wheeled the cart down one row after the other, stopping every few feet to return the morning's take from the book depository to its proper homes.

The Vault by Emily McKay in Young Adult . . .

Hearse and Buggy by Laura Bradford in Mystery . . .

Summer Moon by Jan DeLima in Urban Fantasy . . .

Book by book, she made her way through the library, the necessary yet largely mindless task providing the perfect opportunity to clear her head before she got to work on the expenditure report she was due to give at Thursday's library board meeting. Once that was completed, it would be on to finalizing the next quarter's programming for everyone from toddlers to senior citizens and all age groups in between.

It promised to be a challenging day under normal circumstances. The fact that she'd tossed and turned throughout much of the four hours of sleep she'd managed to get only made it seem all the more daunting.

The Art of Floating by Kristin Bair O'Keeffe in Women's Fiction . . .

For the umpteenth time since she walked out of her home an hour earlier, she found her thoughts straying from Beatrice's tragic night to Leona's verbal lynching and back again, the previous evening's events still hovering in the vicinity of surreal.

"I thought *I* looked tired when I looked in the mirror this morning. But compared to you, Victoria, I look like I slept two nights' sleep in the time span of one."

Tori looked up from the final book on her cart and found the closest thing to a smile she could for her trusty assistant, Nina Morgan. "I take it Lyndon is still working on that new tooth of his?"

Nina nodded, her dark eyes widening. "I thought the bottom teeth were tough when they broke through, but the top ones? Wow. He's just been howling with the pain each night."

Tori pushed the cart down the aisle and shelved the final title, the instant regret over doing so making her laugh. "I almost wish there were another twenty or so titles to put away just so I could procrastinate from the budget report a little longer. Sad, isn't it?"

"More like understandable, if you ask me." Nina leaned her shoulder against the end of the closest shelf and folded her arms across her chest. "So is that why you look so tired? Knowing you had to put together that report today?"

If only it were that simple . . .

To Nina, though, she offered a half shrug. "I don't know, maybe that was part of it on some level . . ."

"And the rest?"

Abandoning the cart, she claimed the shelf directly across from Nina while wishing, instead, for a chair. "Beatrice's governess, from when she was a little girl herself, fell down a flight of stairs last night and died."

Nina's quick and audible intake of air mentally transported Tori back to the previous evening's sewing circle meeting and the moment the young nanny was given the news. "How awful!"

She nodded along as Nina continued to deliver all the appropriate responses about a woman neither of them had ever met yet cared about simply because of the common denominator they all shared.

"Is Beatrice holding up okay? Is she flying back to England to attend the funeral?"

"Miss Gracie fell here, in Sweet Briar," she explained as her focus returned to the present. "She'd literally arrived here the day before, to be the Bradys' new nanny."

Nina covered her generous mouth with her hand and closed her eyes briefly. "That must have been what that siren was about late last night. It woke Duwayne and me from a sound sleep."

"No, Miss Gracie fell *early* in the evening—sometime before our sewing circle meeting started at seven." She thought back to her own late night and the siren that had interrupted her conversation with Milo. "As for the siren I think you're talking about, I heard it, too, and Milo said he saw an ambulance go by his house as we were talking on the phone. I guess it was just a busy night in Sweet Briar."

"It sure sounds like it. Wow, I'm so sorry for Beatrice, and the Bradys. A new nanny was sorely needed in that house, I'll tell you." Then, realizing she'd said too much,

Nina pulled her hand from her mouth and waved it in the air. "Oh, I shouldn't have said that. Please forgive me, Victoria."

Tori pushed off the shelf and stepped closer to her friend. "Stop. It's just the two of us here."

"I still shouldn't—"

"No, please, why did you say that? About the Bradys needing a new nanny?"

Pulling her own shoulder from its resting spot against the opposite shelf, Nina shrugged. "Because the last one they had paid no attention to that little girl. In fact, every night after a lap sit program, I'd go home and tell Duwayne it was only a matter of time before that little girl got hit by a car or fell down a hole or some other awful thing."

"By that little girl, you mean one of the Brady kids, yes?"

"The youngest one, Sophie." Nina inhaled deeply then let it release slowly through her nose. "Such a pretty little thing, Victoria—curly blonde hair, bright blue eyes, and a smile that lifts her cheeks high every time I start reading a book in story time."

"And this former nanny wasn't terribly good?"

"More like horribly awful." Nina shook her head with obvious disgust, her normally calm eyes darkening with restrained anger. "She spent more time texting and playing games on her phone than she did taking care of that baby. And when she *did* have to look up, she wasn't happy about it. Like Sophie being excited to show her something was such an inconvenience, such a tragedy."

"Beatrice pretty much said the same thing about this girl. Only Beatrice's stories involved the Bradys' other two girls." She sighed then gestured toward the information desk and the daily task list she'd compiled before the reshelving had begun. "I guess we better get back to work. Sadly, that budget report won't write itself no matter how much I wish it would."

"Take it to your office." Nina placed her hand on Tori's arm and smiled. "I'll hold down the fort out here. When it's quiet, I'll see how many of the other things on your list I can get done, okay?"

She covered Nina's hand with her own and squeezed, eliciting a smile from her friend that surely matched the one creeping across her own face. "You're a godsend, Nina Morgan, an absolute godsend."

She plugged in the final numbers on the quarter's expenditures and pressed print, the responding whir of the printer as it sprang into action on the other side of her office akin to the sweetest lullaby she could imagine at that moment.

Two hours and a few dozen invoices and receipts later, she was ready to face the board members and any and all questions they could possibly ask about the financial aspect of the library over the past three months. She'd also included a page or two detailing their expected expenditures for the final quarter of the year.

"One dragon slayed," she mumbled to herself as she took in the clock and noted the time she had left to tackle the program calendar. If she put her mind to it, she could get everything done before it was time to join Nina for the day's assorted closing duties.

But even as she pulled out her folder of confirmed authors and patron suggestions, she knew she needed a moment or two to properly transition from the number side of her brain to the creative side. With any luck, a second call to Leona would do the trick.

She pulled the desk phone within easier reach and punched in the familiar number as her mind raced ahead to all the things she wanted to say.

First, she needed to acknowledge that Leona had, in fact, cared enough about Beatrice to leave a message on Tori's home voice mail.

Second, she wanted to know if anything Margaret Louise or Georgina or any of the rest of their sewing circle members had said the night before had gotten through to Leona on any level.

And finally, if it had, she wanted to know if Leona had called Rose to apologize for her egregious behavior Sunday night . . .

Holding the phone tight to her ear, she silently counted each ring—one, two, three, four, five, six.

No answer.

Disconnecting the line momentarily, Tori, instead, punched in the woman's cell phone in the event she was working at the antique shop or batting her false lashes at every eligible bachelor in town.

Once again, she counted—one, two, three, four, five, six.

This time, Leona's voice traveled through the line, her recorded message dripping with the kind of sex appeal one might expect from a twenty-four-year-old hottie.

"Hello there, you've reached Leona. I'm sorry I missed your call but I'm out enjoying life in the way it's meant to be enjoyed. Leave your name and number and maybe we can enjoy it together for a little while."

Tori rolled her eyes, cleared her throat, and spoke

slowly into the phone. "Leona, it's me, Victoria. I got your message last night about wanting me to call regardless of what time I got back from looking after Beatrice, but you didn't answer. Call me when you get this and I'll fill you in on whatever you want to know."

Setting the phone back on its cradle, Tori allowed the sudden sparkle of her engagement ring to momentarily push all negative thoughts from her head. In eleven days, she would don her wedding dress for real, take her bridal bouquet in her hands, and make her way down the white runner to stand beside Milo and become his wife.

"Milo's wife," she whispered as a smile played across her lips. "Milo's. Wife." Twisting her hand to the left and then the right, she marveled at the way the light caught her diamond.

"It's a pretty ring, that's for sure." Nina took a step into their shared office and then stopped. "And it won't be long before there's another one alongside it."

She pulled her hand back toward her chair and grinned up at her assistant. "Sometimes, I wish the next eleven days would hurry up and go by just so I could look at Milo and say, 'I do.' But then, at other times, I remember all the things still on my list. Like stopping by the jewelry store and picking up the rings, for starters."

"You'll get it done. You always do." Then, sweeping her own hand in the direction from which she'd just come, Nina lowered her voice so as not to be overheard by anyone other than Tori. "Beatrice is up at the information desk and asking to speak with you. She doesn't look good, Victoria. She doesn't look good at all."

Tori shifted her focus to the folder on her left and tried

not to think of the solid hour or so of work it represented—
work she needed to get done before she could even think
about tackling the ever-growing personal list of to-do's
she'd jotted down over breakfast. She was getting married
in eleven days. Not only did she have wedding stuff to
take care of, she also had to make sure all of her *i*'s were
dotted and *t*'s crossed at the library before leaving for her
week-long honeymoon.

But still, it was Beatrice . . .

She tried not to let Nina hear her sigh as she pushed
the folder farther to the side and nodded. "Okay. Send
her back."

"You'll get everything done, Victoria. I know you
will," Nina repeated before she disappeared down the
hallway toward a waiting Beatrice and the library's main
room.

Minutes later, Nina's shy smile and dark hair was replaced
by an even shyer, sadder smile and Beatrice's red-rimmed
eyes. Tori pushed her chair back from the desk and came
around to greet her friend.

"Oh, sweetie, you've been crying again, haven't you?"
She pulled Beatrice in for a hug and did her best to hush
away the sniffles and hiccups the gesture stoked to the
surface once again. "Shh . . . shh . . . I'm here for you,
Beatrice . . . I'm here. I know you're hurting."

Slowly, Beatrice stepped away, wiped her eyes, and
tried to speak. "Miss G-G-Gracie is—is d-dead be-because
of m-me."

Tori gasped. "Because of you? No, no, that's not true,
Beatrice."

"Y-yes it is. She—she c-came be-because of m-me. If
I had not rung her up, she—she would not be d-dead."

"Beatrice, you can't do this to yourself. She came because she *wanted* to come." Wrapping her arm around Beatrice's heaving shoulders, Tori guided the nanny to the folding chair alongside her desk. "No one—not you, not Miss Gracie, not anyone—could have known she'd lose her footing on the stairs. It was an *accident*, Beatrice, a tragic, horrible *accident*."

Cries turned to sobs as Beatrice dropped onto the chair and laid her head atop Tori's desk. "I—I just can't understand why in b-bloody hell she—she fell," Beatrice wailed. "M-Miss Gracie w-was always so—so sturdy . . . so . . . *aware*."

"Accidents happen, Beatrice," she soothed. "Even to people who are sturdy and aware. That's why they're called accidents, sweetie."

"And if it wasn't?" Beatrice asked between sniffles.

She stopped her hand mid–back rub and studied the side of her friend's face. "If it wasn't what?"

Lifting her head from the surface of Tori's desk, Beatrice plucked a tissue from a nearby box and wiped the tears from her cheeks with a hurried hand. "An accident."

"Beatrice, you're not responsible for what happened to Miss Gracie. Sure, you called and told her about the nanny position for the Brady family, but it was ultimately her decision to come and take the position. You didn't force her to say yes. And you're not the one who made her lose her footing on the stairs yesterday evening. It just happened, Beatrice . . . like *accidents* happen."

She watched as Beatrice crumbled the tissue inside her hand and then turned surprisingly dry eyes in Tori's direction. "And if it wasn't an accident?"

It took everything in her power not to throw her hands

up in frustration over her friend's inability to hear her words, but she managed to keep it in check. Beatrice was still in shock, still mourning.

"I know what you're thinking, Victoria, but you're wrong. I know what I'm saying."

Tori took a seat at her desk. "Beatrice, please. None of this is your fault."

Pushing off the chair, Beatrice rose to her feet and wandered over to the window that overlooked the library grounds and their hundred-year-old moss-draped trees. "Miss Gracie came here because of me. There's no rowing about that. But *I'm* not the one responsible for her fall."

Relief pushed a sigh through her lips as she, too, stood. "I'm glad to finally hear you say—"

"Someone else is," Beatrice whispered fiercely.

She forced her jaw back into place and tried to absorb her friend's words. "Wait. What are you saying?"

"I'm saying I need your help, Victoria." Beatrice turned back to Tori, her eyes wide, yet strangely hooded, too.

"My help?" she echoed in confusion. "My help with what?"

"Figuring out who pushed Miss Gracie to her death, and why."

Chapter 7

Try as she might, Tori simply couldn't get Beatrice's words out of her head. She heard them when she was picking through patron suggestion cards and sending e-mails to local authors, she heard them as two more attempts to reach Leona went straight to voice mail, and she heard them as Margaret Louise answered her inquiry about Leona with little more than an audible shrug.

Yet no matter how many times she tried Beatrice's words on for size, they still didn't fit.

Miss Gracie had been at the Bradys' home for just shy of thirty-six hours before her tumble—thirty-six hours that had been spent with three children under the age of nine. Unless one of them was a psychopath in training, the notion that someone had pushed the British nanny to her death was nothing short of preposterous.

Then again, grief had a way of playing tricks on a

person's mind and heart. She knew that as well as anyone every time Rose entered a room and Tori thought, for a split second, it was her great-grandmother.

Sometimes, the heart just didn't want to accept what the mind knew. People on the outside looking in would say her deceased great-grandmother bore absolutely no resemblance to the sewing circle's matriarch and they'd be right. But her heart said something completely different, time and time again.

It was why she'd resisted the knee-jerk urge to wave aside Beatrice's version of Miss Gracie's fall. Instead, knowing what the nanny was going through, she simply insisted Beatrice go home and get some sleep. Arguing with the heart didn't do any good until the heart was better prepared to listen.

Pulling the key from the library's back door, Tori dropped it into her bag and reveled in the feel of the fading sun on the back of her neck. The workday was finally over. At times, she hadn't been sure it would ever happen, but thankfully, mercifully, it had.

Nina, of course, had been a godsend, her expertise with the patrons and the daily closing procedures making it so Tori could finalize the program calendar and attend to a few of the pre-honeymoon tasks that had to be done before it was time to call it quits for the day. Now, as she headed down the library's back steps and toward Main Street, Tori could put aside all thoughts of the upcoming board meeting and concentrate on her wedding list.

She headed east toward the town square and the handful of shop windows that were still lit despite the six o'clock hour. The pull to veer toward the south for a hot chocolate and a brownie was at moments overwhelming in light of her missed lunch, but still, she pressed on, the notion of securing the rings that would signal her marriage to Milo adding purpose to her gait.

Shop by shop, she made her way toward the silver-rimmed sign at the end of the block, each store that she passed earning little more than a passing glance—Calamity Books, Bud's Brew Shack, Shelby's Sweet Shoppe, Elkin Antiques, and—

She paused for a moment outside Leona's antique and collectible shop and peered through the glass, the darkened interior all but confirming what she knew to be true based on the hour anyway.

If Leona had gone into the shop at all that day, she, along with her slate of employees, had hightailed it home for dinner. Why she wasn't returning Tori's call, though, was the real question. Especially when it was Leona who had reached out first.

Digging into her bag, she fished her cell phone from its depths and checked the screen for a missed call icon.

No, it was official. Leona was dodging her calls.

She shook her head and resumed her journey, the remaining shops still standing between her and her destination disappearing rapidly. Her offer to pick up her ring at the same time as Milo's had been debated at first, but in the end, Milo had seen the benefit. He, too, had a list of tasks to get through before the big day, and anything that could be crossed off easily was a good thing.

The front door of Brady's Jewelry opened and closed, spitting out a man in his mid to late forties with a mile-wide smile on his face. His euphoric expression told her he'd been shopping for someone special, while the silver and lavender bag in his hand told her he'd met with success.

"Good evening," he said, tipping his head ever so slightly.

"Good evening." She took the last two steps quickly and pulled open the shop's door, the jingle overhead greeting her at the same time as the clerk behind the counter.

"Welcome to Brady's Jewelry, my name is Ryan and I'm happy to assist you in any way I can. And if you're so inclined to drop a comment card about my friendly service in that drop box by the door when we're done, I'd be most appreciative."

She returned the clerk's smile with one of her own and stepped over to the counter. "I'm Victoria Sinclair. I'm here to pick up a pair of wedding rings my fiancé and I purchased a few weeks ago. You engraved them for us."

"Sinclair . . . Sinclair . . ." he repeated beneath his breath as he unlocked and opened a drawer just out of her line of vision.

"Actually," she corrected herself, "they could be under Wentworth, too." Hiking her bag onto the glass-topped counter, she reached inside and pulled out the receipt. A quick look at the handwritten portion confirmed her change. "Yes, it's under my fiancé's name, Wentworth."

His fingers moved farther back in the drawer to the index tab reserved for names that began with *W*. Seconds later he pulled out a small lavender and silver envelope. "Here we go."

She swapped the receipt for the envelope and slid her index finger underneath its seal, the excitement over its contents making her trembling hands virtually useless. "It's really happening, isn't it?"

Ryan smiled. "If you're buying rings, then yes it is. Congratulations." He took the envelope back and gently poured the rings into his hand, holding out the smaller one for her inspection. "I think it's safe to say this one is yours? Would you like to try it on and make sure it fits?"

She extended her ring finger toward the man and then pulled it back, shaking her head as she did. "Actually, I know it fits and I want my fiancé to be the one who puts it on my finger next."

"Would you like to see the inscription?"

Again, she shook her head. "Would you please check it to make sure it says whatever he requested? I'd rather wait until the wedding to see it for myself."

"Of course. I'd be happy to." Ryan looked from the paperwork to the ring and back again, slowly nodding as he did. "Yep, it says exactly what it's supposed to say."

She picked up Milo's ring and took a peek inside the band, the simple yet powerful inscription intensifying her excitement. "As does this one. Whoever did this did a great job."

"That's our goal. Now, normally I wouldn't let you leave until Mr. Brady had a chance to come out and thank you for your business himself, but he didn't come in today." Taking Milo's ring from her outstretched hand, he placed it on the counter alongside Tori's and then set about the task of polishing away any fingerprints before transferring them to the velvet-lined ring boxes he secured from a nearby cabinet. "There was an accident at his home shortly after we closed last night and he hasn't been back since."

"Oh, I'm sorry to hear that. I hope Mr. Brady and his family are . . ." The words trailed from her mouth as the name, coupled with Ryan's comment, came together in one clarifying instant. "Wait. The Brady of Brady's Jewelry is the same as the family whose nanny just died?"

Ryan placed the boxes inside a shiny silver bag and slid it across the counter toward Tori. "His *new* nanny, yes. She lost her footing and fell down a flight of steps, which seems kind of ironic if you ask me."

"Ironic?" she repeated, her curiosity aroused.

"The whole reason Mr. Brady shipped this new nanny across the ocean was because his wife insisted they needed someone more responsible, more aware. Yet it's this new one who falls down something as routine as a flight of stairs. If you ask me, it doesn't sound like bucking tradition and securing a nanny outside of this area worked all that well for them."

She wrapped her fingers around the handle of the bag yet left it in place as she digested his words against the backdrop of limited information she knew about Miss Gracie's predecessor. "The previous nanny was Cynthia, right? Cynthia . . . Martin?"

"Marland," Ryan corrected. "Yeah . . . why? Did you know Cindy?"

Something about the flash of surprise in the clerk's eyes made her wish Beatrice and Luke had lingered at the playground Saturday evening rather than rushing back home to play ship. If they had, she might be able to throw out a few more facts that made her sound as if she were more in the know than she really was. Yet as she noted the ongoing energy shift in the clerk, she realized she didn't really need more details.

Those, she could find on her own from a young man who obviously knew more about his employer's nanny than just her name and the reasons behind her job loss . . .

"I saw her the other night at the park." She stopped, took a deep breath, and hoped her blabbering sounded

even semi-intelligent. The fact that she was taking liber-
ties with the truth, however, certainly called for a little
self-examination in the very near future. "She seemed . . .
upset. Maybe even a little mad."

Ryan stopped wiping down the counter long enough
to offer a show of solidarity for Cynthia Marland.
"Wouldn't *you* be mad if you were removed from your
job because the people around you believed the sky was
falling when it wasn't?"

"You think she was a good nanny?" she asked.

"She was never late, and she never left before the parents were home." Ryan returned to his task, wiping at a
particularly stubborn fingerprint with a vengeance. "She
made sure they ate, too. Beyond that, what else is there?"

"Making sure they're safe at all times, for one."

"Cindy did pretty good at that. Forgetting to tell the
one kid's school about her seizure meds could've happened to anyone if you think about it."

Not someone hired specifically to take care of a child's
every needs, she thought. To Ryan, though, she merely
nodded and hoped the simple gesture came across as
commiseration for Cynthia's plight. "You two are friends,
I take it."

"We date from time to time." With the last of the fingerprints finally off the glass countertop, Ryan tossed the
cloth into a box behind his feet and eyed the clock above
the door, his sales floor smile morphing into one befitting
someone who was ten minutes away from bidding his
workday good-bye.

"Was she angry when the Bradys let her go?"

"She was livid. In fact, when she called to tell me, she
cursed so much one of my friends—who could hear her

on the phone with me from the opposite side of my living room—asked if I could find a truck driver for him to date, too." Ryan laughed at the memory and then scooted Tori's bag to the edge of the counter in preparation for the shop's pending closure. "But then, when she was still harping on it a week later with every bit as much intensity, he told me not to bother."

"She was that angry, huh?" She didn't bother to see if he nodded, her mind already on to the next question her mouth was reluctant to utter. Instead, she went for a more mundane way of getting the kind of information that could prove useful in regards to Beatrice's claim. "Why didn't she just get another nanny job?"

"This is Sweet Briar we're talking about, yes? There's only so many families looking for nannies at any given time. Add in the fact that my boss's wife was telling everyone in her circle that Cindy was inept, and you can understand the problem."

"That makes sense, I guess." Gathering her bag and her purse together, she backed away from the counter, her desire to learn more about the Bradys' former nanny losing out over the pull to get home and check in on Rose, Beatrice, and even Leona. "I imagine you want to get home so I better head out. Thanks for your help with the rings. They look great."

He reached underneath the counter, extracted a slip of paper, and slid it—along with a pencil—in Tori's direction. "If you wouldn't mind, I'm kind of hoping a few of these in the box might convince Mr. Brady to give me a raise."

She retrieved the pencil from atop the paper, checked off the appropriate boxes for the service Ryan had provided, folded it in two, and then carried it over to the box beside the shop's front door. "Good luck with your raise, I hope you get it."

"So do I." His smile stretched wide across his narrow face as she pushed the comment card through the narrow opening on the top of the box and yanked the door open. "Good luck with the wedding, I hope you and your lucky guy are real happy together."

"We are." Stepping onto the top step, she glanced back over her shoulder as Ryan came around the counter to lock the door in her wake. "And I hope your sometimes girlfriend finds a job again real soon."

"If she lays low and lets the talk die out, she'll be fine."

Chapter 8

She hadn't planned to stop at Debbie's Bakery before heading home, but knowing Milo was tied up at a school board meeting for most of the evening made the pull of her fellow sewing circle sister's baked treats even more overpowering than normal. The fact that she could sit down and relax for the first time all day while eating that baked treat made the decision to stop a veritable no-brainer.

Now all she had to do was pick what she wanted . . .

A salted caramel brownie?

A giant chocolate chip cookie?

A peanut butter and chocolate tartlet?

A white chocolate mousse pastry puff?

A piece of caramel drizzled cheese—

"You could always have one of each, Victoria. I won't tell."

She looked up from her love affair with the bakery case to find Debbie Calhoun eyeing her with naked amusement. "And even if you didn't, everyone would know because I'd be dead."

"I think I should be offended by that, don't you, Emma?" Debbie nudged her chin in the direction of the college-aged girl who ran the register at the bakery most days.

Emma grinned and nodded. "It sure sounds like someone is doubting your baking ability, boss."

Tori shot her hands up in the air and waved them from side to side. "Wait. You misunderstand the reason for my death."

Debbie's left brow lifted nearly to her hairline. "Oh?"

"If I ate one of everything in this case," she said, pointing, "Rose would kill me."

"Rose? Why?"

"Because I wouldn't be able to fit into that gorgeous wedding dress she spent the past six months making for me . . ." She glanced back down at the case and pointed at the top treat on the left. "I'll take a salted caramel brownie and a promise of baker-client confidentiality while I'm at it."

"You got it." Emma slid open the case and reached inside for the largest of the six brownies. With expert hands, she placed it smack dab in the middle of a doily-draped plate and set it on the counter beside the register. "Would you like a drink to go with that?"

"She'll take a hot chocolate with extra whipped cream," Debbie interjected with nary a look over her shoulder as she set about preparing the drink. "And they're both on the house."

"Debbie, please, you don't have to do that."

"I know I don't, but after taking care of Beatrice the

way you did last night, I *want* to." The bakery owner held the powder blue ceramic mug under the milk steamer and gestured toward the seating area with her chin. "Why don't you take your brownie and I'll join you with your drink as soon as I'm done."

"Sounds good." Holding an index finger to her lips for Emma to see, Tori plucked a five-dollar bill from her already-open wallet and stuck it in the tip jar beside the register. When the money was safely inside with Debbie none the wiser, she liberated her plate from the counter and carried it across the room to the quaint seating area on the other side.

As the only person in the bakery at the moment, Tori had her pick of tables, and as was usually the case, she gravitated toward the four-top closest to the front window. There, she could enjoy Debbie's sinful creations while reading, chatting with friends, or watching the comings and goings of her Sweet Briar neighbors.

She had just settled herself, her phone, and her brownie at the table when Debbie slid into the opposite chair. "A hot chocolate for you . . . and a much-needed coffee for me."

Reaching for her cup, Tori narrowed her eyes on her friend. "I'm surprised you're here at this time. I thought you always left the dinner hour to Emma so you could go home and eat with Colby and the kids."

"I do. But Colby took the kids to Tom's Creek to catch a fellow author's talk at one of the independent bookstores. I thought about going with them but decided I'd use the opportunity to get some work done so I can spend more time at home tomorrow afternoon and evening." Debbie propped her elbows on the edge of the table and wrapped her hands around her own mug, her eyes nearly rolling back in her head as she did. "I've been working the books all afternoon and I can't tell you how good it is to sit down."

"Actually you can," Tori muttered. "The library board meets on Thursday night so I spent my whole afternoon doing the same thing."

Debbie scooted her drink into the middle of the table and then lifted it into the air. "Then to us! And a well-deserved break."

"To us." Tori lowered her hot chocolate enough to take a sip and then still farther until it was back on the table next to her brownie. "Have you, by any chance, talked to Leona since the meeting last night?"

A cloud of something resembling disgust rolled across the thirty-something's normally cheerful features just before the grunt that preceded her verbal answer. "No. And I don't intend to. What she did to Rose on that TV show of hers Sunday night is unforgivable."

It was hard to argue against Debbie's words, even harder to entertain the notion of defending Leona, but Margaret Louise's twin was their friend, too, prickly exterior and all. "I agree, and I think, on some level, even *Leona* knows she was out of line."

"I don't know how you can say that when she was as belligerent as she was at our sewing circle meeting."

Tori closed her eyes briefly against the memory of Leona, hands on hips, facing down her accusers the previous night, her initial confusion over the planned attack quickly giving way to a defiance that hadn't helped her case in the slightest.

"That woman is mean ninety-nine percent of the time, Victoria, and she seems almost proud of that fact."

There was a part of her that knew Debbie's description of Leona wasn't far from the truth. After all, Leona's claws came out often. But there was also the part of her that had seen glimpses of a very different Leona throughout the past two-plus years. It was *that* Leona she adored, and *that* Leona she simply had to try and defend . . .

"She left a message on my answering machine last night. She wanted to check in and see how Beatrice was doing." She knew it sounded lame in light of the horrific humiliation Leona had inflicted on Rose, but at least it was something. And if need be, she could always remind Debbie of the baby rabbit Leona had bestowed on Rose the previous year. The gift of Paris's unexpected offspring surely had to count for something, didn't it?

"She left a message? Well, whoop-de-do." Debbie reached behind her head, pulled the ponytail tie from her hair, and let her dark blonde hair rain down over her back for just a moment before gathering it into its previous hairstyle once again. "And I suppose, when you called her back, she spent a nanosecond listening to your update on Beatrice and the rest of the time talking about her manicure, her clothes, her latest date, and the shortcomings of everyone in Sweet Briar except, of course, her own."

It was the first time since Tori had moved to Sweet Briar and met Debbie Calhoun that she'd ever seen the woman truly angry about something. She'd seen her friend upset and scared during that time, but angry to the point of making her pale blue eyes dark as night? Never.

"Actually," she half whispered, half mumbled, "she didn't answer when I returned her call—last night or either of the times I tried today."

Debbie shook her head as her previous grunt returned

with a more snortlike edge. "So what you're saying is Beatrice didn't even *get* her nanosecond. Hmmm, how very caring of Leona."

"I don't know, Debbie. Maybe something came up with Annabelle."

"If Margaret Louise's mother was ill, I'd know." Debbie took another sip of her coffee and then gently swirled the remaining liquid around inside the mug. "No, Leona is doing exactly what Leona always does, which is why I'd much rather talk about someone who has earned our concern by being an absolute sweetheart since the moment she arrived in this town. So how *is* Beatrice?"

Beatrice . . .

Oh, how she wanted to keep the subject on Leona in an effort to find a way to undo some of the damage the self-proclaimed hottie had brought down on herself, but it was no use. Debbie and the rest of the circle would need proof of Leona's goodness from Leona herself. When that would happen was as much Tori's guess as anyone else's.

"I tried to call her once this afternoon, but her line was busy."

She forced herself to focus on the conversation that was happening rather than the one that wasn't long enough to acknowledge Debbie's statement. "Depending on when you tried to reach her, that busy signal may have been during one of the times she called me."

"Is she holding up okay, the poor thing?" Debbie pointed at the untouched brownie on Tori's plate and made a face. "You can eat and talk at the same time, you know."

Suddenly, the caramel drizzle that graced the delectable-looking brownie wasn't cutting it for her anymore. In fact, the gurgling in her stomach that had propelled her to stop at Debbie's in the first place was now absolutely silent. Still, Tori took a bite if for no other reason than to keep from hurting Debbie's feelings. When she was done chewing, she posed a question of her own. "Have you heard anything about Miss Gracie's fall around town this morning? Anything that might give a clearer picture as to how it happened? Chief Dallas didn't have much to say other than she fell."

Debbie glanced around the empty seating area and then back at Tori, her shoulders pitching forward across the table as she did. "I ran into someone at the school this morning who was there when it happened. She's the mother of one of Jackson's classmates."

"She was there?"

A quick nod gave way to more information. "It seems Julie Brady had a pot luck dinner with a few women—mostly moms of kids in Reenie's and Kellie's classes. Wealthy moms like herself who employ nannies to look after their children. Anyway, from what I heard, Julie was gushing about Miss Gracie and how she was amazing with all three girls . . . attentive, encouraging, gentle, you name it. By the time she was done, Julie was giving out the phone number of the agency in England where Beatrice and Miss Gracie were both found. And she did this with some of their current nannies, and her sister-in-law, in the next room!"

Tori stopped picking at her brownie and met Debbie's wide eyes with her own narrowed ones. "I don't understand."

"The kids of these women were there, too. In the playroom with Julie's kids. Of course, their assorted nannies were there, too." Debbie flung herself back against her chair and sighed. "Can you imagine being there—doing your job—and hearing your employer discussing the many benefits of hiring someone else for your position? Even if you have to know you're not very good?"

"Not very good?"

"This is Sweet Briar, South Carolina, Victoria. Most of the really good nannies want to work in New York City or L.A., and for one of the reputable agencies that can get them those assignments. The ones that stay here and work out of the Nanny Go Round Agency really have no aspirations beyond the paycheck and a chance to hobnob with some of Sweet Briar's more well-to-do families."

She tucked the information aside and brought the conversation back to the previous night's tragedy itself. "Do you know why Miss Gracie was going down to the basement during all of this?"

Debbie stopped mid-shrug to smile at a customer who came into the shop with a gaggle of kids. To Tori, she said, "Oh, this is going to be a big order. I probably better go help Emma. Maybe we can chat more later if you're still here when they're done?"

She looked from her near-empty mug, to her half-eaten brownie, to her still silent phone and shook her head. "Actually, I better be wrapping this up. I've got one more stop to make before I head home for the night."

"Does this stop happen to include a handsome third grade teacher who is just eleven days away from marrying one of my best friends?" Debbie teased.

Slipping her phone back into her purse, and the last bite or two of brownie into her mouth, Tori stood and brushed a parting kiss across Debbie's cheek. "If only I could say it did."

Chapter 9

"One . . . two . . . three . . . four . . . *Leona*," Tori
said as she pulled to a stop outside the condo Leona shared
with her long-eared, nose-twitching daughter, Paris. Like
the four units to its right, and the single unit to its left, the
brick face of Leona's building was a ruddy red color with
wide steps leading to the half-glass/half-mahogany front
door.

Tori knew the interior layout well, including the narrow staircase that had all but sealed the fate on Leona's
decision to take in her aging mother. Yet the fact that the
sewing circle's current arch enemy had even offered had
to say something about Leona's underlying spirit, didn't it?

"Stop it, Tori," she mumbled. "Stop trying to plead
Leona's case. She got herself into this mess and it's her
job to get herself out."

It was the same mantra she'd told herself throughout

the day as call after call went unanswered, and neither Margaret Louise nor Debbie seemed to care. Still, her heart was having a difficult time getting in sync with her brain. After all, she knew there were good sides to Leona—special sides that made her worthy of a second chance and the nagging sensation that something wasn't right.

Sliding her hand forward, she slipped the gear shift into park and contemplated her next move.

If she knocked on the door and out and out told Leona she was worried about her, Leona might get the mixed message that what she did to Rose on Sunday night was somehow okay. And it wasn't. Not by a long shot.

Then there was the reward for bad behavior aspect. Leona had been nasty, plain and simple. It was why Dixie, Georgina, Debbie, and Leona's own sister, Margaret Louise, had all but shunned her the previous evening. Would stopping by to make sure she was okay be akin to Tori undermining her sewing sisters' clear and concise message that nastiness would no longer be tolerated?

Conflicted, she let her gaze travel up the partially lit exterior steps to Leona's front stoop and the morning newspaper that sat, untouched, outside the woman's front door. Something inside her gut twisted ever so slightly and she reached for the handle of the driver's side door, only to let her arm drop back down.

No. She knew the game Leona was playing and she refused to indulge the attention-monger.

When Leona finally admitted she'd been cruel, apologized to Rose, and cared enough about Beatrice to actually *hear* whether she was okay or not, they would speak again. Until then, Tori would focus on Milo and her

wedding and the friends in her life that treated one
another with respect and kindness.

Her mind made up, she placed her foot on the gas and
headed toward the next and final stop on her list.

Block by block she made her way across a darkening
Sweet Briar. Streetlights clicked on, porch lights shone
brightly, and streets cleared of playing children as another
day bowed to the promise of a new one.

At the entrance to one of the town's older neighbor-
hoods, she turned left and then right, slowing the car to
a crawl as she reached her final destination. Like so many
of its immediate counterparts, Rose's home was small—
maybe twelve hundred square feet, but the second-to-none
landscaping attended to by the eighty-something woman
herself made it the most enviable place on the block.

The hint of light on the other side of the living room
drapes told her what she needed to know: Rose was
awake. Or at the very least, propped up in a chair in front
of the television dozing.

This time, when she slid the car into park, she followed
it up by cutting the engine and stepping out onto the road.
The promise of some alone-time with the woman who'd
become like a surrogate great-grandmother helped
quicken her steps all the way onto the porch and over to
the front door.

Rose answered on the fourth knock.

"Good heavens, Victoria, how many times do I have
to tell you you don't have to knock?"

She stepped into the house and turned to match the
elderly woman's reprimand with one of her own. "Probably as many times as I remind you to lock your door
whether you're awake or not."

"That door hasn't been locked in the sixty years I've owned this place and I'm not about to start locking it now." Rose leaned her tired body forward, planted a kiss on Tori's cheek, and then shooed her into the tiny living room. "So did you get the wedding rings?"

"I did." Tori crossed the carpet that separated Rose's favorite chair from the love seat on the other side and sat down. "They're out in the car."

"Which is locked, I hope." Without waiting for a reply, Rose moved on, her words bringing Tori's mental checklist into the foreground. "And the minister? He's all set for the big day?"

"I'll check in with him tomorrow. I'm taking the morning off to go through as many things on my list as I can."

Rose lowered herself onto her chair, wincing as she did. "You'll get it all done, I'm sure."

"Rose? Are you okay?" she asked as the woman's eyes closed tightly for the briefest of moments. "Is something hurting?"

Slowly, Rose opened her eyes and focused on Tori with a sadness that was impossible to miss. "That question implies there are things that don't."

In a flash, Tori was off the love seat and crouching beside Rose, her hand finding her friend's and holding it tight. "Is there anything I can do? Do you want me to get you your medicine? Or some hot tea?"

Rose returned the squeeze and then released it long enough to wave the questions and their accompanying worry aside. "You can visit with me like you came to do. And hear me out about this ridiculous business of me being in your bridal party."

"You're in my bridal party, Rose." She took a moment

to study the soft wrinkles that lined the woman's face, the lifetime of joy and anguish that had created them not much different than the highways and byways that came together to make up a treasured road map. "I wouldn't want it any other way."

Silence fell around them as Rose dropped her focus to the afghan she'd tucked across her lap within seconds of sitting down. "But fifty years from now, when you look back at your album with Milo, I don't want to be the one who stands out for looking ridiculous."

"Rose," Tori said, swallowing over the lump created by her friend's words, "fifty years from now, when I look at my wedding album, you will stand out. Of that, I have no doubt. But it won't be for something as absurd as you looking ridiculous. It'll be because of how truly special you were to me, and how incredibly blessed I was to have you in my life."

A single tear from each eye made its way halfway down Rose's pale cheeks before being wiped away by a trembling hand. "I don't want to throw off the look of your wedding. I—I'm too old and hunched over to be anything more than the old woman seated in the front row—the one who doesn't get the concept of a mirror."

"The one who doesn't get the concept of a mirror?" Tori echoed. "Wait. That's what Leona said the other night on that stupid show of hers, isn't it?"

Rose's silence was all the answer she needed.

Rising to her feet, Tori began to pace around the room, five strides one way, five strides the other. "So many times I've heard everyone comment on how mean-spirited Leona can be, and sure, I saw it at times. I tried to push that aside and instead focus on the *good* she did. But just because she gave you a bunny and me a sewing box that reminded me of my great-grandmother doesn't really change her heart, does it?"

Rose stamped her foot on the ground then pinned Tori with a stare. "That woman may have a fuzzy knowledge of what love is, Victoria, but she loves you every bit as much as she loves Paris."

Heat rose up Tori's neck and into her face as she sank onto the love seat once again. "I can't believe you're defending her after what she did to you the other night."

"That betrayal she experienced at the hands of her best friend and her fiancé shortly after college hurt her deeply. I have no doubt that experience is responsible for so much of the Leona we see now—the one who pushes people away with her words and her actions."

Oh, how she wanted to believe Rose, to finally have what she needed to justify her lingering warm feelings for Leona, but—

"What she said about you the other night was awful. There's no way you can tie that to a forty-year-old hurt."

"You don't think so?" Rose challenged. "All Leona wanted back then was to marry the love of her life, with her best friend looking on. It didn't happen. Now, it's happening for the one person who sees something good inside her. She can't lash out at you, so she lashes out at the easiest target she can find."

"With the easiest target being you, I take it?"

"Of course. There's no way on God's green earth I'll ever be able to show her up. I'm too old, too wrinkled, too tired." Rose shifted in her chair and then leaned her head against its upholstered headrest. "Oh I'll give her what-for when I can, but in the end, we all know she's right. I *am* an old goat. I *am* fashion-challenged. And I *don't* consult a mirror."

She tried not to laugh, but it was hard. Here was this woman who'd been on the very public receiving end of Leona's meanness, pleading Leona's case. From anyone other than Rose, it would be impossible to comprehend.

"You are amazing, Rose Winters. You really are," Tori mused. "And *that* is why you will put on that gorgeous Harvest Wheat–colored dress with your silver flats and stand beside me as my matron of honor when I marry the love of my life in eleven days."

Rose rolled her eyes skyward, releasing an exhausted sigh as she did. "That woman is right, you know. You don't listen." Then, with a pained shrug of her frail shoulders, she moved on, all talk of Leona now in her rearview mirror. "Now tell me about Beatrice. Margaret Louise told me what happened to her governess and that you drove her home after the meeting. How is she holding up?"

"She is beside herself with grief . . . and guilt."

"Guilt?" Rose repeated. "What on earth does that one have to be guilty about besides being too much of a doormat?"

For the first time since arriving, Tori allowed herself to relax, going so far as to kick off her shoes and pull her stocking-clad feet up and onto the comfy cushion. "She keeps saying Miss Gracie wouldn't have come if it wasn't for her."

"And maybe that's true. But that doesn't mean she's responsible for the woman losing her footing and tumbling to her death."

She grabbed one of the throw pillows from the far end of the love seat and pulled it against her chest as she compared Rose's words against the ones she herself had shared with Beatrice. "And I told her that. But now all she keeps saying is that Miss Gracie didn't lose her footing."

"She fell, didn't she?" Rose snapped.

"That's the version the police have given, yes." Resting her chin against the top edge of the pillow, she allowed herself to close her own eyes for just a moment. "But Beatrice isn't buying that version."

"What other version is there?"

She opened her mouth to share the ludicrous notion Beatrice had dropped on her earlier that day, but something inside her made her stop.

Cynthia Marland staring at Beatrice and Luke across a playground . . .

Cynthia Marland's inability to find another job in Sweet Briar for the time being . . .

Could Beatrice be right?

"What other version is there?" Rose asked a second time.

"Beatrice's version," Tori finally answered. "The one that has Miss Gracie being *pushed* to her death."

Chapter 10

Tori stopped at the base of the church steps, pulled her leather-bound planner from her purse, and flipped it open to the list of items she needed to check off before relieving Nina in time for lunch.

Pastor Watkins was all set for the wedding with the lone exception of the vows she and Milo pledged to have in the man's hands by the end of the week. Hers were almost done, save for a few final tweaks. They'd been both easy and hard to write—easy, because her feelings for Milo ran deep, but hard, too, because she wanted to word everything just right. He deserved that.

Uncapping her pen with her teeth, she made a check next to *pastor* before skimming her way down the rest of her list for that morning.

Check in with Margaret Louise about favors.

Check in with Dixie about reading.

Get miniature pillow to Leona.

Go over parking for reception with Georgina.

She glanced at her wristwatch and noted the time—the post-breakfast hour—and the fact that it was a Wednesday, making it entirely possible she could kill all four birds with one stone. Her mind made up, she recapped her pen, slipped it into her purse along with her notebook, and headed toward the once-a-month Super Seniors meeting at Johnson's Diner.

At the end of the block, she turned left, and then right, Waters Hardware and Southern Style Gifts melding into each other as she nodded a greeting to several familiar faces along her route. When she finally reached the diner, she was more than relieved to recognize the powder blue station wagon parked beneath a weeping willow tree on the south side of the lot. If nothing else, Margaret Louise was still inside.

She took the steps at a rapid pace, stepping aside as she reached the front door to allow a threesome of white-haired residents to exit the diner, the smiles on their faces proof that getting out among peers was good for the soul no matter what the age. And when she heard the laughter as she finally made her way inside, she couldn't help but wish, if only for a moment, that she, too, could be a part of the group.

"Well, would you look who's here," bellowed a familiar voice just beyond the half wall that separated the waiting area from the dining room. "Why, it's Victoria, 'bout thirty years early, but no less welcome!"

Waving at her polyester-clad friend, Tori made her way over to the table that stretched across the center of the room. She bent down, kissed the top of Margaret Louise's head, and then nodded at the latest addition to the woman's sweat suit collection. "New color?"

The grandmother of eight beamed. "It was a birthday present from my grandbabies. They took a vote and it was six to two in favor of navy with a hot pink pinstripe."

"Suggested, no doubt, by Lulu," Tori guessed as an image of Margaret Louise's now-eleven-year-old granddaughter flashed before her eyes.

Dixie, who was seated on the opposite side of the table, twisted her mouth around for a moment. "You expect us to believe that the baby voted, too?"

"He did. Jake Junior said so." Margaret Louise peered down at her outfit then back up at Tori. "They put three colors in front of him and waited for him to touch one with his little hand. Course, when Matthew touched this one, he got it wet with drool, but that's no bother. Makes it extra special that way."

"Yes it does." Tori gestured toward the empty seats at her friends' end of the table. "Is it safe to say your meeting is all but wrapping up?"

Dixie nodded then patted the empty spot at the end. "Is everything okay at the library?"

"Everything is fine. Nina is holding down the fort for me until lunch so I can get a few more things done before the wedding."

"Ten more days, can you believe it?" Dixie mused softly. "Sometimes it seems you just got here, Victoria."

She waited for the inevitable reminder that her arrival
in Sweet Briar had signified the end of Dixie's forty-plus
year reign as head librarian, but it didn't come. Instead,
Dixie continued on, a hint of moisture in the corners of her
eyes. "And now, you're set to marry Milo Wentworth."

"I hope you're jotting this down, Margaret Louise."
Georgina scooted her own chair closer to their end of the
table. "Because a moment like this really should be docu-
mented for posterity."

"A moment like what?" Dixie snapped.

"I reckon Georgina is referrin' to you not remindin'
Victoria that she stole your job out from under you like
you've been remindin' her 'n everybody else ever since."

Dixie's eyes widened behind her bifocals only to disappear behind her palms. "Have I been that bad?"

"Yes," Georgina and Margaret Louise chorused.

Tori reached across the corner of the table and gently
squeezed Dixie's upper arm. "Dixie, that's all water under
the bridge. Has been for a long time. You know that."

"We're just ribbin' you, Dixie." Margaret Louise
leaned back in her chair and folded her arms across her
ample chest. "So what brings a youngin' like you to a
meetin' like this, Victoria?"

Dixie's hands slowly lowered to the table as she turned
her still red face toward Tori. "I've narrowed my selection
of poems down to two. I'll know which one I'm going to
read at the wedding by the weekend."

Tori hiked her purse onto her lap and fished out her
notebook and pen once again. Flipping it open to the
correct page, she moved the pen down to the appropriate
line and placed a check to its left. "You don't have to tell
me at all if you don't want to. Just make sure to get the

title and author of the one you select to Nina by Sunday. She and Duwayne need it to finalize the wedding booklet for the church service."

"I'd like that," Dixie whispered. "That way it can be a surprise for you and Milo on your special day."

"We'd like that, too." Tori took in her list and moved on to Georgina. "Will parking be a problem with your neighbors? I can't imagine they'll be all too excited about having as many as six dozen cars lining their street."

"They could always call the mayor and complain," Margaret Louise quipped, clearly pleased with her joke. "Oh. Wait. You *are* the mayor, ain't you, Georgina?"

Georgina waved aside Tori's worry with a quick hand. "I've already talked with my neighbors. What cars don't fit on my own circular drive will be parked in my next-door neighbor's driveway while they're on a cruise."

Hijacking Tori's pen from the table, Dixie leaned over and placed a check next to that item. "There. That's one more thing done." Then, pointing at Margaret Louise, Dixie added, "We've only got about another twenty or so favor bags to go, right?"

"Lulu just did three more last night, so I think we're down to sixteen if my count is correct." Margaret Louise tapped her chin with her forefinger and then nodded. "Yep, sixteen to go. I imagine we'll have 'em done by Friday."

Dixie placed a check next to that line, too, then shoved the notebook away with a look of disgust. "Frankly, if it were *my* wedding, I'd un-invite that one. She doesn't deserve to come as far as I'm concerned."

Margaret Louise sat up tall, pulling the notebook into view, her face falling with a mixture of disdain and sadness in short order. "I wish I could argue with Dixie, but I can't. Not after what she did to Rose."

"I haven't laid eyes on her since our circle meeting on Monday night and I can't say I'm sad about that." Georgina fidgeted with the rim of the straw hat she'd draped across her lap, the snarl she wore across her mouth evident in her voice as well. "The fact that she could sit there and act as if she did nothing wrong just blows my mind clear out of my head. I mean, I know she didn't learn that kind of meanness from Annabelle."

"She sure didn't," Margaret Louise mumbled. "And she didn't learn it from Daddy, either. Though lookin' back, I s'pose the way he spoiled her has somethin' to do with all her struttin'."

It pained Tori to hear them talk about Leona with such disgust, it really did. Because as wrong as she knew the woman had been, she also knew Leona had a good heart, too.

"So nobody has talked to her since the other night at your house, Georgina?" she asked.

All three heads shook side to side in unison. After a moment, Margaret Louise looked up and pinned Tori with a tired stare. "I take it you haven't, either?"

"I've tried to. Several times. But she hasn't answered any of my calls."

Georgina harrumphed.

"Why bother trying? She doesn't deserve a friend like you . . . or any of us, for that matter," Dixie declared. Then, softening her tone, she offered an apologetic shrug in Margaret Louise's direction. "I swear, Margaret Louise, I don't know how on earth the two of you could have been born from the same parents, let alone on the same day. You two are as different as night and day—the nice, kind twin, and the mean, evil one."

Her heart ached for the heavyset woman with the heart of gold. Sure, Margaret Louise knew her sister was flawed, but flawed or not, Leona was still her sister.

"Those calls I've been trying to make to Leona?" she said to Dixie and Georgina, while looking at Margaret Louise. "They're because she called me to inquire about Beatrice. And she made that call because she *does* care."

"She cares?" Dixie echoed. "Oh, please."

Tori grabbed the notebook from the table, closed it, and stuffed it back into her purse. "Look, I won't argue that what she did to Rose on her show Sunday night was wrong. And deep down inside, I think she knows it was wrong, too. But I'll tell you this much: If Rose can see past the infraction to the hurting soul behind it, I think we should be able to try and do the same."

When they said nothing, she added, "There's some good in Leona, too, you know."

"Good that's becoming harder and harder to find, if you ask me." Dixie drummed her fingers atop the table and then pointed at Tori's bag. "So do you have the pillow in there?"

"I do."

"Can we see it?"

For a moment, she considered saying no. After all, there had been enough Leona bashing for one day. But finally, she reached into her bag once again and pulled out the small satin and lace pillow she'd made for Paris and held it out for her friends to see. "See the two ties on top? Those will hold our rings in place. The larger tie on the bottom will secure around Paris's neck."

"I still can't believe you're actually going to let that woman's bunny rabbit be your ring bearer," Georgina said. "Excuse me, let me rephrase. I can't believe you're actually going to let that woman's bunny be your ring *girl*."

Tori held the pillow out for an extra second or two, and then, when she was sure Margaret Louise and Dixie had seen it, too, she plopped it back into her bag and stood. "Paris has been part of our group since not long after I came. And believe it or not, Leona has been a big part of my life here in Sweet Briar. It seems only right that both she and Paris are a part of Milo's and my day."

Tori was nearly to the road when Margaret Louise caught up, her labored huffing and puffing nearly drowning out her pleas for Tori to wait.

"Margaret Louise?" she asked. "Are you okay?"

"I—I'm . . . fine . . . you just walk fast . . . is all." The woman leaned against a nearby tree and took a moment to catch her breath, wiping a few droplets of sweat from her brow as she did. "I . . . I wanted to thank you for . . . what you said back there."

"What I said?"

Margaret Louise gave a long, slow nod. "About Leona."

"I said what I feel, Margaret Louise. Because Leona is my friend. She always will be."

"She's lucky to have you, you know."

She considered her friend's words then gave the only response she could. "I'm lucky to have her, too. I mean, she tries my patience, sure . . . but I know she's always there when I need her, and that says something in my book."

"I wish I could find some of that positive thinkin' 'bout my twin right now, but I can't."

"You really haven't spoken to her since the circle meeting the other night?" she asked.

Margaret Louise shook her head and puckered her lip as she did. "Not a word. Don't have nothin' to say to her 'cept that I'm spittin' mad. Which I reckon she knows without me sayin' a gosh darn thing."

A snap of something that felt a lot like worry started in Tori's chest and wound its way into the pit of her stomach. Where was Leona? Why hadn't she returned even one of Tori's dozen or so calls to date? Was she sulking after the verbal attack she suffered Monday night? Was she deliberately trying to erase anger from everyone's minds by replacing it with worry?

She supposed anything was possible with Leona. But still, she couldn't quite shake the nagging feeling that something wasn't right. Leona liked to hear herself talk way too much to just drop off the grid without some sort of dramatic exit.

A vibration against her hip caught her by surprise and she reached into her pocket in the hopes that Leona was finally calling. A check of the Caller ID screen, however, revealed a different name.

"I'm sorry, Margaret Louise, I need to take this. It's Milo, and I need to bring him up to speed on wedding things," she said as she paused her hand atop her phone and smiled apologetically at her friend. "I'll give you a call tonight after I get home from work, okay?"

"You can try, but I'll be watchin' my grandbabies while Jake and Melissa go to a meetin' 'bout Jake Junior's soccer team. There's no tellin' whether I'll be able to hear you over the noise that will be fillin' my house with all them youngin's, but we can sure try." Margaret Louise meandered away from the tree and over to the driver's side of her station wagon. "Give my love to Milo."

"I will. And give mine to the kids when you see them." Holding the still vibrating phone to her ear, she reveled in the smile that accompanied the knowledge that her soon-to-be husband was on the other end. "You have a real knack for knowing when I need to hear your voice, do you know that?"

"Wouldn't that be always?"

Her smile gave way to a laugh as she tried desperately to come up with a clever retort, but she came up empty. Milo was right. She always needed to hear his voice. "Guess what?"

"You love me?"

"That's an easy guess . . ."

"You're counting down the days until we're finally married? Which, by the way, is ten in case you're not."

"Oh, I'm counting, all right . . ." She stepped onto the sidewalk that bordered the front of Waters Hardware and continued walking. "I crossed four out of five things off my wedding prep list this morning."

"Four out of five?"

"Uh-huh." She turned right at the end of the block and hurried toward the library, the approaching noon hour signaling the end to her personal time. "I reconfirmed with the minister and told him we'd have our vows to him by Saturday at the latest, Georgina is confident parking at the reception won't be an issue with any of her neighbors,

Dixie has narrowed down her reading to one of two and I'm confident it will be perfect, and Margaret Louise said she's only got about sixteen favors to go."

"Sounds like a productive morning."

"And I picked up our rings last night—although I didn't look at mine. I want the next time I see it to be when you slip it onto my finger during the ceremony."

"Which can't come soon enough, as far as I'm concerned." He took a breath then continued, his words quickly confirming his superior listening skills. "So what's the one item you didn't get to this morning?"

Her pace instinctively slowed as she stepped onto the grounds of the library and noted the five minutes or so she had left of her morning. "I wanted to give Leona the pillow for Paris."

"And?"

She wandered over to one of the trio of picnic tables strewn around the grounds and took a seat on the edge of its bench. "I haven't seen her yet today."

If he picked up the tension in her voice, he didn't let on. "Any word on how Beatrice is doing?"

Beatrice . . .

She looked again at her watch. There was no time to check in on the nanny before relieving Nina, but maybe, if she found a quiet moment or two in the second half of the workday . . .

Without waiting for her to answer, Milo continued, his voice taking on an odd tone. "Kellie said something strange during science this morning."

"Kellie?" she repeated.

"Yeah. The oldest of the three Brady kids."

"Okay . . ."

"We were experimenting with sound and how it travels. One of the boys in my class asked Kellie if she heard Miss Gracie falling down the steps."

She sucked in her breath. "Oh no. Did she get upset?"

"I guess, a little. But kids this age are all about the story as much as the emotion, you know? So while the thought of someone falling to their death on the stairs in her home might spawn a number of nightmares in the not too distant future, in class, all she really worried about was answering Timmy's question as it related to our discussion on sound."

"So she *did* hear her fall then?"

"She heard Miss Gracie shout, but by the time she went to see what was wrong, it was already too late."

"How awful." She took a moment to digest the situation as it related to an eight-year-old little girl and then allowed herself the sigh it demanded. "How frightening to hear someone yell for help and not be able to do anything."

"But that's just it. Miss Gracie didn't yell for help."

She pulled her gaze away from the moss-draped trees that canopied the picnic table and fixed it, instead, on the stairs she knew she should be starting to climb but couldn't. Not yet anyway. "Then what did *she* yell?"

"She yelled 'stop.' "

"Stop?"

"That's what Kellie said," Milo confirmed. "I guess Miss Gracie was trying to will her body to do something gravity wouldn't allow."

"I guess," she murmured.

"Hey, art class is over so I better get back to my room and relieve Mrs. Niggle. But I'll see you tonight, right?"

Tonight . . .
Tonight . . .

"Tori?"

She startled at the sound of her name. "I'm sorry, what was that?"

"I was just saying I'd see you tonight. At my place, remember? We talked about ordering a pizza around six thirty or seven and maybe watching a movie on TV as a way to detox from all of this last-minute running around we've been doing."

"No, I remember." She scooted her purse back onto her shoulder and stood, the beginning chimes of the town square's midday bell propelling her feet toward the front steps of the library and the co-worker that was no doubt eager for Tori's return. "I just got distracted there for a minute. But trust me, I'm all for the idea of slowing things down for a few hours just so long as the next ten days can still go fast."

Chapter 11

"Stop it! That's my book!"

"But I wanna look at it, too!"

Tori looked up from the computer screen just as Nina's quiet voice filled her left ear. "Can I just say how glad I am Lyndon isn't that age yet?"

She bobbed her head to the left to afford a better view of the tug of war taking place in the middle of the self-help aisle.

One tug toward the dark-haired four-year-old . . .

One tug back toward the slightly lighter-haired three-year-old . . .

One tug toward the dark-haired four-year-old . . .

And finally, a book grab from their mortified mother . . .

"When the two of you start fighting over a book that neither of you have the slightest interest in, it's time to head home." The woman slammed the object of her children's disagreement down on the closest shelf and then grabbed both boys by the hand. "Let's go! Now!"

"But what about our cookies from the bakery?" wailed the younger child.

"You should have thought of that before you decided to argue in the middle of the library after I specifically told you to keep quiet."

Hushed and not so hushed whining accompanied the threesome to the front door before disappearing from the library once and for all. Straightening her shoulders, Nina made her way around the information desk and toward the now vacant aisle and its misplaced book. "And to think I was actually starting to give some thought to the notion of a little brother or sister for Lyndon in the near future."

Tori pressed save on the notes she was making for the rapidly approaching board meeting and then stretched her arms above her head. "Siblings fight. It's part of growing up."

"I get the occasional disagreement, I really do, but when it's over something that doesn't matter to either one of them to start with, that's when I'm not sure I'll have much patience." Nina retrieved the offending book from the shelf and held it up for Tori to see. "Because two kids under the age of five really need to argue over who gets to hold a book about finding your inner spirit."

"They were probably just tired." Tori peeked up at the clock above the front door and let out a sigh of relief. "Looks like it's time to call it a day. So what's your evening looking like?"

Nina smoothed her hand over the book's cover and then placed it on the correct shelf by author's name.

"Duwayne and I are taking Lyndon over to Duwayne's mama's house for dinner."

"Sounds good. Especially since it means you won't have to cook after being here all day." She shut the computer down, neatened the stack of scratch paper and bin of pencils utilized by patrons inquiring about specific titles, and slid off the stool she'd inhabited for the past hour. "Milo and I are ordering pizza and watching a movie on TV as a way to chill for a little while. I think we really need a few moments of that before we get into the final week leading up to the wedding."

"You're going to be a beautiful bride, Victoria," Nina mused. "Real beautiful."

She pushed her stool flush against the counter, smiling as she did. "Thanks, Nina. Rose did an amazing job on the dress, that's for sure."

"Are you sure you want Lyndon at the wedding? He's quite the babbler these days."

"Yes, I want him there. I want Melissa and Jake's kids there, too." Tori emerged from behind the information desk and headed toward the bank of computers designed for public use, shutting off each monitor as she passed. "Thanks for covering for me this morning. I managed to get quite a few things crossed off my list."

Nina returned to the desk and the wheeled cart that held the half-dozen books that had been returned over the past hour. Grabbing them into a single stack, Tori's assistant took off around the library, returning each title to its proper home. "It was my pleasure. This whole day has been eerily quiet around here . . . except, of course, for the stop-it boys just now."

"The stop-it boys?" she echoed in amusement.

"That's right. And I suspect they have some sisters in our teen book club."

She laughed. "You mean Dana and Donna Wilkins?"

Nina stopped in the last aisle, widened her eyes, flared her nostrils, and placed her hands on her rounded hips. " 'Didn't I tell you to stop sitting next to Bobbie?' . . . 'I don't have to stop anything, Donna Sue! He's my friend, too.' "

"Ah yes, the trials and tribulations of teenage girls." Tori finished with the computers and then took in the library's main room in its totality. The straightening she and Nina did throughout the quiet day had made it so a number of their closing tasks were already done. "I think we're good to go. Why don't you lock up the front on your way out and I'll shut things down in the office and let myself out the back way?"

"I'll do that." Nina returned to the counter just long enough to retrieve her purse and lunch sack from an interior-facing drawer and then headed toward the front door, keys in hand. "I'll see you back here tomorrow."

"See you then, Nina." She listened for the pair of distinct locking noises in her friend's wake and then turned in the direction of her office, flipping off the lights in the main room as she went. Once in her office, she collected her own belongings, straightened a few piles she'd made little headway on, and then checked her phone.

No missed calls from Leona or anyone else . . .

"Where are you, Leona?" she whispered. "Why aren't you returning my calls?"

Scrolling through her contacts once more, she stopped on Leona's name and pressed dial. Six rings later, she ended the call at the familiar sound of Leona's recorded voice.

"Okay, Leona, you don't want to answer my calls?" she muttered en route to the back door and the car she'd left in the lot prior to her many wedding-related tasks that morning. "That's fine. There's more than one way to skin a cat."

For the second time in less than twenty-four hours, Tori's gaze traveled through the windshield and up the front steps of Leona Elkin's condo. When she reached the front mat, she noted that the previous day's rolled-up newspaper now had a mate.

Hmmm . . .

Perhaps Leona had simply escaped the sewing circle's crosshairs and taken a little trip. After all, next to caring for Paris and flirting with uniform-wearing younger men, traveling was among the woman's favorite pastimes.

Tori moved her field of vision upward, to the windows that faced the front road from the first floor of Leona's unit. There, she found even more evidence to back up her latest theory on the whereabouts of Leona Elkin, including an utter lack of any discernible light coming through or around the carefully drawn curtains.

She knew she should be irritated that her friend had simply taken off for parts unknown with nary a consideration for those who might worry, but she wasn't. Not really anyway. If Leona was stomping around a city like Charleston, or sunning herself on one of its nearby beaches, it meant she was okay. And when it came right down to it, it was the not knowing whether Leona was okay that had been eating away at Tori's last nerve.

A flash of something out of the corner of her eye made

her turn in time to see an unfamiliar male figure taking Leona's steps two at a time. Surprised, she leaned around the steering wheel for a closer look. In the man's left hand was a key. Tucked under his right arm was . . .

"Paris?" she gasped.

Sure enough, two long ears peeked out from around the man's arm and twitched in rapid succession.

"What on earth . . ." The words disappeared into the air as she yanked open her door and stepped onto the pavement. "Excuse me . . . Can I ask what you're doing with my friend's rabbit?"

The man turned as he reached the top step, a crop of disheveled sandy blond hair draping itself across his left eye. "You know Leona?"

She pushed the door shut, came around the front of the car, and stopped at the base of the steps. "I know Leona well enough to know she doesn't go anywhere without that rabbit."

The lack of any visible movement of his hair as he nodded gave her pause.

Hairspray, perhaps?

Or maybe hair gel?

Shaking the odd side thought from her head, she waited for something that would explain the unexplainable. Beyond, of course, the fact that Paris was being held by an attractive man in his late twenties . . .

"I took a bit of a chance letting Paris"—he engaged eye contact with the nose-twitching bunny for a split second—"into the ambulance in the first place, but at least I put my foot down about the emergency room."

"Emergency room?" she repeated. "Wait. What are you talking about?"

He repositioned Paris inside the crook of his arm and peered down at the papers by his feet. "Damn. I knew I should have tried to get over here yesterday but I was too busy keeping up with Leona's instructions." An ineffectual rake of his key-holding hand through his hair confirmed her earlier suspicions. "I had no idea looking after a bunny could be so all-consuming, you know?"

"Stop! Go back to the emergency room part. Please."

"Can I just bring her inside first and get her one of the treats Leona is insisting I give her before bed tonight?" Without waiting for her answer, the young man inserted the key in the lock and pushed her friend's front door wide open. "If you're a friend of Leona's, I'm sure she'd be fine with you coming inside, too."

Tori jogged up the stairs and followed him into Leona's front entryway. "The treats are in there," she said, pointing into the rarely used kitchen. "Leona keeps them in the third drawer down, to the right of the fridge. Underneath the pile of take-out menus."

When he located the bag of bunny treats, he pulled out a few choice morsels and held them out for Paris to sniff and nibble, the animal's wide eyes a near-perfect match to the confusion Tori still felt. "Okay, she's had her treat. Now where is Leona? And why do you have Paris?"

"My partner and I got the call about her fall while we were playing cards at the station Monday night." He stroked his wide hand down Paris's back and then leaned over to set her free. "I'm Sam, by the way, and I'm also an EMT in case I didn't mention that."

"You didn't, but go on . . ."

"Leona fell right over there." Sam took three steps out of the kitchen and waved his hand toward the overturned throw rug and scattered knickknacks on the far side of the otherwise pristinely kept living room. "I'm guessing she lost her balance on the stationary step she was using to exercise and went down on her left side."

Paris froze in response to Tori's gasp, terror making the rabbit's nose twitch even faster. "Leona fell?"

"She did. But fortunately, she'd been waiting for a call back from some friend of hers and her cell phone was within reach. That's when she called us."

"And this happened when?" she asked.

"Monday night. Somewhere between ten and eleven."

The night of the sewing circle meeting and Miss Gracie's fall . . .

"You said Leona was waiting for a call back from a friend when this happened?"

"That's what she said."

Monday night . . .

Between ten and eleven . . .

If she was remembering correctly, she was probably on the phone with Milo when Leona fell and called for help . . .

"Wait. I think I heard the sirens that night," she said as two and two began to come together.

"They were blaring, that's for sure."

Tori leaned against the nearest wall to offset the sudden weakness in her legs. "Was—was she in a lot of pain?"

"I can't imagine she wasn't, but she seemed to do an amazing job of holding it at bay."

"How is she now?" she asked over the increased thumping in her chest. "And *where* is she now?"

"She's at Tom's Creek General at the moment. She was pretty tipsy the first twelve hours or so, but the nurses had her up and taking a few steps not long after her surgery yesterday."

"Surgery?"

Sam nodded. "She fractured her hip. Which I could tell almost the second I saw her that first night." Paris hopped over to his foot and twitched, bringing the story back to her in much the same way Leona would do under similar circumstances. "We were halfway out the door with Leona when I saw this little one hopping after us."

"And she talked you into taking care of Paris these last few days?"

"No, I *offered*. Leona is an amazing woman. Beautiful, too. Heck, even my roommate who thought I was nuts for looking after Paris changed his tune when I took him to meet Leona. She's spectacular, you know?"

Despite the throbbing ache near her temples and the nagging guilt associated with learning of Leona's fall two days too late, Tori couldn't help but smile.

Leona, Leona, Leona . . . Even in a weakened state, you still know how to turn on the charm . . .

"Quick question, Sam. Do EMTs wear uniforms, by any chance?"

"Of course. Why do you ask?"

"No reason, really." She shifted her focus to Paris and lifted the small rabbit into her arms. "I can take this one home with me if that would be easier."

Sam's face lit up with unrestrained hope. "Seriously? Wow, that would be awesome. I mean, it's not that I don't want to help Leona out, 'cause I do, but, well, I'm getting ready to start the next of three twelve-hour rotations tonight and I kinda get the sense Paris is used to company."

"Because she is." Tori smoothed the rabbit's ears back

then watched as they shot straight up once again. "But thank you . . . for looking after Paris these last two days, and for taking care of Leona when she fell. I'm sick at the thought that she was all alone when it first happened but grateful you got here so quickly."

"It was my pleasure, ma'am." He reached across the empty space between them and gave Paris a quick scratch along her short neck. "As for you, Miss Paris, with any luck I'll be seeing you again just as soon as that gorgeous owner of yours is back on her feet."

Chapter 12

Casting a sidelong glance in the direction of the passenger seat, Tori pushed through the guilt to find the smile she owed her fiancé. "I'm very aware of how lucky I am, by the way."

He stopped drumming his hands to the background beat on the radio and puffed out his chest. "Yes, yes you are." Then, as quickly as the posturing arrived, it disappeared behind a laugh. "Why are you saying that? What did I do?"

"You understood when I said I needed to pass on our pizza and movie date. And with little more than seconds to absorb the out-of-left-field why."

"What's to absorb? Leona is in the hospital. We'd be pretty awful if we reacted to that by ordering a large pepperoni pizza with a side of breadsticks."

Carefully, she maneuvered the hairpin turn a few miles

outside Sweet Briar and then turned left on Route 25 toward Tom's Creek. "Still, I know you needed a night to chill."

"As did you. But Leona didn't ask to fall and fracture her hip."

The road twisted to the east and then the south as they approached the town limits of Sweet Briar's most metropolitan neighbor and the increased traffic that came with the title. "I'm still lucky," she quipped. "Lucky *and* hungry."

"I vote we check in on Leona and see if she's eaten. If she hasn't, I'll track down the hospital cafeteria and see what they've got." He pointed toward a large rectangular-shaped blue sign and its telltale white *H*. "Here we go. Looks like the visitor parking is over there to the left."

She followed his verbal clues and promptly found a spot close to the entrance. Ten minutes later, they were poking their heads inside Room 245.

"Leona?" Tori called. "Are you up for some visitors?"

A rustling of sheets was followed by the sound of a sleepy Leona. "Who's with you, dear?"

"Milo."

A second rustling was quickly followed by the distinct sound of a drawer opening and closing and a zipper being opened.

"Leona?"

"One minute. I just need to . . ." Her friend's voice died out as whatever had been unzipped seconds earlier was rezipped and placed back in a drawer. "You can come in now, dear."

"Shall I turn on the light?" Tori asked as she led the way into the room with Milo no more than a step or two behind. At Leona's garbled assent, she flipped the switch beside the door and blinked at the rapid answer of the fluorescent fixture affixed to the ceiling. "Whoa, that's bright."

"Tell me about it." Leona patted her hair self-consciously as Tori and Milo came into view, her freshly applied lipstick a dead giveaway to the reason behind the zipper sounds. "I spoke with the president of the hospital this morning and made a suggestion or two they might want to implement with their accommodations."

Tori resisted the urge to roll her eyes and instead took a long, hard look at her friend and the dark circles that lined the underside of her bloodshot eyes. "Leona Elkin, why on earth didn't you call me when you fell?"

"I *did* call you, dear. You just chose not to call back in the ongoing pack-style punishment being inflicted on me because of something that lasted less than five seconds."

Ignoring the watered-down version of the truth, she opted to focus on the lesser of two arguments she could wage. "If you'd called me back and told me you'd fallen, Leona, I'd have dropped everything."

"I don't believe in begging, Victoria. If you don't know that by now, you don't know me at all."

"You wouldn't have had to *beg*, Leona. We are friends, aren't we?"

"I thought we were," Leona sniffed.

Aware of Milo standing just over her left shoulder, she took a deep breath and moved on to the only thing that really mattered at that point. "How are you feeling? Are you in pain?"

"A bit less now that I'm in one place, but when Sam had to lift me onto the gurney and then from the gurney to the bed in the ER, it was awful. It was the same when the nurse had to bring me down for the X-rays."

"You were very fortunate to have an EMT like Sam, that's for sure."

Leona's left eyebrow inched upward. "You know Sam, dear?"

"I met him this evening. He's how I learned you'd fallen." Tori lowered herself to the edge of Leona's bed, only to jump back up in reaction to her friend's wince. "I'm sorry, I'm sorry. I didn't mean to hurt you."

Leona's eyes drifted closed for a few seconds then opened slowly. "My pain just then had nothing to do with you, Victoria. Sit. Please." Then, gesturing toward the chair on the opposite side of her bed, she mustered a pain-free smile and a seductive blink for her male visitor. "Milo, how sweet of you to come."

"There's nowhere I'd rather be right now, Leona." Milo looped around the bottom of the bed and took the seat reserved especially for him. "And just so you know, my neighbor is looking after Paris while we're here."

"Your neighbor?"

Tori perched a bit farther from Leona's leg and reached for the woman's hand. "Sam's work schedule the next few days would have made it hard for him to care for Paris, so I took her. Once Milo and I get back this evening, I'll retrieve her from the neighbor's house and bring her home with me."

"Thank you." A rare burst of uncertainty had Leona picking at the fabric of her hospital blanket. "I miss her terribly."

"As I'm sure she misses you."

"Where did you see Sam?" Leona asked after a dramatic pause to wipe at her eyes.

"At your condo. He came by to get some treats for Paris."

"Hmmm. So not only is he attractive and strong, he also follows directions. Very nice." Leona snuggled her head back against her pillow and again closed her eyes, this time opting to leave them that way while she continued talking. "He's going to take me to dinner once I'm back home."

"When will that be?" Tori asked. "Sam said you had *surgery*?"

"I had a pin put in my hip but I'm told I should heal nicely. Unfortunately, with my incredibly unfair placement on everyone's most hated list, I will probably be going to rehab for a while before I can go home to Paris."

"Rehab?"

Leona's never-before-seen mascara-less lashes parted to reveal hazel eyes that seemed more stricken than dramatic. "The doctor insists that I will need a little bit of . . . help . . . for a few days, while I recover."

"Oh, Leona, I think you're going to need help for more than a few days," Milo interjected. "One of my mom's friends broke her hip last year and it didn't go very well."

"I didn't break my hip. I merely fractured it."

"But you're also sixty-five, Leona," Tori protested, earning herself a death glare in the process.

"Do you know what I was doing when I fell, dear?"

She rewound her way through her evening until she was able to recover something that sounded vaguely familiar. "Um, something with a footstool, I think?"

"It was a stepper, Victoria. As in, a piece of workout equipment that one uses to *work out*." Leona softened her gaze as she swung it toward Milo. "I will rebound from this like any other *forty*-five-year-old would."

"You still had major surgery, Leona," Milo reminded her not unkindly. "Which means you need to take things slow in order to fully rebound. Go too fast and you'll only hamper your recovery in the long run."

"I have to get better quickly. For Paris. And Sam."

Tori tried to stifle the laugh before it made its way past her lips, but she wasn't entirely successful. "S-Sam?"

"He's smitten, dear."

It was a sentiment she couldn't argue, not after hearing the worship the EMT had for the woman. Instead, she asked, "If someone was at your home with you, could you go there instead of a rehab facility?"

"I could. But other than Paris, I have no one."

"You could ask Margaret Louise."

Leona lifted her chin to afford her fully opened eyes a view of the ceiling, shaking her head as she did. "You saw my sister the other night. She despises me."

"Stop it, Leona. Margaret Louise doesn't despise you. She's just upset over what you did to Rose."

A flash of pain skittered across Leona's face followed by a heartbreaking groan.

"Leona?" She reached for her friend's hand again and held it tightly. "Are you okay? Should I get a nurse?"

"No. I—I'll . . . be fine. I'd rather take the pain meds a little closer to bed." Two deep breaths later, Leona was in command of the conversation again. "I won't be asking my sister for help."

"I could help," Tori whispered.

"No. You're getting married in ten days."

"But I don't want you going to a rehab facility," she protested.

"What other choice do I have, dear?"

Milo rose to his feet, retraced his original steps, and came to stand beside Tori. "You could hire someone to stay with you for the first week or so. Someone who can help you get in and out of the shower, in and out of bed, and whatever else you need."

"Are there people who *do* that sort of thing?" Leona asked.

"Sure."

Tori looked up at Milo. "You mean like an in-home nurse?"

"She could get someone like that, I guess. But I'm thinking more along the lines of someone who can simply be there with her, morning, noon, and night, until she's okay to be on her own again."

Leona pulled her hand free of Tori's and reached for a small pad and pen on the wheeled nightstand to her left. "Where would I find someone like that?"

"We could ask Beatrice," Tori suggested suddenly.

"She has too much on her mind, dear." Leona uncapped the pen and hovered it above the paper. "I think I'll call the chamber of commerce first thing in the morning. If there is someone who fits the bill, they'll—"

A second, longer grimace of pain stole the rest of Leona's sentence and brought Tori to her feet. "Okay, I can't handle seeing you in this kind of pain any longer. I'm getting the nurse."

Chapter 13

Tori stopped in the doorway of the children's room and took in the face of each and every two-year-old seated atop a carpet square listening to the antics of a little brown mouse. In their expressions she saw the same wonder that had drawn her to books as a small child and still kept her enthralled as an adult.

"I can't help but wish I was two again. If I was, Miss Gracie would still be alive."

Startled, Tori pushed off the door frame and glanced over her shoulder to find Beatrice standing mere inches away. "Oh. Beatrice. I didn't see you standing there," she whispered as she took hold of the nanny's arm and led her across the hall and into her office, where they could speak without disrupting Nina's story time. "How are you doing, sweetie?"

"I'll be better when I bloody well know the truth behind Miss Gracie's fall."

"You still think someone else was involved?"

"I don't *think* it, Victoria, I *know* it." Beatrice's focus drifted back across the hall, only to return to Tori with raw intensity. "Especially after what Kellie said."

"I heard about that from Milo. But I don't understand how Kellie's recollection proves anything."

"If Kellie had heard her yell, 'no,' I might be able to consider it an accident. But she yelled, 'stop.' "

"I don't understand."

Beatrice paced from one end of the office to the other, frustration fairly dripping from her pores. "If you were falling, what would you yell, Victoria?"

"I don't know. I don't know I'd yell anything."

"I think I'd yell for help. But that's not what Miss Gracie did. She said, 'stop.' " Beatrice paused mid-step and turned to face Tori. "People only say 'stop' to someone else—stop talking, stop hitting, stop being mean, stop *pushing*."

She felt her head jerk backward from the punch of Beatrice's words and the barrage of recent conversations they recalled . . .

"Stop it! That's my book!"

"Stop trying to plead Leona's case. She got herself into this mess . . ."

"Stop it, Leona. Margaret Louise doesn't despise you . . ."

She covered her mouth with her hand as more and more conversations utilizing the word *stop* played their way through her thoughts, each and every instance involving another person.

Was Beatrice right?

"Wow. I—I don't know what to say, Beatrice."

"Say you think there's a chance she didn't fall. Say you think there's a chance someone pushed her down that staircase."

Ten minutes earlier, her answer to her friend's plea would have been very different. But it wasn't ten minutes earlier.

Tori swallowed against the lump slowly rising in her throat and let the edge of her desk serve as a prop for legs that were suddenly weary. "Let's say you're right, Beatrice. That someone pushed Miss Gracie down those stairs. Who would want to do that? And why? She'd only been in town for thirty-six hours at that point, right? Is that really enough time to cultivate a murderous enemy?"

"I think that would depend on the why, wouldn't you say?"

She took a moment to study the young nanny and the fiery determination that lit the young woman's normally dull eyes. "You're convinced she was murdered, aren't you?"

"I bloody well am."

"Do you have any suspects?"

"One."

"And that would be the nanny she replaced, yes?"

"Cynthia Marland," Beatrice confirmed. "She was furious over being fired by Mrs. Brady. She honestly believed that Reenie's seizure at school wasn't her fault and that she should have been given another chance."

"Why? So she could kill the child next time?" Tori mumbled.

"Precisely what Mrs. Brady was trying to prevent."

"But if Cynthia was fired, would she have even *been* at the Bradys' house when Miss Gracie fell?"

Beatrice fidgeted with the hem of her blouse only to release the fabric from her fingers with a determined shrug. "She wasn't invited, but that doesn't mean she wasn't there."

"Did anyone mention seeing her?"

"I haven't asked yet. But the only people that could tell me would be the one or two nannies from the Nanny Go Round Agency, who wouldn't tell me even if I asked."

"Oh? Why not?"

"Because they're afraid I've started a trend toward British nannies. Which is silly, of course. If there's a trend, it's in the Nanny Go Round Agency having inferior nannies."

"Are the nannies from this local agency really that bad?" Tori asked.

"I can only say that the families who employ help from Nanny Go Round get what they pay for."

"These nannies come cheap?"

"If the paychecks I've seen at the park are any indication, they make little more than a pittance."

Tori drew back. "Then why do they do it?"

"The perks, I suppose. A bedroom in a fancy house . . . use of a car . . . that sort of thing." Beatrice shoved a piece of her hair off her face. "From what I have been able to gather, it's a way to live like they haven't and probably never will on their own."

"And that's the case with Cynthia, as well?"

Beatrice crossed to the window and looked out over the library grounds. "You know those houses you pass as you head out on Route 25? The very last ones before you leave Sweet Briar town limits?"

She mentally put herself on the road that led to Tom's Creek and willed herself to see her surroundings rather than the road itself.

"There's about a half dozen or so of them there on the left and—"

"Wait," she said, crinkling her nose. "You mean those dilapidated ones? With the appliances and stuff on the front porches?"

"Cynthia lives in the green one with her parents. Her grandparents live in the brown one, her older brother and his girlfriend in the yellow one, and some other sort of relative in the blue one. Some of the other nannies live on that same street, too."

Tori drummed her fingers against the cool metal of her desk as she tried Beatrice's words on for size. "So living in a home like the one Mr. and Mrs. Brady own is literally like being in a different world."

"One she wasn't too keen on leaving."

"What you're saying doesn't make sense, though."

Beatrice turned. "Why not?"

"Hear me out, okay?" Pushing off the edge of her desk, Tori wandered over to the drink station she and Nina had set up on a cart by the door and held out a bottle of water to Beatrice. When the nanny declined, she twisted off the cap and took a quick sip. "You were the one who suggested Miss Gracie to the Brady family, right?"

"Yes."

"Then it stands to reason that any resentment Cynthia felt would be aimed at *you*, not Miss Gracie."

"And that is why she followed me and Luke around—

to the park, the school, the market, and on walks. But once Miss Gracie was actually here, no amount of bullying would put Cynthia back in the Brady home. Only Miss Gracie's death could do that."

"In her dreams perhaps." Tori took a second, longer sip, then recapped the bottle and set it on the cart next to the coffeemaker.

"No, Victoria. In reality."

She froze as her friend's words took root. "Wait. Are you saying Cynthia is working for the Bradys again?"

"She showed up Tuesday morning, offering to help bridge the gap until they found a replacement for Miss Gracie."

"And did they take her up on the offer?"

"I don't know," Beatrice said. "I couldn't listen to talk of replacing Miss Gracie. It was far too painful."

Tori tried to think of something to say, something that could erase the grief from Beatrice's face while simultaneously giving the young woman solace, but she came up empty.

"Tell me you see what I see," Beatrice implored. "Tell me you think Miss Gracie's fall wasn't an accident."

Tori retraced her steps back to her desk, only this time she went straight for the notepad and pen she kept in her top drawer. "I can't deny this whole business with Cynthia feels off."

"It does, doesn't it?"

"I'll make a call or two this afternoon." She retrieved the notepad, flipped past the pages devoted to the remaining items on her wedding list, and stopped on the first empty page she could find, her mind instinctively prioritizing the things they needed to do even before the tip of her pen had made so much as a dot on the paper. "Maybe try to see what I can find out about the Nanny Go Round Agency and its hiring practices."

A half sob, half laugh echoed through the room as Beatrice lurched forward and wrapped her arms around Tori's neck. "Oh, Victoria, I knew you'd see it my way. Thank you! Thank you for helping me catch Miss Gracie's killer. You are truly a wonderful friend."

As if guided by some unseen force, Tori's gaze left the notepad and traveled across the room to the wall calendar and the multicolored circle that was now just nine days away . . .

No, I am truly an idiot.

Chapter 14

Tori stared down at the budget figures she'd painstakingly compiled earlier in the week and tried to focus on the report she'd be giving at the board meeting that night. But no matter how hard she tried, there wasn't a program she was proposing or a subscription she was being forced to cancel that could keep her thoughts away from Miss Gracie.

Was Beatrice right? Had the British woman been pushed to her death?

And if so, had it been Cynthia Marland who'd done the pushing?

Focus, Tori, focus . . .

The part of her brain that embraced reason knew any hijinks associated with the nanny's death were for the police to worry about. After all, Tori had enough on her own plate with a board meeting and her wedding to Milo.

But it was the other part of her brain—the part ruled by reality—that knew there wouldn't be any investigation. Chief Robert Dallas was a nice enough man, but to him, police work was merely a funding tool for his two favorite pastimes. Ruling Miss Gracie's death an accident was easy and freed up his time for fishing and hunting.

The real question, then, was whether to convince Beatrice to let her suspicions go, or do a little behind-the-scenes sleuthing to determine whether her friend was right.

Finish your report for the board . . .

"Victoria?"

She glanced toward her office door and sent up a mental prayer of thanks for the distraction that was Nina. "Hey, I have to tell you, that story time you did today was adorable. You had those little ones eating out of the palm of your hand."

"They were cute today, weren't they?" Nina agreed before moving on to her reason for momentarily abandoning her post at the information desk. "I know you told me to hold your calls for a while, but Ms. Elkin is on the line and she doesn't sound very good."

Dread propelled her hand toward the phone and the blinking red light that indicated Leona was on line two. "Thanks, Nina, you did the right thing." Her assistant nodded and disappeared in the direction of the main room as Tori brought the phone to her ear. "Leona? Is everything okay? Did you have a setback?"

A faint sniff greeted her questions, followed by a second, louder sniff.

"Talk to me, Leona, please," she pleaded.

The sniffing gave way to a series of rapid hiccups before a tear-choked voice filled her ear. "I—I miss Paris."

She rolled her chair back a few inches and peeked over the edge of her desk at the brown box Milo had helped her secure for the purpose of housing her friend's rabbit during work hours. "She's right here, Leona, and she's doing fine. Munching away on one of her favorite organic carrots as we speak."

"Is she munching quickly or slowly?"

"I don't know. Slowly, I guess."

The sniffing resumed. "That means she's depressed, dear."

Rolling her chair free of the desk, Tori closed the gap between her and Paris with two short scoots. "I think she's just full, Leona."

"She's without her mama. She's depressed."

"I don't know how you can say—"

"Look at her ears."

"Okay . . ."

"They're drooping, aren't they?"

Tori leaned forward, eliminating any chance the edge of the box inhibited her view. Sure enough, the ears that were normally ramrod straight were, in fact, a bit droopy.

"And her beautiful brown eyes are half-mast, yes?"

Wedging the phone between her shoulder and her ear, Tori reached into the box and lifted Paris into her arms, taking note of the animal's eyes as she did.

Yup, half-mast . . .

"She could just be tired," she posed weakly.

"This is Paris's awake time, dear. She's depressed."

Tori cuddled the animal to her side, kissed the spot

between her droopy ears, and secured the phone with her hand. "Okay, so what's your plan?"

"Smuggle her into the hospital to see me."

"I can't bring Paris into a hospital!"

"I have a private room, dear," Leona reminded her in a voice that suddenly sounded far bossier than it did tear-filled. "If you are stealthy enough, no one has to be the wiser."

She considered the various implications of doing as Leona asked but was thwarted from sharing them by Leona herself.

"If you do this, dear, you are absolved from your hideous treatment of me this week."

"*My* hideous treatment of *you*?" she echoed.

"Of course. How else could you describe the way you stood by and said nothing when my sister and her posse attacked me so viciously the other night? Had you said something in my defense, I wouldn't have turned to a workout to counteract my grief when I got home . . . And if I hadn't gotten on that stepper in such a compromised state, I wouldn't be lying here, writhing in pain, while my precious Paris sinks into utter despair."

"Wait. You actually blame *me* for your fall?" Paris's ears perked up in reaction to Tori's shrill voice, but drooped again almost immediately. "You can't be serious."

"Please, Victoria, I need to see Paris."

Oh, how she wanted to tell Leona to take a hike, to call her on her below-the-belt guilt tactics and refuse to buckle under their pressure, but she couldn't.

Leona was, well, Leona . . .

She looked down at Paris and said the only thing she could. "If Nina is okay with closing on her own, we'll be there by four thirty. But we're only staying for a little while. I have a board meeting tonight."

She reached into the tote bag and shifted the travel magazine to the side just enough to afford a momentary peek at her nose-twitching contraband. Already the rabbit's ears were more upright, and her eyes a bit wider, as if somehow she could sense who she was about to see.

"Now, when we step off the elevator, we have to make it past the nurses' station as inconspicuously as possible, okay, Paris?" At the bunny's answering twitch, Tori repositioned the periodical across the top half of the tote bag and waited as the elevator doors swished open at Leona's floor.

"Can I help you?"

Tori stopped in front of the nurses' desk and offered as natural a smile as she could muster for the woman seated on the other side. "Uh, hi, I'm just stopping by to visit my friend, Leona Elkin. She's in Room 245 and she's expecting me."

"Miss Elkin has asked that I hold all visitors here at the desk until she's done with her therapist."

She resisted the urge to groan and, instead, tightened her grip on the handles of the bag. "Oh, okay. Um, she didn't mention a visit with her therapist when she asked me to stop by."

"She must have forgotten," the nurse said around a yawn. "It happens sometimes."

A sudden jolt at the bottom of her bag earned her a lifted brow and more attention than the pair needed. "If your bag is getting heavy, you could set it here on the desk with me."

As if . . .

To the nurse, Tori simply said, "No, it's okay. Holding Leona's favorite magazines is actually a really good workout for my arms." She shifted her weight from her left foot to her right and took in Room 245's closed door. "Um, do you happen to know how long her therapist will be in with her?"

The nurse's shoulders heaved upward as she returned to whatever she'd been typing on her computer when Tori stepped off the elevator. "I would have expected her session to have been over ten minutes ago, but like yesterday, he seems to be spending a little extra time with Miss Elkin."

She felt the knowing smile as it moved from one end of her mouth to the other. "This therapist is a male?"

"Is he ever." The nurse bobbed her head around the left side of the monitor to reveal cheeks that were suddenly flushed. "There's not a nurse in this hospital who doesn't secretly wish to be me just so they can watch that one come in and out of the rooms on this floor—oh, shhh, here he comes now."

She turned in time to see a tall, blond man emerge from Leona's room, a heart-stopping, dimple-accompanied smile gracing his thirty-something face. Suddenly, any question she may have entertained as to why Leona's therapy session ran longer than expected two days in a row was gone, in its place an answer born out of experience.

"Almost makes me want to mop my kitchen floor for the first time in months just so I can slip and break my hip," the nurse whispered in Tori's direction while her gaze remained fixed on no one but the therapist until he disappeared inside the elevator at the end of the hall. "Oh yes, that is one fine, *fine* man."

Switching the Paris-inhabited tote from one hand to the other, she bade farewell to the infatuated nurse and slipped into Leona's room, closing the door behind her as she did.

"Who's there?" Leona called out.

"It's me. Victoria—the person you called and asked to come for a visit, remember?"

"Oh. Yes. Give me one moment, please."

She waited through several odd sounds before she was invited all the way into the room and patted over to the bed. "Did you just arrive?"

"I've been here for about ten minutes but your nurse said you were with your therapist." Setting the bag on the ground next to the bottom edge of the bed, she lowered herself onto the unclaimed portion of the mattress. "She was wondering why your session was running late. For the second day in a row, no less."

"Dustin's therapy is very . . . *thorough.*"

"When it extends from your hip to your mouth, I must agree," Tori mused.

A sly, almost devilish smile appeared as the woman plucked a handheld mirror from the wheeled cart to her left and examined her collagen-enhanced lips. "Mmmm, yes, I really must find a lipstick brand that can withstand being kissed, mustn't I?"

Without waiting for a response, Leona returned the mirror to its spot and pointed toward the bag. "Give her to me."

Tori contemplated the mileage she'd get from teasing the woman but decided it wasn't worth the risk to her own personal safety. Especially when she was expected to don a hand-sewn wedding dress in nine days . . .

Leaning forward, she pulled the bag onto the bed, pushed aside the magazines, retrieved Paris from its base, and carefully set the rabbit atop Leona's stomach. Instantly, Paris's eyes widened and her ears perked.

"Oh, my sweet, precious baby. Mama has missed you so very, very much."

Tori blinked against the sudden misting in her eyes, but drew the line at the sniffles that threatened to blow her cover. "She seemed to know it was important to keep it quiet as we came into the building. I was afraid the nurse might notice my bag moving, but she was too busy drooling over your therapist."

"How did she sleep for you last night?" Leona asked, gazing down at Paris.

"She did fine."

"I think she looks a little tired. But that's to be expected, of course, when she has been so sad and confused over my tragic circumstances." Leona's hands glided over Paris's back, only to start the process all over again when she reached the bunny's little white cottontail. "But that's all about to change come tomorrow when I get to go home."

"You're going home tomorrow?"

"Technically the doctor said *Saturday*, but I got him to agree to tomorrow afternoon if I can promise that someone will be there to take care of me for at least the first week or so."

Her shoulders sagged with relief. "So Margaret Louise is going to come and stay with you then?"

A flash of pain made its presence known in Leona's eyes

before bowing to a snort. "Unless you went against my wishes and told my sister about my fall, she doesn't know yet. She'll find out when she gets off that Rose-before-family bandwagon she's been driving since Sunday's show."

There were days she wished she could reach out and throttle Leona with her bare hands. But that urge would have to wait. Besides, there were far too many people around who were trained to revive her at a moment's notice . . .

"Margaret Louise is your *sister*, Leona. She should know what's going on."

Leona stopped stroking Paris long enough to pin Tori with a stare. "Yes, Victoria, she is, and she should. The fact that she has denounced me is *her* cross to bear."

"Leona, please. You're not seeing this situation for what it is."

"Oh, I see it for exactly what it is because it's the way it's been for years. Rose Winters is perfect. I'm not. But it all comes down to jealousy. I'm beautiful, desirable, and well traveled. Rose is . . . old." Leona looked down at Paris and smiled. "No, I'm going to be able to return to my Precious Paris tomorrow thanks to that hunk you're marrying in nine days, Victoria."

"You hired someone to stay with you?"

Leona nodded. "I hired a young girl from the Nanny Go Round Agency. She'll be there when Sam brings me home in the ambulance."

Tori swiveled her body to afford the best unobstructed view of Leona possible. "The Nanny Go Round Agency?"

"That's right."

"I thought they were a nanny agency. For families with young children . . ."

"And I think they are, for the most part. But after you and Milo left last night, I telephoned a few colleagues. One of them suggested I try the Nanny Go Round Agency. So I called and left a message on their after-hours machine and the owner called me back first thing this morning to make the arrangements." With careful fingers, Leona inched Paris up her chest until they were nuzzling noses. "There, there, my most precious angel. I know it sounds like an eternity, but you only have to stay with Victoria for twenty-four more hours."

Chapter 15

Tori had never been gladder to see a board meeting come to a close than she was at that moment. Sure, her budget report had been well received with only a small amount of nit-picking from the board members, but to know that such a brain-numbing task was behind her as she approached her last pre-wedding week was exhilarating.

Now, with the exception of her day-to-day tasks at the library, Tori's complete focus could finally be the wedding. No longer would she have to shake herself from her daydreams about becoming Mrs. Milo Wentworth to punch numbers into a computer or bang her head against a wall.

Yet as she drove out of the parking lot behind the trio of board members and the handful of local residents who attended the meeting, she couldn't help but give the nagging non-wedding thoughts their due.

First, there was the business with Leona not telling Margaret Louise about her fall. On the one hand, she knew it wasn't her place to spill those beans—especially when she'd been sworn to secrecy. But on the other hand, she had to consider the very real possibility that Margaret Louise would be furious with Tori if she found out from anyone else.

Leona's ultimate goal perhaps?

She did her best to shake the disturbing possibility from her thoughts but it didn't go far.

And then there was the pesky feeling that Beatrice's suspicions about Miss Gracie's fall were true. Oh, how she tried to tell herself it wasn't her problem either way, but every time she did, reality brought her back to the same thing: If she didn't snoop around, who would?

"Concentrate on the wedding, Tori," she muttered aloud as she came to a stop at the end of the lot. "Plan your honeymoon outfits, help make the favors, go home and call Milo."

They were all good reasons to turn right toward home, but in the end, she turned left, her destination as foggy as her post-meeting brain.

Maybe she just needed a drive to get her head back on track . . .

Pushing on the radio, she turned the dial until she got to the eighties station and the music her older cousins had painstakingly exposed her to in the hope of shaping her musical tastes. How pleased they'd be at the wedding reception when they realized how their efforts had withstood the test of time.

The ending notes of one song led into the beginning of another and she did her best to focus on the lyrics and the catchy beat. Yet five blocks later, she returned the car to silence.

What on earth was with her?

Why couldn't she just relax?

They were two very good questions for which she wished she had no answers. But she did, even though they weren't the ones she should have nine days before her wedding.

No, her preferred answers would be: *Nothing, I'm fine*, and *I'm just excited to get married to Milo*.

Instead, they were: *I have to fix this thing between Margaret Louise and Leona*, and *How can I relax when Beatrice's childhood governess might have been pushed to her death?*

She headed out toward the southern edge of town, the tiny homes and cottages that had lined her view thus far giving way to the kind of homes one might find in a magazine. Georgina's house was up ahead and to the left and allowed her thoughts to stray toward the reception for a few glorious moments. But as she cleared the mayor's street and turned down another, her thoughts immediately returned to the whole business with her friends, especially as her travels took her past the home Debbie and her author husband shared with their two children.

If she was honest with herself, Margaret Louise wasn't the only person in their circle who was fed up with Leona's antics. Debbie, Dixie, Melissa, and Georgina were all showing signs of having hit a Leona-threshold, as well. It was certainly an issue that needed to be dealt with for the overall health of the sewing circle, but the breakdown between sisters was far more troubling.

She loved Margaret Louise, loved her generous spirit,

her hearty laugh, her adventurous soul, and her happy-go-lucky disposition.

But she also loved Leona for all the things the woman kept hidden just below the surface. Things like generosity, a listening ear, and the willingness to share life lessons when Tori least expected them yet needed them most.

She crossed through the next four-way stop and slowed as she approached a mailbox marked BRADY.

Sure enough, the home where Cynthia Marland had once worked was a far cry from the dilapidated bungalow she grew up in on the opposite side of town. Here, in place of appliances on the porch, there were Adirondack chairs grouped together on one side, and an inviting swing swaying in the night's gentle breeze on the other. Instead of two dirty windows facing the road, there were nearly a dozen large picture windows perfect for seeing and being seen.

A pair of two-seater sports cars parked in the circular driveway hinted at the kind of furnishings and gadgets that filled the home—furnishings and gadgets Cynthia had likely only heard about from classmates growing up.

It wasn't a lifestyle Tori needed, yet it was one she could imagine some seeing as their ultimate brass ring.

The question, though, was how difficult it would be to let go of that ring after touching it for several months . . .

Tori couldn't imagine killing to reclaim possessions, but then again, she hadn't grown up the way Cynthia had.

The vibration of her phone echoed against the cup holder where it resided, prompting Tori to pull alongside the curb and check the Caller ID screen.

Margaret Louise.

With a single tap of her finger, she took the call. "Good

evening, Margaret Louise, isn't this a nice surprise? How are you?"

"I think the real question is how are you? Did you survive another meetin' with Winston?"

"Winston and the rest of the board were fine. Nothing awful to report."

"I got the rest of the weddin' favors done this evenin'. Lulu helped," Margaret Louise chuckled although the sound seemed a bit forced to Tori's trained ear. "That's another thing crossed off your list, Victoria. It won't be long now, huh?"

She pulled her attention off the Bradys' home and focused it on her friend. "I'm hearing something in your voice. Is everything okay?"

"Everything is fine. I had a nice dinner with Jake and Melissa and those grandbabies of mine and I stopped in for a visit with Mama on the way home."

"How is Annabelle?" To anyone listening in, the question might seem rather generic, but when it came to Margaret Louise and Leona's mother, it was far more specific than it sounded.

"The nurse on duty said Mama only took two things from the man sittin' next to her at dinner. But he didn't mind none. In fact, he said she could keep 'em."

"Is this the man who they say is smitten with your mama?"

"One of 'em."

Tori savored the first real laugh she'd had all evening then summed it up in a quick sentence for her caller. "So Leona came by her ways honestly, I see."

"Can we not talk about my twin? She has a way of ruinin' many of my conversations this week."

"Oh?"

"Jake pulled me aside after dinner this evenin' to tell me I needed to make amends with Leona. Can you imagine? *I* need to make amends with *her*?"

She seized the opening Margaret Louise's story gave her to side with the woman's son. "I don't think he's saying you're at fault for what happened at the circle meeting, I think he's just reminding you that Leona is your sister and family has to get past the bumps."

"I can't forgive her for what she did to Rose on that TV show of hers. I reckon those two will keep fightin' until the day Rose dies, but it's always been confined to our meetin's . . . where there are plenty of us to step in and call Leona on her ways. But on Sunday, she did it in front of the entire county in a way that had everyone but us laughin' at Rose!"

It was the same point she'd used as a reason to delay calling Leona back after their meeting Monday night, and for driving past her home without really stopping the next night. Yet it was a point that receded into unimportance the moment she'd learned of Leona's accident.

Because when push came to shove, Leona mattered to Tori. And Tori knew Leona mattered to Margaret Louise.

"I talked to Rose the day after our circle meeting," she shared as a lead-up to the news that had to come out. "I vented my frustrations over Leona's behavior just like you're doing with me now. And you want to know something?"

"What's that, Victoria?"

"Rose actually defended Leona." The sharp intake of air in her ear told her to keep going. "I could hardly believe it. In fact, I even tried to argue with Rose about it, but she was the bigger person, as always."

"There's no excusin' what my twin did. No excusin' at all."

"I agree. I truly do. And I believe we're all going to need to sit down with Leona when she's well again and help her understand that what she did was wrong—"

"Well again?"

Tori paused in confusion. "Excuse me?"

"You just said we're goin' to need to sit down with my twin when she's well again."

So I did . . .

"Right now, I think Leona is dealing with too much to have us shove her face in what she did. But in a few weeks, when she's up and moving around again, it'll be time to talk. In the meantime, I have to agree with Jake. Leona is your sister—and my friend—no matter what she's gone and done."

Margaret Louise's normally boisterous voice dropped to a tortured whisper. "Tell me, Victoria, what happened to my twin?"

Tori nestled her cheek against the seat back and gazed out the passenger side window at the Bradys' home once again, the welcoming porch light doing little to illuminate the path of the figure exiting the door off the left side of the darkened home . . .

Jerking upright, Tori narrowed her eyes in an effort to make out any details of the figure that would confirm his or her identity, but it was difficult in the dark.

"Please, Victoria, I have to know."

The figure slunk along the hedge line that bordered the western edge of the Bradys' property then took off in a run toward a parked car on the other side of the road that Tori hadn't noticed until that moment. But as she watched, the figure looped around to the passenger side of the waiting car and yanked open the door, her identity and that of the driver visible for one illuminated moment before the occupants sped away.

"Victoria?"

"Huh? What?"

"What's wrong with Leona?"

Leona . . .

Leona . . .

She willed herself to focus on the voice in her ear even as the image recorded by her eyes seared itself into her thoughts. "Leona fell after the meeting the other night. She fractured her hip and had to have surgery. She's at Tom's Creek Hospital and in a fairly decent amount of pain, but she's being released tomorrow and she's positively giddy at the notion of going home to Paris."

Under different circumstances, she might have been offended by the wordless hang-up that followed her announcement, but considering she'd just witnessed Beatrice's prime suspect sneaking out of the Bradys' house and into her boyfriend's car, she decided to let it slide.

Chapter 16

Tori was just shelving the last of the returns from the overnight drop box when Georgina Hayes paraded her way through the front door and over to the information desk. Dropping a large manila envelope onto the counter, the statuesque woman pulled her trademark straw hat from her head and looked around.

"Hello, Nina. Is Victoria in her office by any chance?" Georgina nudged her chin in the direction of the envelope and then covered it with her hat. "I've got something I'd like to discuss with her if she is available. It shouldn't take long."

Tori exited the self-help aisle and winked at her assistant. "I don't know, Nina, should I find some time to spare for our mayor?"

Georgina spun around, knocking her hat and the envelope to the floor as she did. "Oh. Victoria. I didn't know you were there." The woman reached down, retrieved both items, and placed them back on the countertop. "I heard the board meeting went well last night."

"It did." Tori stepped through the opening in the semi-circular desk area and tapped Nina on the shoulder. "If you want to take your lunch now, I'll hold down the fort. But be sure to check the shelf below the coffeemaker first. I stopped at Debbie's on the way in this morning and bought you a treat."

Nina's eyes widened with unrestrained hope. "A blueberry scone?"

"How'd you guess?" she teased.

"Mayor Hayes, if that envelope contains a list of signatures from residents demanding you institute a Victoria Sinclair Day in Sweet Briar, I'd like to add my name." Nina vacated her stool, squeezed Tori's hand, and then headed in the direction of their shared office across from the children's room.

"Nina has a point, you know. Victoria Sinclair Day would be good for local businesses," Tori joked as she claimed Nina's stool and smiled up at her sewing circle sister. "Especially Debbie's Bakery and Shelby's Sweet Shoppe. In fact, in celebration of my day, it could be a rule that folks *have* to eat chocolate."

Georgina tried her best to bite back a smile, but she wasn't fast enough.

"Admit it, Mayor Hayes . . . you're considering it, aren't you?"

"I'll see what I can do." Georgina grabbed hold of the envelope again and came around the desk to claim the second stool. "I was hoping you might consider being a part of the Buy Local Task Force I'm trying to get off the ground."

"A task force, huh? That's usually a code word for meetings," Tori quipped, only to backtrack when Georgina's expression fell. "I'm not saying I'm opposed to it, but there's only eight more days until my wedding and then I'm gone for a week for my honeymoon."

"Bless your heart, Victoria, I'm not talking about right now. I'd be a fool not to realize how busy you are. But I was hoping you might help me after you're back home and settled in with Milo." Georgina worked the metal clasp at the top of the envelope but stopped short of removing its contents. "And I'm not talking about five meetings a week. No, I'm talking about a meeting once a month. Tops."

"Once a month might be doable." She glanced toward the front door as it swung open and then waved as Lana Turner, owner of Turner's Gifts 'N More, stepped inside. "Welcome to Sweet Briar Public Library, Lana."

Lana's smile widened as she acknowledged Tori and then Georgina. "Mayor Hayes, I didn't expect to see you here."

"Why? I read," Georgina joked. "Though I will admit that my standard reading material is far less exciting than anything you'd find here."

Tori swiveled around on her stool and positioned her hands atop the keyboard. "So what can I help you find, Lana?"

Ducking her head to the left and then the right, the platinum blonde scanned their immediate surroundings before finally reengaging eye contact with Tori. "I know I'll probably be stoned for admitting this out loud, but here goes. I've fallen behind on Colby Calhoun's books and I really should catch up before I'm at a party and someone outs me."

"Your secret is safe with me." Tori pulled her hands back off the keyboard and pointed toward one of the most requested shelves in the entire library thanks to the home-grown author's standing in the community. "I think his most recent title is still checked out, but all his others should be there."

"Thanks, Tori."

"Lana, could you hold on a minute?" Georgina requested as she reached into the envelope and pulled out a piece of paper with black-and-white pictures, captions, and text boxes. "I was planning to stop by your shop later this afternoon to show you the mock-up for my Buy Local brochure anyway, so showing you now will save me a trip."

With quick hands, Georgina folded the pamphlet as it would appear to a reader and handed it to Tori. Then, reaching into the envelope a second time, she pulled out another copy and did the same for Lana. "I was hoping you both could give it a quick look and tell me your first impressions—you know, what speaks to you, what doesn't, what might be a good addition or point to hit, that sort of thing."

Tori set the pamphlet next to the computer and took in the whimsical font used to encourage people to keep their money in Sweet Briar. "I think this font puts an almost-too-playful aspect on the message and I'm not sure that's what you're really trying to do, is it?"

Georgina rested her chin on tented fingers. "Absolutely not. Encouraging folks to spend their money here, as opposed to Tom's Creek or Reed's Corner, is serious business."

"Then find a serious font."

"While I agree with Tori, I do think you can find a font that is both serious and inviting." Lana pointed at the picture beneath the opening title and scrunched her nose. "But this picture on the cover? It *has* to go."

Tori studied the picture of the well-dressed man standing halfway up the steps of Brady's Jewelry. The snapshot itself was a good one, although another round of cropping might not be such a bad idea . . .

"I could move it inside, I suppose," Georgina mused, "but I thought it was good because you can see some of the other shop signs in the background."

"Oooh, you're right. I can actually make out Shelby's Sweet Shoppe behind him, and a little bit of Calamity Books beyond that." Tori readied her hand to move onto the inside section but looked at the picture one last time. "Yeah, I think it's a good shot for the cover."

"For me, this picture makes me want to toss the whole thing in the trash without reading any further." Lana pulled her focus from the pamphlet and the offending picture and fixed it instead on Georgina. "I realize that not everyone will see this picture as hypocrisy at its finest, but *some* will. And that, right there, is reason enough to remove it entirely if you're even remotely serious about this whole Buy Local initiative."

Tori caught the look of shock on Georgina's face and knew it surely mirrored her own. But it was the mayor who questioned it first. "Hypocrisy? What are you talking about, Lana? Jim Brady has kept his business in this town despite the availability of storefronts in areas with far more foot traffic than we see in Sweet Briar."

Lana gazed back down at the pamphlet, gave the inside and backside a precursory look, and then handed it back to the mayor with a shrug. "I'm not questioning Jim's loyalty to this town as a business owner, Mayor Hayes. I'd be a fool to think something like that, let alone voice it."

"Then what's the problem?" Tori asked.

"This brochure is about keeping our money in Sweet Briar, yes?" Lana twisted the ends of her stylish bob between the fingers of her right hand then released it to point at Tori's pamphlet in response to Georgina's nod. "How can we expect our residents to do something the man on the front of the brochure doesn't do? I mean, it's like my grandfather always said, 'If it's good for the goose, than it's good for the gander.'"

"Are you saying that Jim doesn't keep his money local?" Georgina questioned. "Because if you are, you're off base. I see Julie at Leeson's Market almost every time I'm in there. And it wasn't more than a week or two ago that I saw Jim coming out of *your* store, Lana, with a series of gift bags in his hand."

"I'm not saying he doesn't shop in town, because I know he does. But I also know he and his wife just bypassed a local company in order to patronize one overseas."

Suddenly, Lana's words made sense, even if they were more than a little misguided. "Normally, I'd stay out of something like this simply because I don't feel I have enough information to weigh in," Tori said. "But on this particular subject, I think I do."

Turning her body to face Tori, Lana leaned her elbow

atop the counter for support. "Okay, enlighten me. Please. Because I will never understand taking work away from one of our own in order to give it to someone overseas."

"From what I've heard from multiple sources, the Bradys have always hired their nannies locally. Perhaps even from the same local agency."

"The Nanny Go Round Agency. That's right here in Sweet Briar," Lana confirmed. "And yes, that was my understanding about the Bradys as well. Until recently anyway."

Tori rushed to correct the image of a family she really didn't know. "Keep in mind that only changed because of a life-or-death situation they encountered with the last nanny from Nanny Go Round. Their kindergartener almost died on the second day of school this year because of an allergy Cynthia failed to mention to the teacher. That's a serious screwup, Lana—one that had the potential to end that little girl's life."

"Wow. I didn't realize . . ."

"And even my assistant, Nina, mentioned how inattentive this particular nanny seemed to be with the youngest Brady, too." Tori dropped her voice to a near whisper despite the absence of any patrons at that moment. "Nannies aren't supposed to be that way. It's their job to be on top of everything where their employer's children are concerned."

"Okay. It certainly makes more sense now, but why couldn't they just hire a different nanny from that agency? Why bring one in from another country?"

"First of all, I believe it was Julie who made that choice. At least that's what our friend, Beatrice"—she pointed between herself and Georgina—"told me. But regardless,

I think it's a little understandable that a parent wouldn't want to chance their children's well-being with another nanny from the agency where they hired Cynthia."

Georgina slipped Lana's pamphlet back into the envelope and stood. "In Jim and Julie's defense, I can see why a suggestion from Beatrice Tharrington in regards to a suitable nanny would be taken seriously. Beatrice has been with the Johnson family for years now and she's not only been a wonderful companion for their son, Luke, but she's also been a tremendous asset to our community, helping to sew costumes for our Memorial Day parade each and every year."

"And now that this British woman is dead, will they go back to Nanny Go Round?"

"That will be their decision, of course," Georgina cautioned. "But if they *don't*, I can't say I wouldn't do the same under similar circumstances."

Lana shot her hands up in defeat. "Okay, okay, I stand corrected. But you have to know that if I had that impression when I saw your brochure, it's likely others will, too."

"And they'll be wrong," Georgina interjected.

"But will they be standing next to someone who can tell them that when they look at your brochure and contemplate throwing it in the trash?" Lana tapped her hand on the top of the counter and then turned toward the shelf containing Colby Calhoun's books. "It's something you need to think about if nothing else. In the meantime, I'm going to get caught up on my reading—which, I'm pleased to point out, is in support of a *local* author."

Chapter 17

Tori was just setting a gift bag and box of chocolates on the floor of the passenger seat when she heard the familiar squeak and hum of Margaret Louise's car as it pulled up alongside her own. She turned and waited as her friend rolled down the window for conversational purposes.

"Hey. I'm on my way over to Leona's to make sure she's settled in with her caregiver and to bring her a few things to keep her busy."

Margaret Louise stuck her pudgy hand through the open window and shooed Tori from her field of vision. "What's in the bag?"

Tori backed herself against the side of her car and did her best to give a verbal inventory of the gift bag's contents. "A few romantic comedies she can watch on the DVD player in her room, a few travel and antique magazines, those gummy bears she refuses to admit she likes, a cross-word puzzle book, and a carrot for Paris."

"You're wastin' your money if you think my twin is goin' to eat those chocolates." Margaret Louise pointed toward the rectangular-shaped box beside the bag. "If there's one thing I know 'bout Leona, it's that gettin' her to eat chocolate is like gettin' her to smile at anyone who falls in the diaper-wearin' demographic."

"Oh, I know that, but she likes to *receive* them. Once she does, though, she's more than happy to hand them off to someone else."

A fleeting grin brought a much-needed, albeit short-lived, interior light to her friend's eyes. "Now don't you go eatin' that whole box by yourself, Victoria. You've got a weddin' dress to wear in eight days and you don't want to be lookin' like me."

"I wouldn't want to have a beautiful smile and eyes that dance when I talk about everything and anything?"

A hint of crimson rose in Margaret Louise's cheeks, prompting the woman to cover them with her hands. "I was referrin' to my jigglin' belly but thank you for sayin' such nice things."

"It's easy to speak the truth." She pointed between her car and her friend's. "You want to come to Leona's with me? We could say the chocolates are from *you*."

Margaret Louise shifted in her seat and brought her hands back to the steering wheel. "No. I've got somethin' of my own to do right now."

Something in the woman's voice brought Tori up short and sent her internal radar pinging. "You haven't called her yet, have you?"

When her question was met with silence, she reached over, shut the door on Leona's gifts, and stepped away from the car. "Margaret Louise, you're going to regret this one day. Leona may have made a mistake on her show last week, but she's still your sister. And you know as well as I do that there's one positive for every not-so-positive where your sister is concerned."

Margaret Louise shrugged and then shifted her car back into drive. "I reckon you're right 'bout that. But I'm still digestin' and decidin'."

"Digesting and deciding what?"

"I'm digestin' what she did to Rose, and decidin' what I want to say to my twin."

Tori closed the gap between their cars and leaned her head through the open window. "Don't wait too long, okay?"

When Margaret Louise said nothing, Tori went for the most persuasive tactic of all. "Once you've figured out what to do with all of this, let me know, because I could use your keen eye on a little matter I promised Beatrice I'd look into."

Like a dog alerted to the scent of a tasty bone, Margaret Louise shifted her wagon back into park. "Is this a matter that needs a little investigatin'?"

"It's looking that way," Tori teased while doing her best to maintain a straight face.

"And this has somethin' to do with Beatrice?"

"It does."

Reaching up, Margaret Louise scratched at her hairline. "Wait! The only time we've done any investigatin' is when there's been a body."

"*Almost* every time, yes . . ."

"The only body havin' anythin' to do with Beatrice is her Miss Gracie."

Tori retreated from the window and took a few steps back toward her own car. "Yes. That's right."

"Miss Gracie fell down a flight of stairs, Victoria. What kind of investigatin' can we do with—" Reality dawned across Margaret Louise's face, widening her eyes and gaping her mouth as it did. "Wait. Are you tellin' me you're thinkin' she didn't fall?"

Tori looped around the hood of her car and answered her friend across its roof. "Everything I've got so far is circumstantial, I know, but there's a pretty good chance Miss Gracie's fall was as a result of someone's hand."

"Count me in, Victoria!"

Tori yanked her door open, slid into place behind the steering wheel, turned the key in the ignition, and pressed open the passenger side window. "I'd love to have you ridin' shotgun with me on this, Margaret Louise, but I think you're too distracted with this whole Leona thing."

"I ain't any more distracted by my sister and her mean ways than you are with your weddin' . . . which, I will remind you again, is in eight days, Victoria!"

"I've got the wedding under control at this point. And having someone helping me get to the bottom of this woman's death will make everything a whole lot easier."

"Let me help you, Victoria," Margaret Louise pleaded in a voice thick with saliva. "Please."

"Sure thing. Just turn your car off, hop in here with me so we can visit your sister, and then we'll talk about how we proceed with our investigation." She glanced down at her dashboard clock and then back up at her friend. "It's only five thirty, Margaret Louise. We can fit a whole lot of investigating in between now and bedtime."

Margaret Louise's gaze dropped to what Tori assumed was her own dashboard clock and then disappeared behind closed lids. "I can't right now, Victoria. I've got somewhere I need to be in less than twenty minutes."

"Okay. Well, when you see fit to work things out with Leona, give me a call and we'll talk motives and suspects then." She applied just enough pressure to the window button to raise it halfway. "Unless, of course, I've figured out the truth all on my own by then . . ."

She was still chuckling to herself when, arms full, she was forced to use her elbow to ring Leona's doorbell.

Half a minute later, the door swung open to reveal a familiar face. "Oh, hey, it's you—the one who stepped in and saved the day with Paris before I had to go to work the other night."

"Sam, right?" she said by way of response as she accepted his gestured invite inside. "Leona told me you were probably bringing her home today."

He swept a hand through his disheveled hair then cast a longing glance toward the living room and the tired, yet always stylish woman seated in a straight-back chair in front of the fireplace. "Unfortunately, as you can see"—he pointed inward at his EMT uniform—"I'm still on the clock, which means I have to run out of here the second a call comes over the radio."

"How's she doing?" she asked, lowering her voice. "Was she able to handle the move without too much pain?"

"She's an amazing woman," Sam gushed. "I've never seen anyone come out of a hospital after hip surgery looking like that."

Tori followed his gaze back to Leona and the facial pallor that painted a different picture for anyone in the know. She supposed she might see things the way Sam did if she didn't know Leona so well, but after the barrage of makeup and posture talks she'd been given by the man-magnet over the last two-plus years, she knew there was more to the story.

"Is her caregiver here?"

Sam nodded and pointed to a young woman in her mid-twenties typing away on a handheld device, seemingly oblivious to everything about her surroundings, including Leona.

"Huh. Okay."

"Hey, I've gotta step outside and check in on my partner. If he's still content out there with his sandwich and his magazine, I'll get to stay a little longer. Either way, though, I won't leave without saying good-bye to Leona."

"Sounds good, Sam. Thanks for getting her here safely." She watched as he walked through the door he'd just held open for her and then turned and made her way into the living room. "I see you made it home, Leona."

Setting the gift bag and the box on the end table to Leona's left, she stepped close enough to her friend to whisper a kiss across her forehead. "You're in pain, aren't you?"

"Whatever . . . gave you that . . . idea, dear?"

"You mean other than the way your voice buckled just now?" She glanced toward the girl in the corner, still typing away on her device, and then plucked a blanket off the back of the couch and draped it across Leona. "Well, for starters, you seem chilled. Next, there's a paleness to your skin that your makeup simply isn't hiding. And finally, there's the row of lashes you missed with your mascara brush. Since I've never seen any of those things in all the time I've known you, and you've never fractured your hip before, I can only deduce they're related."

Then, hooking her finger over her shoulder while Leona grabbed for the mirror on the edge of the table, she lowered her voice so only Leona could hear. "And what's with this one over there? Is she being paid to look after you and your needs, or to keep up with her friends on social media?"

Leona turned the mirror every which way before resting her head against her seat back with a groan. "I can't believe I left the hospital looking like . . . well . . . looking like *you*, dear."

"Why, thank you, Leona. I always know where to go for a slice of humble pie."

Waving her words away, Leona addressed Tori's most recent question. "I think it's best she stay buried in her technology while Sam is here."

"Why?" Tori asked, only to receive her answer in a second, longer look at Leona's temporary employee.

Distracted or not, the girl was beautiful in the way twenty-somethings tended to be—full of life (even if it was lived on social media), void of wrinkles, and shapely without trying.

Leona released a second, but no less frustrated groan, successfully reclaiming Tori's focus in the process. "I don't eat chocolates, Victoria. You should know this by now. It's why I look like this. Or rather, like I do every other moment except this one."

"I know you don't eat chocolate, Leona. But I do."

"Which is why you look like that, dear . . ."

Tori laughed off the anticipated response and lowered herself to the edge of the couch closest to Leona. "But I think you'll enjoy what's in the bag. It'll certainly help keep you busy.

"Oh, and there's a carrot in there for Paris, as well." She took in their immediate surroundings and even snuck a peek around the back side of Leona's chair. "Are you ready for her to come back home or do you think it would be wiser for her to stay with me for a while?"

"I can't stand being away from her for another night."

"Then I'll give Milo a call and ask him to swing by my place and pick her up."

"Thank you, dear. It's nice to know I can count on *someone* from that group of women who believe lip service about loyalty and friendship is all that matters."

The front door slammed shut behind them, prompting Leona's head to part company with the back of her seat at the same time her plumped lips turned upward in a flirtatious smile. "Oh, good, I was hoping you hadn't left, Sam."

"There's absolutely no way I would leave without saying good-bye to you, Leona."

"I didn't think so," Leona purred before reaching for the chocolates. "I got you a little something in advance of the more"—Leona batted her partially made-up eyes at the uniformed man—"*thorough* thank-you that will be coming your way very, very soon."

Chapter 18

Tori took advantage of Leona's flirting to cross the room and engage the caregiver who, until that moment, had yet to even look up at the injured woman.

"Hello. I'm Victoria Sinclair, Leona's friend." She held her hand out and waited as the twenty-something slowly lifted her head to pin Tori with a bored stare.

"Hey."

"And you are?"

"The live-in help for the next week or so." Relocating her handheld device to her lap, the young woman gathered her long dark hair into a high ponytail, secured it, fussed with it, and then let it cascade over her shapely shoulders once again. "But this should be an easy gig because that lady over there"—the girl pointed past Tori—"told me I'm really only here to make her doctor happy."

It took everything she had not to pull the girl to her

feet and usher her straight toward the front door. But she couldn't. Leona was an adult. She didn't need Tori questioning her choices.

On the other hand, as Leona's friend, she also couldn't sit by and say nothing . . .

"I think we need to start this conversation over, which we can do by you shutting that off." She guided the girl's eyes to the still illuminated device and waited.

"But I'm snap chatting with my BFF."

She waved aside the girl's protests while simultaneously working to tame her own rising anger. "For the next week or so, your primary focus is *that lady over there*"— she pointed her finger at Leona—"who, by the way, is Miss Elkin. When Miss Elkin is sleeping, or otherwise occupied, you can check in on your BFF."

"She looks pretty occupied to me," the girl said, reclaiming a wad of gum from whichever molar it had been attached to prior to that moment.

"Miss Elkin just got home, and you just got here, too, isn't that right?" At the girl's nod, she continued, "Which means you really should be spending this time familiarizing yourself with her home and the doctor's instructions for her care this next week or so."

"You really think I'm going to be doing that much? I mean, she's what? Seventy-five or something?"

The hair on the back of Tori's neck stuck out as she waited for the gasp from the other side of the room. Fortunately, neither Leona nor Sam seemed to hear the caregiver's words. As the cloud of fear passed, Tori focused on the still unnamed girl once again. "Miss Elkin fractured her hip. That alone means you're here to make sure she doesn't re-harm herself by moving around prematurely."

"My boss said there will be a therapist and a home health nurse coming in to make sure Miss Elkin is moving around, so I think she'll be fine."

"What is your name?" Tori asked pointedly.

"Rachel. Why?"

"Because that's usually an important piece of information to give a person when you're speaking." She heard the sarcasm in her voice but felt no need to soften it. "Miss Elkin has hired you to look after her needs until she no longer needs you to do so. That means, you get whatever she asks you to get, and you help her with whatever she needs you to help her with. If she tells you she's got it covered, you essentially stand nearby to make sure that's true."

"Okay, okay. Sheesh. Are you her granddaughter or something?"

This time, her shoulders lurched upward toward her ears as she braced for impact, but once again, there was nothing.

Sam might be worth keeping around . . .

She shook the part amusing/part very real thought from her head and answered the girl's question. "Leona is one of *my* BFFs."

Rachel looked from Tori to Leona and back again as surprise widened her previously half-mast eyes to something actually resembling circles. "Yeah, but you're like forty and she's like—"

She waved her index finger in front of Rachel. "I'm not forty, and Miss Elkin is not"—she lowered her voice to a whisper—"seventy-five. And if you want to keep your job, I suggest you start by refraining from guessing her age.

"Beyond that, I'll tell you that age doesn't make or

define a friendship. *Caring* about one another does. Which is why I'm here now, and why I'll be stopping by often to make sure Leona is doing okay."

"Is she at least nice?" Rachel asked.

"Depends on who you ask, I guess." She glanced over her shoulder at her friend and willed herself to see past the pale skin and tired eyes to the Leona she knew and loved. "She can be sharp-tongued and impatient as all get-out, but I wouldn't trade her for anything."

Rachel looked down at her now blackened screen and then set the device on the closest flat surface. "I guess I can do this for a week or so."

"I take it you prefer working with little ones?"

The girl snickered. "Uh. No. I've stood in for a few of the other girls on occasion and all that nose-blowing and homework-helping is enough to drive me insane."

"Well, if you don't like working with kids, and you don't seem to be particularly interested in the infirm, can I ask why you're working for the Nanny Go Round Agency at all?"

"Honestly, this is the first true assignment I've been on for Tara in over a year. She needed an actual body this time and I didn't really have anything else to do." Rachel twisted her mouth to the left. "My boyfriend, or should I say *ex*-boyfriend, up and took off for California last week."

"Who is Tara?" she asked.

"Tara Reed. She's the owner of the agency. She went to school with my dad. That's how Jeanine got in, too. Only I think Jeanine's mom and Tara are real tight, which is why she's not dealing with this kind of interrogation."

She filed the name away for further inspection at a later date and moved on. "Jeanine?"

Tonguing her gum from one side of her mouth to the other, Rachel chewed through her answer. "The one I was trying to snap chat when you came over."

Ahhh, the BFF . . .

"Does she work as a nanny for little ones or as a caregiver like you are?"

Rachel tapped her chin for a moment as she pondered Tori's question. "You know, I think most of her gigs go down as kids. Which, I guess, makes sense since she actually talks about being a kindergarten teacher one day."

"Did she study education in college?"

"Jeanine didn't go to college. But you don't really need college to be a teacher, do you? I mean, as long as you know how to tie your shoes and wipe your nose, you can teach a five-year-old."

She stifled the second half of her snort with a quick hand. "It's a bit more complicated than that, Rachel."

"Oh. Well, then maybe she can be a teacher on paper, too. After all, the money doesn't change much if you actually *do* it, so why bother."

"People don't get into education to be rich, Rachel. They get into it because they love children."

Rachel's brows dipped forward in confusion, only to resume their normal position with a quick shrug. "If you ask me, there's way too much to keep track of with kids. Just ask my friend, Cynthia."

She swallowed. "Cynthia? As in Cynthia Marland?"

"Yeah. You know her?" Then without waiting for a response, Rachel continued. "She got railroaded on her last real call. She forgot to tell the school about some problem one of the kids had and they didn't have the medicine they needed when the kid started twitching and shaking and stuff. But c'mon, are you telling me Cynthia is supposed to keep track of *everything*?"

"When you've been hired as a nanny? Yes. That was her *job*, Rachel."

Rachel crossed her arms and stopped just short of stamping her foot. "What*ever* . . . Mrs. Brady didn't have to threaten the rest of us, too!"

"The rest of you?"

"Me. My friends. *Everyone* on the agency's books."

Her curiosity aroused to an all new level, Tori stopped herself mid-lip-lick. "Hold on a minute. Are you saying Julie Brady threatened to sue the agency?"

"I wouldn't know it even if she did. That kind of stuff is discussed above my pay level, as my father would say." Softening her stance somewhat, Rachel yawned. "Cynthia just needs to make it right. If she does, none of us have to worry. If she doesn't, and she decides to get all high-and-mighty, we're all in trouble."

Pointing toward the hallway off the condo's main rooms, Rachel yawned a second time. "I'm thinking I might take a nap for a little while."

"You can nap when Miss Elkin naps." Tori swept her hand and Rachel's focus toward Leona and the man she was currently offering a rather fond farewell. "Which, judging by the approaching dinner hour, won't be happening anytime soon. Why don't you see what she wants for dinner instead?"

Like a deer caught in the glaring headlights of a pickup truck with a well-appointed gun rack, Rachel froze. "Wait. You mean I have to *cook*, too?"

Chapter 19

As excited as she was to be marrying Milo, Tori couldn't help but feel a little nostalgia for her cottage and the various details that had come together to make it a true home. Sure, the plaid armchair she'd bought at a thrift store within days of moving to Sweet Briar would be coming to her new home along with all of her other belongings, but there, at Milo's, they'd look different.

"Penny for your thoughts?"

She looked up from the box she was in the process of sealing shut and offered her fiancé what she hoped was a genuine smile. "I'm beyond excited at the fact that we're getting married in seven days and that we'll finally get to begin our life together."

"But . . ."

"Am I that transparent?" she asked, dropping the tape roll onto the floor.

"I'd like to think I just know you." Milo handed her the black marker they'd been sharing to label each box and then added, "As I should, don't you think?"

She jotted the contents onto two different sides of the box and then capped the marker and set it back on the floor. "I guess I'm remembering the move into this place. How excited and nervous I was all at the same time. I mean, I was determined to start fresh, but that meant everything being new. It was a little scary."

The overhead light caught the amber flecks in Milo's eyes and made them dance against their dark brown backdrop. "From what I can see, you jumped in with both feet and made Sweet Briar your home. Everyone in this town loves you, baby."

"And I love this town and everyone in it." She leaned her head against the wall and quietly surveyed the stack of boxes to her left and the handful of scattered boxes to her right. "When I made the decision to move here, all I truly focused on was finally getting to be a head librarian. I knew I wanted to make friends and fit in, but the thing that made me actually leave Chicago was the job."

"Then I guess I owe Winston and the rest of the board members a thank-you note or something . . ."

Pulling her knees upward, she rested her chin atop them and smiled. "They'll be at the wedding so you can thank them then if you're so inclined."

"I am, and I will."

"When I put that there"—Tori pointed at the corner cabinet between the living and the dining rooms—"I figured I'd put knickknacks and things on those shelves. But instead, I found myself filling them with amazing moments I never would have had if I hadn't taken this job."

Milo lifted his own finger to indicate the first of the half-dozen or so yet-to-be-packed picture frames that never ceased to bring a smile to her face as she passed from one room to the other, regardless of mood or hour. "I love that picture of you and Rose on that red-and-white-checked blanket of yours. That was one of the summer evening concerts, wasn't it?"

She managed to blink away the sudden moisture in her eyes, only to have the same emotion make its presence known via a tightness in her throat. "There was something about Rose that grabbed hold of my heart during my very first sewing circle meeting. It was like she gave me back some of the best parts of my great-grandmother—not in a way that replaced her, but in a way that has helped me to see she's always close by."

Rising to his feet, Milo crossed the sea of boxes between them to sit beside her and hold her hand. "I wish I could have met your great-grandmother, Tori. Especially knowing that she's such a huge factor in the amazing person you are."

"I do, too, Milo." She squeezed his hand and then brought it up to her lips for a quick kiss. "She would have loved you. Of that, I have absolutely no doubt." Then, lowering their hands back to her lap, she took in Rose's photograph once again. "But if I can't have my great-grandmother at my wedding, Rose is the next best thing."

"I'm glad. I know she thinks the world of you, that's for sure. And your being here has given a noticeable lift to her life, as well."

"I hope so. I can't even entertain the notion of her not being here one day." She swatted the thought away with her free hand and, instead, pointed to the next shelf and the first of the three frames it held. "You've known Margaret Louise longer than I have, but have you ever known her to be unhappy?"

"When her husband passed, I guess, though even then, she opted to focus on her memories rather than the fact that he was gone."

"Anytime I'm feeling grouchy, I look at that picture and remember the moment she won that contest with her sweet potato pie. She was so tickled with her win, you'd have thought she'd hit the lottery."

"Because to Margaret Louise, pleasing people with her recipes *is* a lottery win."

"And did you ever think the day would come that Dixie would actually *like* me?" she joked as her gaze moved on to the next picture, and the recognition ceremony Tori had insisted the board host upon Dixie's last turn as a volunteer at the library.

"Considering we're talking about *you*, yeah, I knew it would happen." He turned, leaned across the small gap between them, and lingered a kiss against her temple. "How could it not?"

Her attention zoned in on the next picture—a selfie of her, Leona, and Paris during their first girls' night slumber party. Thinking back to the moment they snapped the photo, she couldn't help but giggle at the wrestling match that had ensued when she'd tried to angle the camera in such a way as to document what the always polished Leona was wearing. Leona, of course, had won, but the simple fact the woman had worn footie pajamas around Tori spoke volumes about the trust they shared.

"I wish everyone else could see the Leona I know," she whispered.

"Don't you think Margaret Louise does?"

Tori considered Milo's question and found that even she was surprised by the answer that left her mouth. "I'm not entirely sure Leona *lets* her sister see her vulnerable sides."

"But they're close . . ."

"As close as two people who are as different as night and day can be anyway," she conceded. "Or at least they were, before this whole Rose fiasco—a fiasco that Rose herself seems more willing to overlook than Margaret Louise or anyone else in the circle."

"It's still that bad?" Milo asked.

"As of last night, Margaret Louise still hadn't reached out to Leona about her fall." She extricated her hand from his and used it to cradle her forehead. "When anyone in this town so much as stubs a toe, Margaret Louise is on their doorstep with a pie . . . or four. Yet after what Leona did on that show of hers, Margaret Louise hasn't even picked up the phone to *check* on her sister let alone bake a pie for her."

After a moment or two of silence, Milo scooted away from the wall and turned his whole body so they could be face to face. "If you're worried about friction at the wedding, I have no doubt everyone will behave that day if for no other reason than because they love you."

"And us," she reminded. "But honestly, until you just said that, the wedding aspect hadn't even entered my mind. I just hate knowing that this group that has been so wonderful to me these past two-plus years is beginning to fray at the seams—no pun intended."

"They'll get it together," Milo reassured her. "There's way too much history there to throw it away over some really bad judgment on Leona's part."

"It might help if she *admitted* she used bad judgment."

"She hasn't?"

Tori made a face. "We're talking about Leona, remember?" Pushing off the ground, Tori rose to her feet and wandered over to the window that overlooked her small backyard. "Which means I'm the only one keeping an eye on Rachel."

"Who is Rachel?"

"She's the one Leona hired to stay at the house with her instead of going to rehab," Tori explained as she took in the cozy outdoor gathering place Rose had helped her visualize and execute right down to the morning glory–wrapped arbor that served as its entry point. "This girl is no more than twenty-three and has absolutely zero interest in doing anything resembling work."

Milo snickered. "And Leona is okay with that?"

"When I left last night, Leona had been so busy flirting with the EMT, I'm not sure she actually exchanged more than a sentence or two with this girl. But honestly, even if she's realized it by now, I think she'll let it slide simply because her main objective is to be home with Paris."

Even without the sound of his footsteps, Tori could sense Milo's nearness before his arms came around her shoulders and drew her close. It was a gesture she adored and one she looked forward to adoring for the rest of her life. "Leona isn't going to let anyone mistreat her, Tori. You know that as well as I do."

She unlinked his hands from in front of her chest just enough to turn around and face him, her own hands linking together behind his neck. "You're right. Leona isn't one to stay silent on any subject for long. If she needs me, she'll call."

He kissed her forehead, her nose, and finally her lips, only to pull away and smile down at her with both dimples on full display. "I finished my vows last night and I'm pretty proud of them if I must say so myself."

The warmth of his smile sent a shiver of excitement through her body. "I can't wait to stand there, in front of all our friends and family, and say everything I want to say to you and hear everything you want to say to me."

He loosened his hold on her just enough to be able to see into her eyes. "So? Any word yet on when your parents are coming in? Will they be here for the rehearsal dinner?"

"Their flight comes in from South Africa on Saturday morning, about two hours before the wedding. And they'll fly back out around ten that evening."

"That's only thirteen hours," he protested.

"It's thirteen more hours than I've gotten in years, Milo." She leaned forward, kissed the tip of his chin, and then stepped out of his arms and headed into the kitchen for a glass of water.

He followed her and then nodded as she held up a glass in lieu of words. "Wow, Tori, I'm sorry. I know how disappointed you must be."

Holding his glass against the water dispenser in the refrigerator door, she rushed to squelch the anguish she heard in his voice. "Milo, you need to understand that this is the way it is with my parents. I suppose some kids could have seen it as a reason to have resentment or to act out, but it's all I ever knew. To me, my parents were always superheroes, saving kids in poor countries with hugs and kisses. Maybe I would have felt cheated if they hadn't entrusted me to my great-grandmother's care . . .

but they did. And I had a wonderful childhood complete with great-grandparents who adored me, and parents who loved me every bit as much. They sent me postcards and letters all the time, and when they were able to fly home and see me, we made every second count."

He took the glass from her outstretched hand and held it without taking a drink. "I know, but I guess I was hoping they'd carve out a little more time leading up to the wedding so I could get to know them . . . especially with your great-grandmother being gone and all."

After a quick sip of her own drink, she put her glass down on the counter and set Milo's down next to it as well. Taking his hands in hers, she smiled up at him. "One of the things my parents taught me was that family is more than just bloodlines. It's that, too, of course, but it's also the people you meet in life who change your world for the better and accept you for who you are. For them, that caveat has always included the children they've met on their mission trips around the world. For me, once my great-grandmother died, that caveat became Rose, Leona, Margaret Louise, Debbie, Melissa, Beatrice, Georgina, and Dixie. They're my family, Milo. They're *our* family along with my parents and your mom. Having them all there in witness to our marriage will be wonderful. That said, the most important person at that wedding for me is *you*."

Once again, he pulled her into his arms and held her tight, the warmth of his breath against the top of her head lifting her spirits and chasing away all residual worry that had clung to her heart since leaving Leona's house the previous evening. "I love you, Tori."

"That's good, because I love you, too." She broke free

to reclaim her glass and to take a second, longer sip. "Which is why I must insist you take your tape roll and your marker and hit the road, mister."

His left eyebrow arched in amusement. "That doesn't sound like a whole lot of love to me."

"The guys from your men's group are taking you out for your bachelor dinner at five, aren't they?" At his nod, she continued. "It's almost four now. So go home, get yourself cleaned up, and go have a good time. We can do more of this packing stuff tomorrow."

"What are you going to do?"

"I'm not sure. I might take a bath and read . . . or I might give Leona a call and see if Paris needs a carrot or something."

Chapter 20

Tori waited until Rachel disappeared inside the guest room across the hall before she plopped into the reading chair beside Leona's bed and finally asked the million-dollar question.

"So? How's it going with Rachel?"

Leona carefully folded the edge of her satin sheet down across her lap and nestled her head against the pillow Tori had positioned against the headboard. "With proper direction—given slowly and repeated often—she's doing . . . okay."

Tori pinned her tired friend with a pointed stare. "She's dreadful, isn't she?"

"You have no idea, Victoria." Leona reached up, pulled a row of false lashes from her upper right lid, and then moved on to the left. "A *GQ* model could walk right past her and she wouldn't have a clue."

"She's rather fond of her electronics, isn't she?" Tori posed without really needing an answer. "You could always call the agency back and demand they send someone else—like maybe someone who actually gets the whole concept of work."

Leona placed her lashes into a tiny container beside her bed and then reached for the cold cream jar to its left. "I'm not going to need any help by the end of the week, so why bother? She eventually does what I need her to do."

"I'm not so sure about the end of the week, Leona. You looked mighty uncomfortable when Rachel brought me in here."

"Nothing my little pain pill can't take care of." Leona stuck three fingers of her left hand into the jar. "Though I'm already trying to wean myself off them."

"If you need them, you should take them." She leaned closer to Leona, took the jar from her hands, and recapped it while the woman applied the cream to her cheeks, her chin, and her forehead with the help of a handheld mirror. "Rachel told me your in-home nurse stopped by today and that you were in a lot of pain."

Leona pulled a folded white cloth from her nightstand drawer and used it to wipe off all the cream she'd just put on. "Perhaps when you stop by tomorrow, you could bring a muzzle that would fit my young caregiver."

Tori studied her friend for a long moment, noting the woman's tired eyes, pale skin, occasional wince of pain, and the considerable effort put forth to hide those things. "Why are you so determined to make people think you're okay all the time?" she finally asked.

"Because I am." Leona's answer, while firm, lacked

its usual convincing tone. "Why on earth would you think otherwise?"

Tori swapped the cold cream jar for one of the cookies she'd brought along and took a few nibbles. "Hmmm . . . I don't know, Leona, could it be the simple fact that you fractured your hip and you're obviously in a lot of pain?"

"You're assuming that, dear."

"No, I know that." She pointed her half-eaten cookie at Leona and put words to her observations. "You're pale, your eyes are hooded, you try to distract me away from your winces, and you're not snapping at me. All clear indicators that you are not okay despite your best efforts to prove otherwise."

"I do not wince!" A spasm of pain tightened Leona's lips and closed her eyes for a split second.

"I repeat my original question. Why are you so determined to make people think you're okay all the time? I mean, it's okay to be human, Leona."

Leona dropped her cloth onto the corner of the nightstand and stared up at the ceiling. "Do you really think I need to be hit over the head with the knowledge I'm despised?"

"*Despised?*" she echoed. "What on earth are you talking about?"

Slowly, Leona's chin lowered until her bloodshot eyes were trained on Tori's face. "I'd have to be an idiot not to know that if it were Rose or Dixie or Margaret Louise in this bed, under the exact same circumstances, there would be seven occupied chairs in this room right now. Actually, let me change that. There would be *eight* occupied chairs because I would be sitting in one, too."

This time, when an influx of pain closed Leona's eyes,

Tori wasn't sure whether it was from the woman's hip or her heart. Either way, she couldn't help but feel sorry for her friend, and searched for something to say that would be of comfort. "Leona, I'm the only one who knows you fell."

The second the words were out of her mouth, she said a silent prayer for forgiveness. She knew her statement wasn't entirely truthful, but to admit that Margaret Louise knew risked Leona's wrath and heartache—neither of which she wanted to deal with at that moment. Besides, she still had hope Leona's twin would come around sooner rather than later.

"Have you checked in with Margaret Louise this week, Victoria?"

"Yes."

"Have you checked in with Beatrice this week?"

"Yes."

"How about Debbie?"

"Yes."

"And Melissa?"

"Yes."

"Dixie? Georgina?"

"Yes to both."

"How about Rose?"

"Of course."

"Of course," Leona repeated in a whisper. "I rest my case."

"Wait a minute." She polished off the rest of her cookie and stood. "I'm here, aren't I?"

"Your point, dear?"

"I know about your fall because I checked in on you, Leona. Just like I've done with everyone else at some point or another this week."

"Do you think Melissa and Dixie have checked in on Rose? Do you think Georgina has made a call to Beatrice to see how she's getting along?"

Tori saw where the conversation was going and was at a loss for what to say. Instead, she wandered around Leona's bed to the doll-sized canopied version beneath the draped window. There, she found Paris, half sleeping, half listening.

"Face it, Victoria," Leona continued, "you and Paris are not only my true friends but also my *only* friends."

Squatting down beside the animal, Tori reached out, ran a hand down her soft back, and took a moment to compose her response. "Everyone else in the circle is your friend, too, Leona. You just . . . um . . . need to act like one more than you do."

"You mean like giving one of Paris's offspring to Rose?"

She stopped petting.

"You mean like spending my most recent trip to New York City helping you clear Dixie's name rather than shopping and meeting up with old friends?"

Tori stood and turned back to Leona.

"Or do you mean all of those sewing circle meetings I've hosted here in my home?"

She lowered herself to the edge of Leona's bed, shaking her head as she did. "Leona, there's no denying the fact you've done some good things—*friend* things. But you have to be able to see some of the not-so-nice things you've done, too. And what you did to Rose on Sunday night was mean. Everyone is just rallying around her in a show of solidarity."

"Ahh yes, of course. Saint Rose. The one everyone must protect."

"Can you stop for just a moment and put yourself in Rose's shoes?"

"I wouldn't be caught dead in flats, dear," Leona droned. "I simply couldn't do it."

Tori laughed in spite of the seriousness of the subject at hand. "You never quit, do you?" Then, she regrouped and pressed on. "Rose doesn't have many more years, Leona. Every day she seems a bit frailer, a bit slower than she did the day before."

Leona fidgeted with the trim of her sheets but said nothing, the downward cast of her eyes, followed by a distinct swallow or two, the only confirmation Tori's words were hitting their mark.

"Now imagine standing next to women younger than you—women wearing heels and sparkly dresses and moving around without a care in the world. Don't you think you'd have a pang or two of sadness or envy? Maybe even a little uncertainty about whether you fit in?"

"Eighty-two, or whatever the old goat is, is merely a number, dear."

"Maybe you should tell her aging body that the next time her arthritis has her hooked up to an IV pole and too weak to walk."

"I don't do guilt, Victoria."

"Maybe you should."

The chime of the doorbell echoed around the room, effectively bringing their conversation to an end and Leona's hands to her hair. "If it's Sam, you must tell him I'm asleep!"

"But that would make me a liar, Leona," she teased as she stood and crossed to the bedroom door. "You couldn't really ask me to do that, could you?"

"I could, and I did!"

She chuckled her way down the bedroom hallway, past Rachel's closed door, through the living room, and into the front hallway to find two figures standing on the other side of the door's frosted sidelights. A check of her watch, coupled with the overall size and shape of the visitors, all but erased the possibility that Milo was back from his bachelor dinner.

"Are you going to keep standing there, peeking at us through these windows, or are you going to open this door and give me a proper welcome, Miss Victoria?"

Any confusion that accompanied the oddly familiar voice was wiped away by a second voice. "Now Charles, I reckon you just ruined your s'prise talkin' through the door like that . . ."

Grabbing hold of the knob, Tori twisted her wrist to the right and flung open the door, the squeal she let off quickly finding a perfect match from the spikey-haired twenty-something now hopping up and down and waving his hands wildly atop the welcome mat. "I'm here! I'm here!"

She wrapped her arms around the New York City bookstore employee and joined in the hopping. "I thought you weren't coming in until Friday!"

"And miss the chance to attend an official sewing circle meeting? Not. A. Chance." He stepped back, grabbed the first of two large suitcases from the front stoop, and swung it through the open door. With that one safely inside, he did the same with the second and then ran back to Margaret Louise's station wagon for a third.

"Dare I hope you're moving to Sweet Briar?" Tori joked as he huffed and puffed his way back up the steps with the final suitcase.

Charles set the bag next to the others and then loosened the knot on his accessory scarf. "I'm not sure Sweet Briar could handle me, Victoria." He pointed at his hair. "Which is why I dispensed with the red and went with a more natural hazelnut."

"Red? When we saw you in the city, it was purple."

"Oh honey, I've cycled through the rainbow three times since then." He caught sight of himself in the antique mirror on the side wall and brushed a finger across his left eyebrow. "The second time I went with a leprechaun green instead of the neon shade and it was much more flattering."

Tori glanced at Margaret Louise, still standing on the front stoop, and motioned her inside.

The woman didn't budge.

"You can't come this close and not come in and see her," Tori pleaded. "Please. She needs to know you still love her."

Charles swiped his hand across his brow and snapped his fingers in a triangle formation between himself and his airport escort. "What did we talk about on the way here, Margaret Louise?"

"Loving my sister," Margaret Louise replied woodenly.

"First love and then . . ."

Instantly, the roundish woman on the other side of the open door brightened tenfold. "I get to investigate!"

Charles leaned forward until his breath was warm on Tori's ear. "Brilliant use of leverage, by the way."

"Why thank—" A vibration in her back pocket cut her

answer short and she pulled out her phone, the familiar name on the Caller ID screen bringing a rapid hand clap from Charles and an eye roll from Margaret Louise.

Tori pressed the read button.

Remember, I am asleep.

"She thinks you're Sam," she said by way of explanation.

Margaret Louise's eyes gave an encore as Charles's ears visibly perked in tandem with his question. "Who is Sam?"

"The extremely cute EMT who responded to Leona's 911 call when she fell."

Charles looked left, then right, and then brought his lips to Tori's ear once again. "She's taken her makeup off for the night, hasn't she?"

"And her eyelashes," she quipped before widening her words to include Margaret Louise. "I'm grateful the EMTs got here so quickly. Sam and his partner took good care of Leona. Now I only wish they could do something to make the pain go away."

Nodding, Charles brought his hand to the base of his neck. "My across-the-hall neighbor, Gertrude? She broke her hip last year and she hasn't been back to her apartment since. Her son has, which is a whole 'nother story, but she hasn't. Nicole, she's my three-doors-down-on-the-right neighbor, says she's heard Gerty has given up on living."

Margaret Louise stepped through the front door, closed it behind her, and then pushed her way between Charles and Tori, a resolute look plastered across her round face. "C'mon, it's best I get this over with now."

Tori and Charles exchanged a silent high five and then followed the polyester-wearing grandmother of eight down the front hallway, through the living room, and down the second hallway, Charles stopping every few feet to comment on a painting or a particular color scheme.

When they reached Leona's partially closed bedroom door, Margaret Louise stopped. "You go first," she whispered to Charles. "You've traveled much too far not to enjoy her squealin' when she sees you—squealin' that will surely turn to guiltin' and posturin' the second she sees me."

"You got it, girlfriend." Charles stepped around Margaret Louise and guided the door open with his hand.

"So it was Sam then, yes?" Leona said. "He's positively smitten with me—"

"Actually, Leona, it's me!" With one final push of the door, Charles's hands started waving wildly in the air as Leona matched his squeal with one a bit throatier.

"Charles! What a wonderful surprise!"

He jogged over to the side of Leona's bed and planted a dramatic kiss on her forehead before pulling back to study her from head to satin sheet–covered toes. "I hear a hottie rescued you after your fall."

"You have no idea," Leona purred. Then returning the favor, she started her inspection at the top of his hazelnut-colored, spikey-haired head, took it down to his black and gold high-top Converse sneakers, and then returned to her starting point. "I can't believe you came all this way just for me."

Margaret Louise snorted from the open doorway. "He came for the weddin', Twin."

Leona's excitement drained from her face as she

noticed her sister standing in the doorway. "Margaret Louise."

"Leona."

Desperate to see some sort of truce between the sisters, Tori stepped around Margaret Louise to stand in the empty space between them. "Margaret Louise just got back from the airport with Charles"—she looked to the upright sister for confirmation of her words and, at the woman's nod, swung her gaze in Charles's direction—"and Charles asked her to come straight here so he could see you."

"Actually, when you didn't answer your door, Victoria, I called Milo and he said he'd reckon we'd find you here."

Leona's shoulders slumped back against the head-board. "So you're not here to see me . . ."

Charles waved away Margaret Louise's explanation and then positioned his hands atop his hips. "I'm not here to *see* you, Leona. I'm here to *stay* with you."

It was Tori's turn to clap, and clap she did. "You're going to stay here?"

"Little-known fact about *moi*." Charles fluttered his hand at the base of his neck and then plopped down on the bottom of Leona's bed, crossing his legs for emphasis. "For a while, before the bookstore, I entertained the notion of being a caregiver. In fact, I was going to start my own business and call it Care with Flair."

"And?" Tori prompted, laughing.

"I went into the bookstore to do some research and the owners fell in love with me." He pulled his hand away just long enough to flutter his fingers in Leona's direction. "Of course, you understand such a curse, don't you, Leona?"

"I've never known anything different." A flash of pain pushed Leona's eyes shut and nudged Margaret Louise away from the door frame.

"Twin? You okay?"

Slowly, Leona's natural lashes parted to reveal a mixture of emotions Tori could only guess at.

Hurt?

Sadness?

A sprinkle of irritation?

A dash of satisfaction?

"I'll be good as new in no time," Leona finally said. "Knowing I have Victoria, Charles, and Paris caring about me helps."

Charles jumped up from the bed and looked around. "Where *is* Paris?"

Leona and Tori pointed in unison as Margaret Louise backed her way against the door frame. "There'd be lots of people carin' 'bout you if you weren't so mean, Twin."

Lifting her head from its resting place against the headboard, Leona unfolded the edge of the sheet where it rested against her lap and then refolded it just as quickly. "Victoria, I sure do appreciate you stopping by this evening. On your way out with my sister, would you please put a set of clean sheets on the bed across the hall for Charles?"

Charles marched over to Paris, plucked her into his arms, and shook his head. "Oh no . . . I didn't come all this way to be relegated to a guest room. Oh-no-I-did-not. I've heard too many tales of slumber parties from the two of you"—he pointed between Leona and Tori—"not to sleep right here on the floor between your bed and Paris's. Besides, we've got lots to talk about."

A smile lifted the corners of Leona's mouth and nearly stole Tori's breath in the process.

Charles was there . . .

Leona was going to be all right . . .

Tori took a deep breath, savored its calming effect on her nerves, and then moved in to bestow a good night kiss atop Leona's forehead. "Don't stay up all night talking, you hear? You need your sleep in order to heal."

Chapter 21

They weren't even halfway down the front steps when the question finally came.

"So when do we start investigatin'?"

"Investigating?" she asked.

Margaret Louise stopped, turned, and using her elbows and her girth, blocked Tori from going any farther. "You said if I reached out to my sister, I could get in on your investigation."

"And that was reaching out?"

"I went into her room, didn't I? I delivered Charles to her, didn't I?" Without waiting for a reply, Margaret Louise continued, dropping her elbows flush with her sides as she did. "So tell me what we got so far 'bout Miss Gracie and this supposed push."

She swatted at a mosquito on her forearm and another on her hand and then gestured toward their cars parked alongside the curb. "Why don't you follow me back to my house and we can talk over a hot chocolate or whatever I can scare up in my almost completely packed pantry?"

"Packin' your things to move in with Milo?"

She nodded then followed her friend down the rest of the steps and onto the sidewalk. "It's slow going, but I'm getting there. Milo helped a lot this afternoon before he had to call it quits to go to his bachelor dinner."

As they reached the side of Tori's car, Margaret Louise's demeanor brightened immeasurably. "Debbie's is open for 'bout another hour or so. Why don't you hop in my car with me and we can head over there. That way, we can have ourselves a treat while we're hatchin' our plan."

Any momentary disappointment over not being able to put on her slippers was quickly drowned out by the notion of eating something chocolate and sinful. "Okay, you're on."

Five minutes later, when their should-have-been-a-*ten*-minute-drive was over, Tori unbuckled her seat belt and looked across the wide bench seat at her friend, the stepped-up pace of her heart making it difficult to catch her breath let alone think straight. "Um, did Charles say anything about your driving, by chance?"

Margaret Louise's smile widened with pride just before she stepped from the car and met Tori en route to the front door of Debbie's Bakery. "Charles actually said my drivin' rivals that of any taxi driver in New York City. Can you imagine that?"

Tori slid her hand around her neck and did her best to knead away some of the effects of her friend's driving skills. "Wow. That's"—she searched for the nicest way to complete her sentence—"um . . ."

"Flatterin', ain't it?" Margaret Louise finished. "Well, here we are."

The bell-mounted door announced their arrival as Margaret Louise's nose lifted into the air. "Mmmm . . . I smell chocolate and peanut butter. Debbie must be bakin' those tarts you love, Victoria."

"Want to split one with me?" Margaret Louise stopped so suddenly, Tori thumped into her back. "Oh. Hey. Sorry. I wasn't expecting you to stop like that."

"And I wasn't expectin' you to say somethin' like that!"

"What?"

"The splittin' part. Why, as long as I've known you, you've been a girl after my own heart, if not my size, when it comes to eatin'." Margaret Louise held the back of her hand to Tori's forehead, only to pull it away with a frown. "Nope. No fever. Is your tummy hurtin'?"

"My tummy is fine. If anything, it's protesting my request every bit as much as you are." Tori sidestepped her friend and headed over to the glass-fronted cabinet that showcased all of the day's scrumptious desserts. Sure enough, on a doily-topped plate on the left-hand side of the top shelf, were four chocolate and peanut butter tarts. Her stomach grumbled despite the hand she pressed against it in hopes of quieting the sound. "But I have a very special dress I'm supposed to be able to get into a week from today and eating one of those might make it so I'm forced to wear a tent instead."

Debbie emerged from the small office behind the counter with a dish towel in one hand and a plate of chocolate-covered caramels in the other. "And if Victoria is unable to fit in that dress, Rose Winters will have my head for making the treat and *your* head, Margaret Louise, for bringing her here to begin with."

"I'd like to say I ain't afraid of Rose Winters, but I am."

"As am I." Debbie slid open the back wall of the case and deposited the plate of chocolate-covered caramels onto the middle shelf. "Which is why I'll cut one of those tarts right down the middle and plate it that way if you don't want to split one with Victoria."

"*You* could always split it with me, Debbie," Tori suggested. "It's pretty quiet in here for a Saturday evening."

"Which is what I'm going to do, only I have to eat it in back while I wade through a few bookkeeping reports." Debbie pulled out a tart, grabbed a knife from the rack behind her, and cut the tasty treat right down the middle. When she was done, she put Tori's half onto one of the bakery's trademark powder blue plates and handed it to Tori across the top of the counter. "I imagine you want a hot chocolate to go with that, too?"

At Tori's nod, the bakery owner turned her focus to Margaret Louise. "I tried out a new Mississippi mud pie recipe if you're interested."

A few minutes later, plates and mugs in hand, the pair made their way across the dining area to their favorite table in the front corner—a table that afforded both a view of the street, and the dining room as a whole, in the event they ran out of conversation of their own. They were still steps from their seats when Margaret Louise started in. "The whole time I was waitin' for Charles's plane to come in, I was thinkin' 'bout what you said 'bout somebody pushin' Miss Gracie."

"*Possibly* pushing," she cautioned. "This is all just speculation. Remember that."

Margaret Louise placed her Mississippi mud pie and large coffee onto the table and hoisted herself up onto the lattice-backed stool closest to the window. "Victoria, if I've learned one thing 'bout you these last few years, it's . . ." The woman's voice trailed off as a group of twenty-somethings walked into the bakery and sat down at a table on the other side of the dining area, their attention divided between whatever they were whispering about and the temporarily unmanned bakery counter.

"Margaret Louise? Is something wrong?"

"Not yet. But I'm a-watchin'." Margaret Louise turned her attention back to Tori and continued where she'd left off. "Anyway, as I was sayin', if I've learned one thing 'bout you, Victoria, it's that you're a mighty good sniffer."

Tori laughed at the description. "A good sniffer? What on earth does that mean? *You're* the one who knew what dessert I was going to order the second we walked through the front door."

"I'm not talkin' 'bout that kind of sniffin'. I'm talkin' 'bout the kind that has you knowin' somethin' is wrong before anyone else does." Margaret Louise took a sip of her coffee and a forkful of her pie before retrieving the empty fork from her mouth in order to point it at Tori. "If it weren't for your sniffin', we'd have come back from New York City without Dixie."

"Well, that wasn't going to happen." She took a sip of her own hot beverage, savored the caramel sauce Debbie had drizzled across the whipped cream, and then set it back down on the table between them. "And you need to know that I'm not the one questioning Miss Gracie's death. That's Beatrice."

"If you didn't think there was a chance she was right,

you wouldn't be payin' it any mind. But I know you are. I can see it in your eyes."

Tori took a bite of her tart and groaned. "Oh my. This is so good."

"I hope Milo knows the sacrificin' you're makin' to look so purty for him on your weddin' day." Margaret Louise took a few more bites of her pie and then pushed the nearly empty plate off to the side of the table. "But let's get back to our investigatin' and what you're always sayin' 'bout who stands to gain from the death."

"Okay . . ."

"I know from watchin' *Cops and Criminals* on Wednesday nights, it's not always 'bout gainin'. Sometimes it's 'bout other things."

Tori tried to nibble back her amusement so as not to offend but it was hard. Especially when the scrunch of her friend's brow showed just how seriously the matter at hand was being taken. "Go on . . ."

"Sometimes people murder for other things like greed, and jealousy, and even flat-out revenge." Margaret Louise wrapped her pudgy hands around her mug and squeezed it so tight Tori was actually afraid it would explode. "It's the last two of them reasons that seem to make the most sense on why someone might push Beatrice's friend."

She replayed Margaret Louise's list in her head then brought the last two items back into the conversation. "So who do you think was jealous of Miss Gracie?"

"That one's easy." After a lengthy sip of her coffee, Margaret Louise looked back toward the table of twenty-somethings and then lowered her voice to as much of a whisper as her normally booming volume would allow.

"Cynthia Marland. The one who got the boot so Miss Gracie could take care of Jim and Julie's little girls."

"And you think she'd kill because of that?"

"She wouldn't be the first person to get her undies in a bunch on account of gettin' the boot from a job." Margaret Louise took another sip of her coffee and then plunked her cup down on the table with a thud. "Need I remind you 'bout all those nasty looks and comments Dixie made to you after she got the boot at the library?"

"Looks and comments, sure. But that doesn't mean she'd have killed me."

"I'm bettin' she killed you a time or two in her dreams those first few months." Margaret Louise matched Tori's lean and raised it with one of her own. "But Cynthia is cut from a different bolt of cloth than Dixie."

Her interest aroused, Tori shoved her drink to the side and leaned her head closer to her friend. "Do you know Cynthia?"

"I know her people."

"And?"

"They're lazier than a two-legged dog."

"A two-legged dog?"

Margaret Louise waved Tori's question aside and continued on, the excitement in her voice bubbling over into everything from the way she shifted in her seat, to the way she licked her lips in anticipation of sharing everything she'd thought about while waiting for Charles to deplane.

"I don't know if you've seen where she lives, but her room at the Bradys' was probably bigger than her whole house. Goin' back to nothin' after livin' like somethin' would be an awful bitter pill, don't you think?"

It was the same line of thinking she'd already been entertaining on her own, but still, it was validating to hear it from someone else.

"I've been thinking that, too, but every time I do, I come back to the same thing. Killing Miss Gracie shouldn't mean Cynthia would get her job back. I mean, the Bradys fired her for a reason, right?"

"Maybe she just did it for that flat-out revenge I told you 'bout."

"Maybe . . ."

But still, it seemed too easy.

Then again, murder committed in a fit of rage didn't have to be complicated, did it?

The jingle of the front door pulled Tori from her thoughts and turned her attention to a familiar face standing in the doorway. Next to Beatrice stood a little boy with wide eyes.

"Well, lookee who's here." Margaret Louise's hand shot up into the air. "Woo-hoo. Beatrice, Luke . . ."

Beatrice tightened her hand on Luke and made a beeline for their table. "Oh. Victoria. I stopped by your house and you weren't there. So I took a chance I might find you here even though Luke said he didn't see your car in the parking lot."

"That's 'cause I did the drivin'," Margaret Louise proclaimed, patting the vacant seat to her right for Luke, and the one to her left for Beatrice. "Now that you found her, you might as well sit for a spell and visit."

Tori watched as Beatrice made sure Luke got onto his stool safely and then remained standing by his side. "Beatrice? Is something wrong?"

When the nanny didn't answer, Tori followed her wary

gaze to the only other occupied table in the dining room. "Do you know those girls, Beatrice?"

"I do. But that's not why I'm here." Beatrice lowered her voice so as not to be heard by anyone other than Tori and Margaret Louise. "Luke overheard something on Monday night that I think you need to hear."

Something in the way Beatrice spoke made Tori lean toward the pair with her full attention. "Is this about Miss Gracie?"

Beatrice's eyes closed for the briefest of moments and then opened along with a slow nod and a gentle pat on Luke's shoulder. "Go ahead, Luke, tell Miss Sinclair what you shared with me while we were working on your arithmetic lesson this evening. Only let's use our whisper voice, okay?"

Luke peeled his gaze from the last remaining bites of Tori's tart and fixed it instead on Tori, a mixture of apprehension and confusion on his round face. "We wanted to watch cartoons, but Miss Amanda and Miss Stacy wanted to watch a big person show."

"Who are Miss Amanda and Miss Stacy?" Tori asked Beatrice.

"Two of the other nannies from the Nanny Go Round Agency."

"One of which is sittin' right over there." Margaret Louise pointed at the table that had claimed her attention earlier. "Amanda is the redhead and she's a Willey."

"A Willey?" she echoed. "What on earth does that mean?"

Margaret Louise opened her mouth to answer but closed it as Luke continued with his own story. "I know I'm not supposed to watch that kind of stuff, so I whispered to

Reenie to see if she wanted to find some toys to play with and she said yes."

"And this is Monday we're talking about?" she asked Beatrice for clarification. At Beatrice's nod, she smiled at Luke. "So what did you play with?"

Luke's face lit from within and he pulled his legs up under him on the stool. "Reenie said there was a big box of blocks in the hall closet and we could build a whole town if we wanted to."

"Did you?" she asked.

"I built a fire station and Reenie builded a hair place."

Margaret Louise patted the top of her brush-once-and-go hair and winked at Luke. "Sounds like a place I need to visit, don't it?"

All semblance of a smile on Luke's face disappeared. "But Reenie didn't get to finish the whole thing."

"Why not, Luke?"

His eyes widened as he dangled his legs over the edge of the stool once again. "We got scared."

"Scared?" Tori repeated. "Scared of what?"

"I didn't know you could yell and whisper at the same time . . . but you can." Luke traced an invisible line around his section of the table only to look up at Tori when he reached the end. "And then she started to cry."

"Reenie cried?"

Luke shook his head.

"Miss Gracie cried?"

"Nuh-uh, not Miss Gracie, neither. She was in the TV room with the other kids and their nannies."

She looked at Beatrice. "I don't understand."

Beatrice hooked her index finger under Luke's chin

and gently raised it until their eyes met. "Tell Miss Sinclair who was crying."

"Miss Cindy was crying," Luke explained. "She was crying real quiet like she didn't want anyone to make fun of her. But I would have cried, too, if someone was yelling at me. Even if they were whispering it."

"Miss Cindy, as in Reenie's nanny?"

"Her *old* nanny," Luke corrected. "*Miss Gracie* was her new nanny."

Tori heard her own intake of air just as surely as she felt it. "Cindy was at the house on Monday night?"

"We didn't know she was until we heard her whispering with that lady."

"Another nanny?" she asked.

Luke shook his head real hard. "Nope."

"Wait." She took a moment to recollect a conversation with Debbie earlier in the week, one that helped give a little background to the evening Luke was talking about. "Debbie told me there was a potluck or something at the Bradys' house that night and that Julie Brady was singing Miss Gracie's praises and handing out business cards for your agency, Beatrice."

"I wouldn't know," Beatrice said quietly. "It was my night off and I was home getting ready for our sewing circle meeting."

She turned her focus back on Luke. "Was it one of the moms?"

Luke's shrug reached his ears. "No. But she yelled and yelled at Miss Cindy and made her cry," Luke continued, clearly mortified by the incident.

"Did you hear anything they said?"

"Miss Cindy kept saying she was sorry and she'd try

harder next time, but the lady didn't tell her she was forgiven the way Miss Bea does when I do something
wrong."

"What *did* she do?"

"She just kept on yelling."

"Did anyone else hear them besides you and Reenie?"

"No. Just us."

"Did they see you?"

Luke's eyes widened even more as Beatrice reminded
him to keep his voice down. "We took the rest of the
blocks and hid in the closet. But Reenie's foot knocked
the box over and it got real quiet. I told Reenie to hush."

"Did you hear anything else? I mean, besides Cindy
saying she was sorry?" she asked.

"Every time the lady said 'car wash,' Miss Cindy cried
harder and said she was sorry."

Margaret Louise, who was in the process of taking a
sip of her drink at that moment, sputtered her coffee in
several different directions. "Why on earth would someone cry over a car wash?"

"I don't know but it sure made Miss Cindy sad." Luke
looked up at Beatrice and gestured toward the front counter on the other side of the dining room. "Can I have my
cookie now, Miss Bea?"

Tori reached out and rested a hand on Luke's forearm.
"Hold on a minute, Luke. I have just a few more questions
first. How long did you stay in the closet?"

"When the lady quit yelling at Miss Cindy, Miss Cindy
quit crying and went home. I had to cover Reenie's mouth
one more time when the footsteps went by, but then it
wasn't so bad. We even stayed in the closet after the lady
went by because it was kind of fun in there. We pretended

we were in a fort at night and we tried to see what we could build without being able to see a whole lot."

"So then the yelling and the crying were over?"

Luke hopped down off his stool and took a closer look at her tart and Margaret Louise's crumb-ridden plate. "What did you have on that plate?"

"Mississippi mud pie and it sure was delicious." Margaret Louise guided his finger to her plate and one of the larger-sized crumbs. "Go ahead, give it a try."

Luke did as he was told and then looked back up at Beatrice. "Can I have that instead of a cookie, Miss Bea? Please?"

"Yes, Luke, you may. But *after* you answer Miss Sinclair's question, sweetheart."

Tori posed the question again in the event it got lost amid talk of Mississippi mud pie. "So the yelling and crying were all done after the footsteps went by?"

"For a while." Luke shifted from foot to foot, his hands playing with the sides of his jeans as he did. "Until we heard Miss Gracie shout."

She was all too aware of the chill that shot up her spine at the same time Margaret Louise's hand hit the table. "You heard Miss Gracie shout?"

Luke nodded.

"What did she shout?" Margaret Louise interjected.

" 'Stop!' And she said it just like that, 'Stop!' "

It was just as Reenie's big sister had recalled during Milo's science class. Only this time, in context with everything else Luke had shared, Miss Gracie's word took on a whole new meaning.

"And that was the last thing you heard?" Tori rushed to ask.

"Nah, we heard more footsteps . . . only they were running this time."

"That's it? You heard Miss Gracie yell and then you heard footsteps?"

"The footsteps were the *last* thing we heard. But before that, after Miss Gracie yelled, we heard thumps. Loud, loud thumps."

"What kind of loud—" She stopped herself midsentence as the reason for the sounds hit her at the same time Beatrice's eyes fluttered closed in pain.

Slipping off her stool, Tori crossed to Beatrice and pulled her friend in for a hug. "We'll figure out who did this to her, Beatrice. You have my word on that."

Chapter 22

This time, when Tori tried Leona's number and got no answer, she didn't worry. After all, Charles was on the case. No answer when he was around likely meant they were swapping hairstyling techniques or sorting through the latest mound of celebrity gossip in search of what was and wasn't true.

Lowering her phone to the most recently packed box to her left, Tori leaned her head against the wall and allowed herself the sigh that had been dying to come out since she'd opened her eyes that morning. In six days, she'd be marrying Milo. And in addition to her regular job, she still had to make sure her vows were perfect, her out-of-town guests were squared away with their accommodations, the rental company was on target with the tables and chairs for the reception, and countless other details that, if not attended to, could prove disastrous on their big day.

Toss in packing up her entire cottage and trying to finger a killer as she'd stupidly promised Beatrice the previous night, and, well, her proverbial plate was overflowing.

She'd berated herself numerous times throughout the night for vowing to catch Miss Gracie's killer, but as morning had poked its way around her bedroom shades, she knew it was what she wanted to do.

No, she hadn't met the woman.

No, she had no vested interest in learning the truth behind the nanny's supposed fall.

But she knew Beatrice.

And she knew her own gut.

Someone had pushed Miss Gracie to her death in the Brady home the previous week and her money was on Cynthia Marland. Really, could the "who" get any easier? Especially when revenge and greed were both strong motives for murder?

A knock at Tori's back door had her pushing off the floor and crossing to the kitchen just as Margaret Louise entered the room with a familiar powder blue bag tucked under an arm, and a beverage carrier with two lidded cups in a free hand. "I hope you don't mind me lettin' myself in like this, but I could see from the window on the side that you were busy thinkin' and I didn't want to interrupt." Margaret Louise dumped the bag onto the closest counter and then carried their drinks to the small dinette table not far from where Tori stood. "I drove straight to Debbie's after church this mornin' just so I could get us some tummy fuel for the long day ahead."

"Long day?" Tori opened her dish cabinet, took two medium-sized plates from the second shelf, and set them on the counter next to the bag. A peek inside resulted in a loud gurgle from her unfed stomach. "Ooooh, you got four of Debbie's chocolate-dusted donuts. She's always out of them when I stop by there on a Sunday morning."

"That's why I always order mine the night before. I reckon the only reason I was able to add to my order this mornin' was on account of bein' in the right place at the right time . . . not that it'll be appreciated, I'm sure." Margaret Louise stepped around Tori, opened the bag, placed two donuts on each plate, and carried them to the table. "Least I know *you* appreciate my efforts."

"You lost me," she said, following the plates to the table. "Who isn't going to appreciate what?"

"Never mind. I ain't gonna bother chasin' my tail." Margaret Louise took a seat at the table and gestured for Tori to do the same. "When I got home last night, I pulled out season one of *Cops and Criminals* and got myself back in crime-solvin' mode. So let's get to it, Victoria, we've got a lot to do."

Tori took the seat across from her friend and picked up the first of her two donuts, the tantalizing smell combined with the promise of chocolate making it difficult to think let alone respond to anything other than the call of her stomach. "Mmmm. Wow. Debbie really needs to make these a regular menu item seven days a week."

"Debbie knows exactly what she's doin'. As for Miss Gracie, her bein' here was bad for lots of people," Margaret Louise said as she fairly inhaled her first donut and moved on to her second. "Lots of people mean lots of suspects. And lots of suspects mean lots of investigatin' for you and me."

Tori stopped chewing and stared at her breakfast companion. "Lots of suspects? How do you figure that? Near as I can figure, there's only one."

"Don't you go narrowin' the list down to one without me, Victoria Sinclair. I held up my end of the bargain and then some."

"Frankly, I was hoping for more than just you standing in the doorway of Leona's room." She broke off a bite of her donut and set the rest of it back on her plate. "Like maybe some sort of discussion that would put this stalemate of yours to rest."

"Considerin' my sister's predicament, I thought it best not to engage her in front of Charles." Margaret Louise peeled off the lid of her beverage, ran her finger around the edge of the cup, and then inserted it into her mouth with rare hesitancy. "She didn't look real good."

Wrapping her hands around her own cup, Tori met her friend's worried eyes. "Your sister is in a lot more pain than she wants anyone to know. It's why I feel a lot better knowing Charles is there to look after her instead of that Rachel girl. How and why that one got into the business of being a caregiver is beyond me."

"Rachel *Billings*?"

"I don't know. I didn't get the girl's last name."

"Early twenties?" Margaret Louise asked. "Long dark hair? Tiny little earrin' in her nose?"

"Sounds like the same girl."

Margaret Louise turned her focus to her beverage and shrugged. "Well, then the answer to your question is easy. It's the same reason lots of folks get into jobs they don't really like."

"Money," she murmured. "The same reason our one

and only suspect took a job caring for Jim and Julie Brady's kids from what Beatrice says."

"Now wait just a minute. Who are you lookin' at for this?"

"The same person you and I talked about yesterday— Cynthia Marland." She pushed the plate containing her second donut to the side, set her elbows on the table, and rested her chin inside the palm of her right hand. "She had means and she had motive."

When Margaret Louise said nothing, she filled in the blanks with everything she knew. "Miss Gracie was brought in to replace Cindy—at a job she wanted if, for no other reason, than the chance to reside in a house twenty times the size of her own. She was angry at Beatrice for suggesting her former governess to Julie Brady. I witnessed *that* myself at the park last weekend. But harming Beatrice wouldn't have changed Miss Gracie's employment in that house. Harming *Miss Gracie* would. No one else stood to gain from the woman's death."

"I thought that, too, until I got home last night and started thinkin' 'bout who else it could have been since it wasn't Cindy. And that's when I realized that other nannies in the Nanny Go Round Agency had to be feelin' might wary 'bout a British nanny comin' to town. Especially when someone the likes of Julie Brady was singin' her praises. And some of those other nannies were actually *in* the house when the woman fell to her death."

Tori pulled her chin from her palm and signaled a time out with her hands in the air. "Wait a minute. Slow down. You heard Luke last night. Cynthia Marland was not only *at* the Brady house the night Miss Gracie fell, but she was upset, too. And from what I saw the other night when I drove past the Bradys' house, she's still spending time in that house."

"That might be, but there's no discountin' what Luke said 'bout her leavin' before he heard the thumpin' you and I both know was Miss Gracie fallin' down them stairs."

"Luke didn't say that."

"Yes he did. He said Cindy went home after she quit crying."

She rewound her thoughts to the previous night and the details Beatrice's charge had supplied. "But he said he heard footsteps go by the closet."

"Footsteps he heard after Cindy left. Footsteps that had to belong to the one doin' all the whisper-yellin'," Margaret Louise reminded.

"He was in a closet. There's no way he could know whose footsteps were whose."

"Luke is a smart one, Victoria. And I heard nothin' resemblin' guessin' from him last night."

"But no one else makes sense," she protested.

"All the other nannies in the house that night can be considered suspects, too, Victoria." Margaret Louise flipped her hand over and began ticking off names. "And from what Luke said, we know for sure that Amanda Willey and Stacy Gardner were there . . ."

"We do?"

"We sure do. We also know that Jim and Julie Brady are respected members of this community, and, well, if they're happy with somethin', there's a good chance others will want to try it out, too."

Tori broke off another bite of donut and called up a conversation she'd had a few days earlier. "You know, now that you're saying this, I remember Debbie saying

Julie was handing out business cards from Miss Gracie and Beatrice's agency that night. And she said some of the other mothers were actually taking them."

"See? It's just like I said. If Julie Brady was singin' Miss Gracie's praises that night, the other nannies sittin' in that TV room had reason to be worried." Margaret Louise pushed her chair back, stood, and carried her empty plate over to the sink. "So I reckon we just need to figure out which one was more bothered by the singin' than the others. If we do that, I believe we'll find the person who pushed Miss Gracie to her death."

Suddenly the neat and tidy scenario Tori had constructed as to who killed Beatrice's former governess and why didn't seem so neat and tidy anymore. In fact, the more Margaret Louise theorized, the more Tori's head hurt.

"What did I get myself into?" she asked aloud. "I'm getting married in six days, Margaret Louise. I can't be playing detective."

Setting the now clean plate in the dish drainer beside the sink, Margaret Louise flashed a mischievous grin. "I reckon I could do the bulk of the solvin' on my own and I could come to you for any consultin' I need."

She tried to focus on what Margaret Louise was saying, but between the donut she was slowly nibbling her way through and the way her thoughts kept rewinding to earlier parts of their conversation, it was hard. "What do you know about this Amanda Willey? Does her family struggle for money the way Cynthia's does?"

"Amanda works for the Whitehalls, one of the wealthiest families in Sweet Briar."

"I know the Whitehalls," she said. "They contribute a lot of money to the library each year."

"They contribute a lot of money to everything in town. My Jake says they like to see their name on paper but I think it's more real than that."

"What do you mean?"

"I think they know they're blessed and I think they like helpin'. Near as I can tell, that's the only reason they'd have hired a Willey."

"You say that like it's a bad thing." She took a gulp of her hot chocolate and then carried her own empty plate over to the sink.

"One Willey or another is always causin' trouble somewhere in this town. Why, not more 'n a few weeks ago, I remember hearin' Georgina bemoanin' a pothole out on Route 25 that the town has to keep fixin' 'cause the oldest Willey boy keeps doin' somethin' with his four-wheeler that keeps eatin' up the road.

"And it was just last year that my Jake had a problem with Tim Willey over a car-fixin' bill that man refused to pay. Brought the car in to Jake to have it fixed, and then, when Jake did, Tim said there hadn't been anythin' wrong to start with."

"So what did Jake do?"

"He had to take him to small claims court. And he won." Margaret Louise took Tori's plate from her hand, washed it, and placed it in the drainer beside her own. "But don't think that was the end of it for Tim. Oh no, he put a sign outside his yard tellin' people to avoid Jake's garage. It didn't matter much on account of most folks in this town discount much of what comes out of that family's mouth anyway, but it's still a thorn in my boy's side . . . and in my side, too."

Tori returned to her chair and the rest of her drink, her curiosity aroused. "So if I'm hearing you correctly, you think the Whitehalls hired this Amanda Willey as more of a charitable move?"

"Only thing I can figure."

"Is she like the father and the brother?" Tori asked.

"She's a Willey, ain't she?" Margaret Louise wiped her hands on the yellow-and-white-checked dish towel hanging on a hook near the sink and made her way back to the table, too. "Only Amanda ain't so much 'bout troublemakin' as she is gettin' things without earnin' them."

"And why do you say that? Do you know of things she's done or are you just assuming based on her family?"

"I was in a bookstore same time as she was once in Tom's Creek. I saw her come in, empty-handed. Not more 'n five minutes later, she was at the register wantin' to return a book without a receipt. They gave her store credit."

Tori released her hold on her to-go cup and tried to make sense of what she was hearing. "Okay, so what was the problem?"

"That book she was returnin' without a receipt? She just plucked it off a shelf and said it was hers. Like she was *entitled* to do that."

"Oh. Wow." Tori shifted in her seat and then stood, her feet shuttling her around the kitchen with no real destination in mind.

"Every time I see her, she is holdin' court like she's the queen of somethin'. Even last night, when all she was really doin' was whisperin' with her friends, I couldn't shake this feelin' that she was waitin' for food to magically appear on her table, and if it didn't, she'd make a fuss."

"Why would a family like the Whitehalls hire someone like this Amanda person?" Tori leaned her back against the door and waited for her friend's answer.

"Because they like makin' things better—the library, the town square, the annual festivals, even some of the young people."

"Like Amanda?"

"Like Amanda," Margaret Louise confirmed. "But from what Melissa has told me after many school events, this Amanda seems to think her workin' for the Whitehalls gives her Whitehall status in this town."

"Meaning?"

"Meanin' she expects front row seats and special treatment. And she ain't shy 'bout demandin' it."

Tori crossed to the kitchen phone on the counter and pulled open the drawer located just below. In it, she found the pad of paper and pen she wanted. "Any idea whether or not Mrs. Whitehall was one of the women who took a business card for the British nanny agency Julie Brady was giving out Monday night?"

"Six months ago, I'd have said no. But at Back to School Night two weeks ago, I happen to know Carolyn Whitehall got a healthy dose of what folks have been dealin' with where Amanda is concerned for quite some time. In fact, I saw it myself when I was sittin' in Lulu's classroom waitin' on her teacher to start talkin'. Amanda came in with Carolyn and refused to sit in one of the desks until the teacher disinfected it. And when Miss Applewhite did, Amanda insisted the talk be brief because she was, after all, almost a Whitehall. And that's exactly how she said it: almost a Whitehall. Carolyn looked positively mortified, bless her heart."

Uncapping the pen, she jotted Amanda's name down on the top piece of paper and then looked at Margaret Louise. "So I'm assuming you see greed as a motive for Amanda?"

"If wantin' to make sure Mrs. Whitehall doesn't bring someone else into the home to care for the children is greed, then yes I do."

"But how would killing Miss Gracie keep Amanda at the Whitehalls?"

"If Miss Gracie is dead, talk of how wonderful she is dies, too, I imagine."

"Talk of her dies, too," she whispered as she turned to the pad of paper once again. "And this other nanny you mentioned? Stacy something or another?"

"Stacy Gardner. Dumb as a box of rocks, that one. Never did understand how any parent worth their salt would hire that one to look after their children. Then again, the Downings aren't the brightest, either. Their whole life is nothin' but playin' follow the leader. If the other folks in the country club have a nanny, they have one, too."

Tori tapped the end of the pen against her chin and contemplated whether to add Stacy's name. "And she's on your list of suspects because why?"

"She's one of the nannies in that family group so she would have been there if for no other reason than the other nannies were there."

"And her motive?"

"Don't know. I'm still workin' on that."

Tori added the name to the list but placed a question mark beside it on both sides. "So you've got two names for sure."

"Two plus anyone else who might have been worried

'bout the Nanny Go Round Agency goin' belly up if their clients started hirin' from someone else."

"You know, that Rachel girl said something just like that the other night at Leona's." Using her index finger to hold off any potential response from Margaret Louise, Tori worked to recall Rachel's exact words. "In fact, if I remember correctly, she said something to the effect of, 'Cindy just needs to make it right. If she does, none of us have to worry. If she doesn't, and she decides to get all high-and-mighty, we're all in trouble.' "

"From what Luke said last night, it don't sound like Cindy was gettin' all high-and-mighty. Sounds like she was downright sad 'bout everything. Includin' gettin' a car wash."

Something about the combination of Margaret Louise's expression and the mention of Luke's comment made her laugh. "When I was younger, my next-door neighbor friend was always washing cars. It was his parents' favorite punishment whenever he did anything wrong. It almost makes me wonder if washing cars was being used the same way with Cindy."

"And if it was, ain't you a bit curious 'bout who was doin' the punishin'?"

Any residual laughing ceased as Margaret Louise's question took root in her thoughts. "Keep going . . ."

"Accordin' to Luke, someone was hoppin' mad at Cindy. Someone Cindy felt the need to apologize to again and again and again. Aside from Jim and Julie Brady, and perhaps Cindy's own parents, I'm not sure who was in a position to punish Cindy with something like car washin'."

Who indeed . . .

Chapter 23

They were halfway around the outer loop of the park when Milo squeezed Tori's hand three distinct times. It was a tradition they had for saying I love you without words, and as always, it brought a smile to her lips.

Bypassing the usual four-squeeze response, Tori verbalized it instead. "I love you, too."

"I'm sorry I didn't make it over for more packing today."

"Don't be silly. You had lesson plans to work on for our honeymoon week and I get that." Tori slowed their pace as they approached the smattering of picnic tables on the eastern edge of the playground. "Besides, I'd rather use the time we have together to do something like this."

"Agreed. Though getting you packed up means we'll be living together." Milo shifted his hold on her hand in order to help her over the railroad tie that framed the outdoor eating area. Once they'd cleared it, he led her back to the picnic basket they'd temporarily abandoned in favor of a walk. "You checked in on Leona while I was at my bachelor dinner last night, didn't you?"

She tugged the basket toward her side of the table and lifted the lid to reveal the fried chicken dinner she'd been looking forward to all week. "I did."

"And how is she?"

"She's still in a lot of discomfort even though she pretends she's not." Tori pulled out two paper plates, two napkins, and two sets of plastic silverware, and set them at their respective spots.

"Uh, anything else?"

"She liked the crossword puzzle book of travel destinations I gave her."

"That's good." Milo raked a hand over his face. "Anything *else*?"

Tori pulled the plastic container of chicken from the basket and then eyed her fiancé closely. "What are you getting at, Milo?"

"Um, uhhh . . . did you see anyone unexpected while you were there?"

"No, was I—" She stopped as details of the previous evening pushed their way through the on-again, off-again fog that had plagued her brain ever since Margaret Louise arrived on her doorstep with breakfast. "Wait. Yes! Charles is here in Sweet Briar . . . which I'm guessing you already know based on your questions."

He slumped forward against the table in relief and then plucked a chicken leg from the container. "Phew. I was beginning to think you'd missed each other somehow and

I didn't want to blow the surprise for you. Margaret Louise would have had my head on a silver platter if I did."

Reaching back into the basket, she liberated a container of fruit, a bag of chips, and two bottles of water. "This all looks really good, doesn't it?" When he didn't say anything, she pushed the basket aside to provide a more uninhibited view of her fiancé. "I brought brownies if that's what you're thinking."

"What you have right here looks fantastic. But I guess I'm just surprised you aren't more excited about Charles being here. Did everything go okay?"

She uncapped her water, took a sip, and then set about the task of putting food onto their plates. "Finding Charles on Leona's doorstep was a fantastic surprise. It was so good to see him and he's exactly the way I remember him with the exception of his hair. It's now a soft brown, instead of the purple it was in the city."

"Okay . . ."

"And even better, he's going to stay with Leona through the wedding, which thrills me."

He sampled a strawberry and then moved on to another piece of chicken, nodding as he did. "Good. Maybe now you don't have to worry so much about Leona. Charles will take good care of her, I'm sure."

"He will."

"Did Margaret Louise come in with Charles?"

She took another sip of her water and then tried a chip. "She did. Didn't say much to her sister, but at least they acknowledged one another. It's a start if nothing else."

"So is that why you seem more subdued than I expected? Because Margaret Louise is still being standoffish with

Leona?" He set his chicken back on the plate and reached across the table for her hand. "They love you, Tori. They're not going to let this thing between them ruin our wedding, I'm confident of that."

She helped herself to a grape but stopped short of popping it into her mouth. "I'd be lying if I said I'm not sick about the rift between Leona and everyone else. I mean, I know she did it to herself, but I also know she's a good person. And if Rose can find a way to accept what Leona did, then so should everyone else. But I'd also be lying if I said that's what's got me subdued as you say."

"Are you getting nervous about the wedding?" Milo asked quietly.

She tightened her grip on his hand and looked him straight in the eye. "Absolutely not. We're down to six days and I couldn't be more excited. Sure, I'm feeling a little nostalgic about leaving my cottage, but it doesn't even come close to outweighing my excitement over living with you as your wife."

Like a line of dominoes, her words kicked off relief, and then a smile, and then the dimples she loved so much. "Okay. Good. But then what *is* the reason you seem kind of preoccupied and not as happy about Charles's earlier-than-expected arrival as I would have thought you'd be?"

"I guess that's because of what I learned while I was at Debbie's last night with Margaret Louise."

"Learned? About what?"

She extricated her hand from his and took a bite of chicken. With any luck, she hoped it would offset the unsettled feeling in the pit of her stomach. "Beatrice brought Luke by to speak to me. He overheard some things the night Miss Gracie died that gives even more credence to Beatrice's belief the woman was pushed down those stairs."

"Tell me," he prompted as he, too, got back to the business of eating.

"He and Reenie overheard the Bradys' former nanny—Cynthia Marland—being yelled at by another female. Cynthia was crying and saying she was sorry. Whoever this other female was said something about having to wash cars and Cynthia cried harder."

"Wash cars?"

She shrugged. "I know. I found that odd, too. But then here's the kick. Luke said Cynthia left and this other female walked by the closet where he and Reenie were hiding. Not long after that, they heard Miss Gracie yell 'stop' and then heard a bunch of thumping."

Milo cringed. "They heard it?"

"They did. But I'm not sure Luke has really equated the sound to Miss Gracie falling."

"Did he hear anything else?"

"Running. He heard someone running after the thumping started."

"Wow." He looked at the half-eaten chicken leg in his hand and then set it back down on his plate in favor of a chip and a second strawberry. "Wow. So this really should be a murder investigation, shouldn't it?"

"It sure seems that way to me. Only I had my money on Cynthia as the culprit, and Luke's account of that evening makes it so she wasn't even in the house when it happened."

He popped a third strawberry into his mouth and grinned. "So who are you looking at now?"

Tori held her hands up. "That's part of the problem,

Milo. I have way too much on my plate right now to look at anyone. I've got to get some things done in advance at work so Nina won't have any problems while we're on our honeymoon, I have all the normal last-minute details before the ceremony to take care of, I have guests coming in, and a house to finish packing. I really can't be playing detective on top of all of that, too."

"Are you going to tell me Margaret Louise isn't chomping at the bit to help you figure out what happened to Miss Gracie?"

"No," she mumbled. "In fact, she's even offered to take the lead and just use me as a sounding board when she needs one."

"Do you have a suspect list?" he asked, still grinning.

She hesitated for a moment but knew resistance was futile. "We started one this morning over Debbie's famous chocolate-dusted donuts."

"And no Cindy?"

"No Cindy," she confirmed. "All we really have right now are two other nannies that were at the Bradys' house that night."

"And who are they?"

She reached into the back pocket of her jeans and unfolded the piece of paper she'd looked at multiple times throughout the day. "Amanda Willey and Stacy Gardner."

"Hmmm."

"Hmmm?" she echoed as she looked from Milo to the paper and back again. "What does that mean? Do you know these girls?"

"I do. They both have kids in my class. Or rather, the families they work for have kids in my class."

She refolded the paper, returned it to her pocket, and

pushed her plate to the side in order to focus all of her attention on Milo. "And? Your impressions?"

He made a face, his discomfort in answering the question clear. "Stacy is . . ."

"Not terribly bright?" she interjected. At his slow nod, she continued. "Margaret Louise mentioned that this morning."

"That said, though, I just can't see her pushing someone to their death. She's too placid to do something like that."

"Oh?"

"Yeah, she's kind of a pushover, which doesn't help with getting Ronald to do his homework like he's supposed to." Milo took a handful of chips and worked his way through them a chip at a time. "I'm not too sure Stacy is the right fit for a family of two rambunctious boys, but maybe there's something there I'm missing."

"Between that and Cindy and the one taking up a room in Leona's house, it doesn't seem as if Sweet Briar has any real standards for their caregivers."

"It's Sweet Briar, Tori. The employment pool is limited."

"The Johnsons went outside the pool to find Beatrice . . ."

"And Luke couldn't be more squared away," Milo said by way of agreement. "Which is probably why Julie Brady insisted on pulling from *that* pool with her most recent nanny choice."

"And Amanda Willey?" she asked.

"That one you can judge for yourself." Using his index finger, he guided her eyes from his to a red-haired girl basking in the last of the day's sun on a bench in the vicinity of the monkey bars while two still darker-haired boys passed each other at the midpoint.

"She was at the bakery last night, but I was far too focused on Beatrice and Luke to really notice much about her or her companions."

"Well, that's her. With Jordan and Jeremiah Whitehall. Jordan is in my class, Jeremiah is in the grade below."

"I sure would like to meet her. See if I get a feeling one way or the other as to any involvement she may have had in Miss Gracie's death."

"You done with your dinner?" Milo finished his last bite of chicken and a final gulp or two of his water and then set about the task of capping containers, sealing the chips, and placing them all in the basket. When he was done, he gathered up their combined trash and stood. "Come on. I'll introduce you."

She swung her leg over the bench and jumped to her feet. "Anything I should know?" she asked as she trailed him to the garbage can and then over to the playground.

"The more credentials you can provide, the more likely she is to talk to you."

"Credentials?"

"Tell her you're from Chicago, make your apartment sound like it was located somewhere special, and emphasize the fact that you're the head librarian at the library. Do that and you should be good."

"There's only two of us at the library, Milo. It's not like I'm running the New York City Public Library."

"I don't think she frequents the library enough to know the difference so I wouldn't give it too much thought."

She stopped mid-step and waited for him to do the same. "She's not smart, either?"

"No, she's smart. She's just not the type to be interested in reading a book that isn't brand new. You see, being the Whitehall's nanny has given her some interesting expectations of the world around her."

"Margaret Louise pretty much said the same thing."

He encased her hand with his own and led her toward the monkey bars. "Which you're about to discover all on your own in a matter of seconds."

When they reached the monkey bars, the smaller of the two boys let go and landed on the ground mere inches from Milo's and Tori's feet. "Hi, Mr. Wentworth. What are you doing here?"

"Having a picnic with my fiancé." He turned to Tori and smiled. "Jeremiah Whitehall, this is my soon-to-be wife, Miss Sinclair. She works at the library."

The second grader smiled at Tori. "I know you. You were at the book thing with Mrs. Claus last Christmas. You gave me your carpet square because there weren't any left."

"And did you have fun?" she asked.

"Mrs. Claus was cool and she makes really yummy cookies."

"She does, indeed." Tori gestured toward the bench and the girl who seemed oblivious to the fact that two adults were talking to the children in her care. "Is that your nanny over there?"

Jeremiah peeked around the ladder portion of the monkey bars and gave a half nod, half shrug. "Right now she is."

She saw Milo's brow arch in response to the youngster's words and suspected hers did the same. "Right now?"

"Jordan said he heard Mom tell Dad that Amanda is

getting . . ." He cast about for the right word, only to give up and call to his brother. "Jordan, what did Mom say about"—he clicked his tongue behind his teeth and jerked his head in the direction of their sunbathing nanny—"you know who?"

Jordan reached the other side of the monkey bars and let go, smiling triumphantly at Milo as he did. "Did you see that, Mr. Wentworth?" At Milo's emphatic nod, he turned to his younger brother. "You mean when she was telling Dad why she wants to get us a new nanny?"

"Uh-huh."

"Uppity." Jordan climbed back up the ladder and grabbed hold of the closest bar, his body poised and ready to begin yet another journey across the twenty-foot divide from one end of the monkey bars to the other. "Whatever *that* means. But she's only like that because of us."

"Because of us?" Jeremiah repeated.

"Uh-huh. Dad showed me Amanda's real house the last time he took me to get this stupid haircut." His feet came off the top rung of the ladder as his arms took over the job of supporting his weight. "Her . . . whole . . . house . . . could . . . fit . . . in . . . our . . . garage," he said as he moved from bar to bar.

"Sounds a lot like Cynthia Marland," she whispered to Milo.

With his eyes still on Jordan, Milo replied, "They grew up on the same street."

"Jordan! Jeremiah! We've got to go. *Leona's Closet* is about to come on and I don't want to miss it."

Tori turned to find Amanda had not only vacated her bench but was now standing little more than a few feet away. "Amanda? Hi, I'm Tori. Tori Sinclair."

After a thorough once-over that was at times intrigued, and at other times bored, Amanda looked past Tori to smile at Milo. "Mr. Wentworth, I didn't realize that was you."

"You watch *Leona's Closet*?" he asked.

Amanda's eyes widened. "Every week."

Milo draped his right arm across Tori's shoulders and gestured toward her with his left hand. "My fiancé, Tori, is good friends with Leona. In fact, if asked, I suspect Leona would say Tori is her *best* friend."

Suddenly all remaining signs of boredom where Tori was concerned vanished. "You *know* Leona from *Leona's Closet*?"

"I sure do."

"Wow. Just wow." Amanda looked at her watch and then back at the boys, the young woman's struggle between staying and leaving palpable. "I have so many things I'd love to know but they're rerunning an episode I missed a few weeks ago and I really can't miss it again."

She felt her shoulders slump in response and wondered if Amanda noticed. But it didn't matter because Milo did. "I would imagine Tori would be happy to introduce you to Leona if you'd like, isn't that right, Tori?"

Amanda's jaw went slack. "Could you really do that?"

"Yeah, sure. I could probably even get you on the set one day."

The shriek that followed in response brought Jeremiah's hands to his ears and Jordan to the ground. If Amanda noticed, though, she said nothing, her complete and utter attention on nothing other than Tori. "Oh my gosh, that would be so amazing. When can we do this?"

Tori scrambled for an answer that would both appease Amanda and get the girl in front of her once again. "The show is airing a rerun tonight because Leona is . . . a little tied up. I suspect the same will hold true for next week, unless she really goes ahead with the show on my wedding."

"Wait a minute," Amanda gasped. "Was that your wedding party Leona highlighted last Sunday?"

"It was."

"So Mizz Winters is going to be in *your* wedding?"

Something about the girl's mocking tone made her stiffen. "I wouldn't have my wedding without her."

"But she's . . . *old*. And she can't wear heels."

She felt Milo's hand tighten on her shoulder in warning as she geared up for an answer that would likely blow any chance she had of talking to the only viable suspect on her list. Instead, she took a deep breath and gave a nicer version of the retort that was practically burning her tongue. "Rose Winters is one of the most beautiful people I've ever known."

Amanda shrugged then snapped her fingers for Jordan and Jeremiah to get moving. "Come on, boys. We need to go." Then, to Tori, she said, "So when can I meet Leona?"

"How about you and I get together tomorrow to hammer out those details? Maybe we could meet at Debbie's Bakery around noon?"

Chapter 24

Tori reached across the list of books she was slowly cataloging into the system and plucked the phone from its cradle. "Yes, Nina?"

"There's a Charles out here at the information desk and he's asking to see you."

"Fantastic. Send him to my office, would you?" Tori placed the phone back on its base and pushed her chair back from her desk, the opportunity to stand and stretch a welcome one. Then, crossing to the door, she readied her hug.

"Vic-tor-i-a . . . can you believe it? I'm actually here . . . at the Sweet Briar Public Library!" Charles did a little hop before stepping in for his hug. "I heard so much about this place from you that it's almost like I've been here a million times. Only I haven't."

She released him from her arms and stepped back to

give him a thorough once-over. "Can I just say how much I love having you here?"

"Of course you can." Charles's smile multiplied in size and wattage as he peeked his head around Tori and took in her desk, the large window overlooking the grounds, Nina's desk, and, finally, the cart that held the coffee-maker and a smattering of mugs. He pointed at the cart and glanced back at Tori. "Is that where the fire started?"

She nodded and then swept her hand around the completely refurbished room. "But you'd never know we had one in here at all, would you?"

"You sure wouldn't." Charles spun around and grabbed hold of Tori's wrist. "Where is the children's room? I simply *have* to see that."

"Come with me." She led her friend across the hall, flicked on the room's overhead light, and then stepped aside to afford him easy access to her pride and joy. "Well? What do you think?"

Slowly, step by step, Charles made his way through the door and into the children's room Tori had fashioned out of an area previously used for storage. Now, instead of boxes packed high to the ceiling, there were shelves filled with books, a handful of child-sized tables and chairs, and the wooden stage that served as a standing invitation to act out the many stories found inside the room. The walls themselves depicted scenes from classic children's books as seen through the eyes of some of Sweet Briar's younger residents.

She watched Charles's face as he moved into the room and finally stopped to absorb his surroundings. The awe she saw in his eyes warmed her from head to toe as she waited for his verbal feedback.

"Margaret Louise tried to describe this place to me. You tried to describe this place to me. Even Dixie tried to describe this place to me. But as *fabulous* as it sounded, it's a trillion times *more* fabulous in person." Charles spread his arms wide and turned in a small circle. "I would have *loved* this place when I was little . . . heck, I love it now."

"I never tire of hearing that," she admitted before venturing into the room and past her friend en route to the trunk she'd secured from a flea market just days before the room was unveiled for the first time. "Now you need to see one of my absolute favorite parts."

"The dress-up trunk?" Charles asked, clapping.

At her nod, he scurried over to her side and squealed as she lifted the lid and pulled out the bonnet Margaret Louise had made. "Laura Ingalls Wilder," she said, handing the item to Charles. "Sometimes, when I'm in the process of locking up for the day, I come in here and put that on. And every time I do, it reminds me of the little girl who fell in love with books and libraries and knew she wanted them to be a part of her life forever."

Pitching his body forward, Charles began digging through the trunk, periodically holding up various costumes and attributing them to the correct story. He held up crowns and beans and green leafy shoes and more until he found yellow bear ears and a honey pot. "This was my favorite character as a kid."

"How did you know we had those in there?" she asked.

"How could you not?" He pretended to stuff his face with honey and then slowly dropped the props back into the trunk and sighed dramatically. "Don't you wish you could be a kid again?"

She considered his question as she, too, returned the bonnet to the trunk. "Maybe . . . sometimes . . . I guess. But I kind of love where I am right now."

His smile returned and engaged his eyes, as well. "So when do I get to meet Milo Wentworth?"

"You could come over to my place tonight and I could make dinner for both of you."

Just like that, his smile was gone, chased from his face by . . . fear? "Oh no, Victoria, bite your tongue. I did not travel all the way out here—a full week before your wedding—to skip my first ever meeting of the Sweet Briar Ladies Society Sewing Circle."

"Oh, that's right. I forgot."

A scowl formed where his smile had been only moments earlier and he shook a finger at her. "Victoria, you *know* I've been wanting to go to one of your meetings since I saw you, Margaret Louise, Rose, Dixie, Leona, Debbie, and Beatrice on *Taped with Melly and Kenneth*. Besides, I still need to meet Mayor Georgina and Melissa."

She rubbed a hand across her forehead and gestured for Charles to follow her back to her office. "I know. I'm sorry. I guess I just have a lot on my mind right now with the wedding and worrying about Leona and—"

"Leona is going to be just fine. She just needs to accept the fact that she needs to use—" He waved away the rest of his sentence and then went in a different direction entirely. "I have to say, it's a good thing I'm here, Victoria, because that caregiver she has working for her? She's U-S-E-L-E-S-S. Utterly, completely, *useless*."

When they reached her office, she patted the top of the folding chair for Charles and leaned her back against the window. "Before Leona humiliated Rose on cable TV, I have no doubt whatsoever that Margaret Louise would have been at Leona's side every minute in that hospital and at home afterward. But it's different now and it's sad. Very, very sad."

"They'll get through it, Victoria."

"That's what Milo keeps saying, but I'm not so sure. I've never seen Margaret Louise shut down on Leona like this, and if Leona's fall wasn't enough to bring them back together, I'm not sure what will."

"Time," Charles said, simply. "You mark my words, Victoria, all will be well in the Sweet Briar Sewing Circle again."

Tori turned her head and looked out over the library grounds, her focus coming to rest on a man reading a newspaper on a bench beneath the trees. Although the man's back was to her, she knew who it was just as surely as she knew what section he was reading.

That's what Sweet Briar did for her.

It grounded her in its predictability.

It comforted her in its familiarity.

Squaring her shoulders, she turned back to her friend. "I hope you're right, Charles. I really hope you're right."

"I'm Charles, aren't I?" he quipped. "I'm right most of the time, and oh so trendy *all* of the time."

She smiled in spite of the mood she found herself in and pointed at the splash of red beneath his black denim jacket that coordinated perfectly with the silk scarf knotted at his throat. "I see Leona helped pick out your clothes this morning?"

"She consulted."

"How is she this morning?"

"Her therapist is with her now, and then after that,

she'll take a nap. I figure that gives me a three-hour gap before I really should get back to her place."

She left the window to sit at her desk and retrieve the light blue bag from the bottom drawer. Holding it out to Charles, she said, "I picked up a pair of chocolate chip muffins on the way into work this morning. Nina didn't want hers, so it's yours."

He clapped his hands together then liberated the bag from her outstretched hand. "This is from Debbie's bakery, isn't it?"

"It is."

"That's next on my list of must-see Sweet Briar attractions." Charles reached into the bag, pulled out the muffin, and took a little nibble followed by a second and a third. "Oh. My. This. Is. In-cred-ible."

"Wait until you try her salted caramel brownies." She leaned forward, dropping her voice to a near whisper as she did. "Rose would hit the roof if she knew how many of those I've had over the past week or two."

He stopped nibbling and held his hand to his heart. "I can't wait to see Rose at your—I mean, *the* sewing circle meeting tonight." Clearly yet unexplainably flustered, Charles jumped to his feet and shook the muffin bag at Tori. "Lunch is approaching. Can we please go to Debbie's? Please, please, please?"

Her smile froze on her face as she looked up at the clock above the door.

Eleven forty-five.

"Oh, wow, I didn't realize how late it was getting. I have a lunch meeting with a potential suspect."

Charles's mouth gaped open but not before his gasp echoed around the room. "Potential suspect?"

She gathered the papers she'd been working on prior to Charles's arrival and slipped them into their folder. Then, with a few clicks of the mouse, she shut down her computer and stuck a clean notebook and pen into her purse. "Uh-huh."

Leaning forward, Charles clamped his hand atop hers and squeezed. "Does this have something to do with that friend of Beatrice's Margaret Louise was telling me about on the way back from the airport?"

"Miss Gracie," she supplied. "And yes it does."

"So you really truly think she was pushed?"

Oh, how she wanted to say no, to believe with all her heart that Beatrice's former governess simply lost her footing. But she couldn't.

"I do."

Charles released his hold on her hand and rose to his feet to primp and pose in a way that made it impossible to not notice him. "You do remember I was *instrumental* in helping to free Dixie from lockup, don't you, Victoria?"

She knew where this was going. Still, she humored him with an answer. "Of course. And I'm forever grateful for your help."

"Prove it."

By the time they arrived at Debbie's, not only was Charles up to speed on what Luke had overheard moments before Miss Gracie's fall, but he also knew everything Tori did about Amanda Willey at that point.

And like Tori, Milo, and Margaret Louise, he was equally perplexed by the notion that a car wash could incite such tears.

Still, it was good to have a second pair of ears when she sat down with Amanda—especially when those ears belonged to someone as sharp as Charles.

The bell over the door announced their arrival and was followed almost immediately by a deep sigh. "I have spent many a night trying to imagine this place since I met all of you. And even though Debbie has e-mailed me a few pictures as well as a link to the menu, actually standing here, next to you, is like a dream come true."

"A dream come true?" Tori said, laughing.

"A. Dream. Come. True." Charles sashayed over to the glass case beside the register and began pointing. "I'd like one of those . . . and one of those . . . and *two* of those . . . and I'll pass on that because it has strawberries . . . and, oooh, those are your salted caramel brownies, aren't they? I'll take *three* of those . . . and—"

"Charles? Is that you?" Debbie stepped out from behind the counter, dishcloth in hand, and threw her arms around him. "You made it in time!"

Tori took a second to visually peruse the dining area for her lunch date and then, when she came up empty, she turned back to her friends. "And he did it with five days to spare."

"Five days?" Debbie echoed. "No, it's tonight—"

Charles cleared his throat, draped his arm around Debbie's shoulder, and squeezed. "See? Even Debbie knows I was determined to make a *sewing circle meeting*, don't you, Deb?"

Debbie fanned the sudden redness in her face while simultaneously extricating herself from Charles's arm. "It's, um, all he talks about whenever we e-mail." When she was behind the counter once again, she pointed toward the case. "So what can I get the two of you? Are you here for lunch or treats?"

"In our world"—Charles gestured between himself and Tori—"those two words are synonymous, aren't they, Victoria?"

She was about to call them on their odd behavior when the bell jangled atop the door once again and she turned instead to see who was arriving. Sure enough, it was Amanda.

"Is that her?" Charles whispered.

"Uh-huh," she whispered back before closing the gap between herself and the new arrival. "Hi, Amanda. I'm glad you were able to make it."

"I don't have long," Amanda replied, bypassing the counter completely and breezing past two or three tables before landing at one in the center. "I have an appointment for a mani-pedi in twenty minutes."

"I'm sorry. If I'd known, I'd have suggested a different time."

"I just made the appointment three minutes ago."

She felt Charles's amused stare on the back of her head and turned to bring him into the conversation. "This is my friend, Charles. He's in town for my wedding on Saturday and I invited him to join us."

Charles lifted his hand in a wave, only to let it drop back down to his side at Amanda's obvious displeasure.

"I'm here to talk about meeting Leona from *Leona's Closet.*"

"And Charles here is also a good friend of Leona's," she explained. "In fact, he's staying with her at her house while he's in town."

All signs of boredom disappeared from Amanda's

face as she found a smile for Charles, too. "Oh. I didn't realize."

Charles snapped his fingers in his favorite triangle formation and then officially joined Amanda at the table, glancing back at Debbie as he did. "I'll be back to order something in a few minutes, Love."

"Amanda? Can I get you something?"

"Yes. I'd love a latte."

Debbie got to work making the drink while Tori observed Amanda from afar, the girl's sudden interest in Charles purely about his connection to Leona. Milo was right. Amanda was all about status. Working for the wealthiest family in Sweet Briar surely gave her that and more. The only question now was whether the prospect of losing that status could push her to violence.

Push . . .

She closed her eyes against the memory of Beatrice's face upon news of Miss Gracie's death, the utter devastation she'd seen there still capable of sending chills through her body.

"Victoria? Are you okay?"

Opening her eyes, she added a smile to her nod.

When Amanda's latte was ready, Debbie leaned across the counter and lowered her voice so as to be heard by no one except Tori. "I'm not sure why you're meeting with that one, but know that she's only interested in you if she thinks you can get her to the next level in life. And if you can't, you better stay out of her way."

Chapter 25

Tori placed the latte on the table in front of Amanda and sat on the empty lattice-back chair to Charles's left.

"Did you know Charles is from New York?" Amanda asked, breathless. "He works in a bookstore and he sees celebrities all the time!" Without waiting for Tori's reply, Amanda wrapped her hands around her cup and widened her eyes at Charles in rapt interest. "So who is the biggest celebrity you've seen so far?"

Charles straightened his shoulders against the back of the chair and folded his hands atop one another on his knee. "Hmmm. I think that depends on how you define big. Are you talking the biggest soap opera star? The biggest TV star? The biggest movie star?"

"You mean you've seen people from all those things?"

"The biggest soap opera star lives in the building right

around the corner from me. He's been on *Gallant and Gorgeous* for more than ten years now."

"D-Drake Sullivan?" Amanda sputtered.

"One and the same." Charles lifted his chin into the air and then shrugged. "He's much more attractive in person."

"Wow . . ."

Tori nudged Charles's foot under the table and took command of the conversation before she lost her opportunity to a foot scrub and a bottle of nail polish. "So how long have you been working for the Whitehalls?"

Amanda, in turn, took advantage of the change in subject to sip her drink in such a way as to make sure both Tori and Charles noticed the sapphire and diamond ring on her right hand. "I celebrated my one-year anniversary with the Whitehalls last month. They took me to dinner at the Colonnade Room in Tom's Creek to celebrate and gave me this ring, too." Amanda held out her hand. "The sapphire is for my birth month and the diamonds on either side make it all the more breathtaking, don't they?"

"Girlfriend, they must love you," Charles said as he leaned forward to take in the ring. "On my first anniversary at the bookstore, all I got was a piece of substandard cake and a twenty-five-dollar gift card."

"The Whitehalls have a lot of money." Amanda gazed down at her ring one more time and then took another sip of her drink. "They know everybody who is anybody in this town and they're going to take me to Paris with them next month!"

She caught the rise in Charles's eyebrow just before he said, "Ooh-la-la."

Ooh-la-la was right . . .

"Have you ever been to Paris, Amanda?" Tori asked.

"Uh, no. With the exception of a trip to Charleston to see my cousin when I was ten, I've never been out of this godforsaken town."

"So you must be crossing your fingers it really happens . . ."

Amanda eyed Charles with a mixture of something Tori couldn't quite identify. Determination and agitation perhaps? "Oh, it'll happen. Trust me on that one."

Tori could feel the weight of Charles's stare as she searched for the next question she wanted to ask. But it was hard when the only thing she could focus on was whether she'd just uncovered a motive for Amanda to have killed Miss Gracie.

"You know, I just remembered another celebrity I saw last week." Charles uncrossed his legs and brought his hands to the top of the table. "Mark Drury from *Heartbeat*. He looked a lot older in person, but that's probably because of the stress he's under right now."

A kick under the table, coupled with a slight twisting at the corner of her friend's mouth, had Tori asking a question she really had no interest in voicing. "Why's he stressed?"

Charles lowered his voice in conspiratorial fashion and looked from Amanda to Tori and back again. "Word on the street is the show is thinking of replacing him. With someone from another show. Can you believe the *audacity*?"

She tried to conceal her smile as she realized what Charles was doing and jumped in with both feet. "So he steps up his game and proves to them he's a better fit for the role."

"Better yet, he finds a way to get this potential replace-ment off the studio's radar," Amanda suggested.

"Oh?" she and Charles said in unison.

"Out of sight, out of mind, right?" Amanda glanced down at her watch and then back up at Tori. "So, about meeting Leona Elkin . . . Do you really think you can make that happen?"

She wasn't entirely sure how long they sat there, staring at the door in the wake of Amanda's departure, but it was long enough that Debbie left the confines of the counter to snap her fingers in front of first Charles, and then Tori.

"See? This is what you get for passing up food," Deb-bie said. "So what will it be? A sandwich? A bowl of soup?"

Charles was the first to respond, his switch from dumb-founded to eclectic foodie nothing short of impressive. "I remember, in one of your first e-mails after you left the city, you sent a picture of some homemade vegetable soup. Do you still have that?"

"Of course. This place would be boycotted by my lunch regulars if I pulled it off the menu."

"I'd love a bowl of that," Charles said before address-ing Tori. "And what about you, Victoria? A chocolate sandwich?"

She switched gears long enough to make a face. "Ha. Ha." Then, to Debbie, she said, "Actually, I'll take a cup of the same soup."

"And?"

She felt her face warm under the scrutiny and caved

to the pressure. "And a salted caramel brownie—for me, and for Charles."

"Coming right up."

When Debbie disappeared through the swinging doors that separated the sales area from the kitchen, Tori addressed the elephant Amanda left behind. "I think that girl just handed me her motive."

"Handed *us* her motive," Charles corrected. "I'm riding shotgun on this now, Victoria."

"I wouldn't say that in front of Margaret Louise if I were you." She reached out, grabbed hold of Amanda's empty cup, and tapped it against the table. "She claimed that seat a long time ago."

"The backseat works."

She offered what she imagined was something resembling a smile and then moved on. "I would imagine Amanda saw the writing on the wall for her trip to Paris if the Whitehalls brought in a new nanny."

"How could she not?" Charles posed. "It's where my mind would go if I were Amanda."

"Only you'd step up your game as you said earlier, right?"

"I sure wouldn't push an innocent woman down the stairs just to get the thought of a new nanny off my employer's radar if that's what you're asking, Victoria."

She felt her heart rate accelerate in time with Charles's words. "So that's where your mind went, too? To the notion that Amanda pushed Miss Gracie to her death to get the Whitehalls thinking about something other than hiring a new nanny for a while?"

"Living in New York City, you come across a lot of Amanda Willeys. And by a lot, I mean *a lot*. They lie, they schmooze, they bribe, they date, they even *marry* their way into circles they're determined to be a part of." Charles stopped, laughed, and rolled his eyes. "I imagine that sounds rather comical coming from me of all people, doesn't it?"

"I don't understand."

Charles fiddled with the knot in his scarf and then dropped his elbow to the table and leaned his chin against his palm. "Yes, I was smitten with the idea of your circle when I saw you on *Taped with Melly and Kenneth*, but that's because you all seemed so real. So fun. And sure enough, I grew to love all of you once I got to know you. People like Amanda have no interest in getting to the genuine level because they're already looking ahead to the next step."

Hooking her finger beneath his chin, Tori brought Charles's focus squarely on her face. "Not one of us ever saw you as an opportunist. Not ever. As far as we were all concerned, you proved your sincerity the moment you volunteered to help us clear Dixie's name. Your actions, from that point forward, are what earned you a place in not only *my* heart, but everyone else's heart, too."

"I can't believe you want me at your wedding, Victoria," Charles whispered in a voice choked with emotion.

"And I can't imagine you *not* being there."

Chapter 26

Tori grabbed the sewing box and the covered dessert plate from the catch-all table beside her front door and stepped out onto the front porch. Despite the remaining odds and ends still to do before the wedding, knowing she had a sewing circle meeting that night had given her a much-needed boost of energy.

For much of her post-college life in Chicago, she'd dreaded Mondays for all the usual reasons. But once she moved to Sweet Briar and got involved in the Sweet Briar Ladies Society Sewing Circle, the once-despised day had become one of her favorites.

Some could argue the change was due, in part, to the table of homemade treats that were as much a part of the weekly meeting as needles and thread. But even if everyone stopping bringing their favorite desserts, she knew she'd still look forward to Monday evenings every bit as much.

"You look mighty purty in that royal blue top, Victoria," Margaret Louise called out from the driver's side window of her powder blue station wagon. "Mighty purty, indeed."

She hopped off the last porch step and wound her way around the hood of the wagon, the happiness she felt at seeing her friend multiplying tenfold at the sight of the occupant in the backseat. Balancing the plate on her sewing box–holding arm, Tori pulled open the passenger side door and slid onto the vinyl bench seat. "Rose, what a nice surprise. I didn't know you were driving with us tonight. How are you?"

"She has to pee, Victoria, so don't say nothin' 'bout sweet tea or lemonade or water falls until after we get to Leona's." Margaret Louise peered into the rearview mirror as Tori positioned her sewing box on the floor and the dessert plate atop her lap. "Ain't that right, Rose?"

Tori peeked over her shoulder just in time to catch Rose's eye roll. "I bet you even talk in your sleep, don't you, Margaret Louise?"

"Why, Rose, I don't know. No one has ever said nothin' 'bout that."

Rose leaned forward, collected Tori's kiss, and then pointed at the seat belt mounted to the wall between their doors. "Victoria, if you value your life, you'll put on your seat belt."

She started to turn only to freeze as something white and silvery from the trunk area of the wagon caught her attention. "What's that?" she asked, pointing.

"What's what?"

"The white and silver thing in the way—"

Her head snapped back against the headrest as Margaret Louise stepped on the gas and Rose groaned from the backseat. "What did I tell you, Victoria?"

Reaching her left hand across her body, Tori pulled the seat belt down from its resting place and clicked it into the buckle beside her left hip, her heart racing as it always did whenever she was in a car with Margaret Louise. But even as they zipped down one street after the next, she couldn't help but smile as she peeked at Margaret Louise behind the steering wheel and Rose white-knuckling just about everything she could grab in the backseat.

In addition to being an invaluable sleuthing partner, Margaret Louise was an amazing listener and support system. Sometimes she knew what was bothering Tori before Tori herself knew anything was wrong. And whenever Tori had an idea to help the friends of the library raise funds, Margaret Louise was always ready to roll up her sleeves and help.

And then there was Rose. So many times when she found herself missing her great-grandmother, Tori would pick up the phone and call Rose. It wasn't that Rose had replaced her great-grandmother, but rather, Rose had helped to quiet the sorrow and lift her spirits. Knowing that she brought something good to Rose's life, too, made their relationship all the more special.

Margaret Louise turned left at the four-way stop and then right at the next stop sign, their obvious destination both amusing and confusing all at the same time.

"While I know I should be encouraged that you're driving to Leona's, this week's meeting is at Debbie's place, remember?" she teased.

"No it ain't." Margaret Louise elongated her plump body so as to meet Rose's eyes in the rearview mirror.

Tori twisted in her seat enough to be able to see both friends. "Yes it is. Last week we were at Georgina's. After her house it's always Debbie's . . . and *then* Leona's."

"Not this time it ain't." Margaret Louise turned right once again and then mercifully slowed the car as they approached the familiar row of condominiums. "Charles called this afternoon and asked if we'd be opposed to havin' our meetin' at Leona's this week so she could attend, too."

Tori felt her shoulders slump at the thought of no one showing up in retaliation for Leona's latest schenanigans, but they rebounded as Margaret Louise began searching for a parking spot amid a line of familiar cars.

Georgina's . . .

Debbie's . . .

Beatrice's . . .

Dixie's . . .

And Melissa's.

"How come I didn't know about this change?" she asked, swinging her focus back to Margaret Louise.

Again, Margaret Louise looked at Rose before she answered. "I was sure I called you, Victoria. Maybe you missed the message on your recorder?"

"There was no message."

"Well, I'll be darned. I musta called Melissa twice then." Margaret Louise maneuvered her way into a spot directly in front of her daughter-in-law's oversized van and turned off the engine. "If all goes well, my twin will keep her mouth closed tonight and we can get through the evenin' with no fightin' or fussin'."

"I'm sure Leona will be fine. I'm just surprised Georgina and Dixie were even willing to come based on how angry they were at her at the last meeting."

Margaret Louise pulled the key out of the ignition, pushed open the door, and stepped onto the pavement in front of Leona's unit. "We're doin' this for one reason and one reason only."

Tori gathered her sewing box and dessert plate into her arms and then set them on the top of the car so she could assist Rose out of the backseat. When Rose was safely on her feet, Tori retrieved her items as well as Rose's and shut both doors. "And what is that?"

"You."

Stopping midway up the steps, Tori turned to look at her friends, who were little more than a few steps behind. "Me?"

The door at the top of the steps opened to reveal six smiling faces all shouting "surprise" at the same time. "Surprise?" she echoed, resuming her way up the steps. "What are you guys talking about?"

Charles looked at each of the women standing around him, wiggling his eyebrows as he did. "May I?" he asked.

Five heads nodded and then Charles snapped his fingers in his favorite triangle motion. "Welcome to your bridal shower, Victoria!"

"M-my b-bridal shower?"

This time, all six heads nodded in time with the two now standing beside her on the stoop. "That's why we're all here," Margaret Louise explained. "Because we'd all do anything for you, wouldn't we, ladies?"

Tori stepped through the opening made by her friends and stopped to plant a kiss on each and every cheek, and then watched as Charles and Rose reunited for the first time since New York.

"You got rid of the purple, Charles," Rose said, reaching up and touching Charles's spikey hairdo.

He grinned. "Do you miss it, Rose?"

"Surprisingly, I do." Linking her arm inside Charles's, Rose shuffled her way through the crowd and down the hall. "Now where is Leona? I want to see that she's okay."

Tori watched the group's matriarch disappear into the living room and then leaned against the wall. "It sure looks like Rose has forgiven Leona for last week's debacle."

"That may be so, but we sure haven't." Dixie took the covered plate from Tori's hand and peeled back the foil for a peek. "I know it's your shower and all, Victoria, but it sure would be a shame not to put these white chocolate brownies alongside the cake and cookies."

Georgina came in behind Dixie and freed Tori of the weight of her sewing box, too. "And tonight is all about games and presents. No sewing allowed."

"But the favor bags," she protested. "I have to make two more for some last-minute RSVPs that came in from Milo's cousins."

"Melissa and I made four extras in case somethin' like that happened, didn't we, Melissa?" Margaret Louise motioned toward her daughter-in-law yet didn't wait for her confirmation. "So there's nothin' to worry 'bout, Victoria. Nothin' but havin' fun."

An hour and a half into her shower, Tori's face ached from laughing and smiling so much. They'd played

Dixie's wedding bingo with conversation-heart candies, she'd awarded boxes of chocolate to the team who'd created the best toilet paper wedding dress, and learned a few interesting tidbits about each of her friends during Debbie's Guess-Which-Celebrity-I'd-Marry game.

Beatrice, of course, stayed faithful to Kenny Rogers.

Debbie and Melissa both had a fondness for Brad Pitt.

Georgina fancied Tom Hanks.

Dixie was all about Anthony Hopkins.

Margaret Louise laughed at her own choice of Jack Nicholson.

Rose blushed at the mere mention of Paul Newman.

And Charles's choice of Johnny Depp was still sending knowing chuckles around the room. Yet as she followed the laughs with her eyes, Tori became all too aware of the one person in the room who wasn't smiling at all.

She peeked into the hat in search of one final index card and came up empty. "Leona? Where's your card?"

Silence fell across the room as six sets of eyes cast downward, and two sets turned with hers to wait for the woman's answer. "I didn't fill one out."

"Why not?"

"I wasn't *given* an index card, dear."

She felt Rose stiffen at her spot between Melissa and Dixie, and was relieved when Charles jumped up from his preferred seat on the floor to grab a card from the stack beside the pretzel bowl. "Here, Leona. You can fill one out now."

Leona waved the card away with a bejeweled hand. "It's too late now. There would be nothing for Victoria to guess."

"No. No. You don't have to write anything down. Let

me try and guess all on my own." Tori shifted in her seat as a name revealed itself in her thoughts. "Tom Cruise!"

"Too short, dear."

"George Clooney!"

"Although he's very handsome, he's graying too fast."

"Liam Neeson!"

"No."

Charles snapped his finger. "Wait. I bet I can answer this. Channing Tatum!"

Tori prayed her laugh drowned out the snickers that accompanied the thirty-something's name, but as Leona's mouth tightened, she knew she'd been unsuccessful. Still, she tried to focus on her injured friend. "Is Charles right?"

"I'd certainly consider a proposal from Channing, or any of the males from the cast of *Magic*—"

"What do you say we take a break for some more snacks?" Georgina suggested, cutting Leona off. "There's a lot more still to be had besides that amazing cake of Debbie's Tori already cut."

Tori waited as the stampede headed off in the direction of the kitchen and then wandered over to Leona's chair. "How are you holding up, Leona?"

"I'll be fine, Victoria. This night is about you."

"I'm sorry everyone is being so cool."

"Cool?" Leona mimicked. "I rather think they're treating me like a pariah in my own home."

Oh, how she wished she could call the woman on being dramatic, but she couldn't. Sure, everyone had gone out of their way to make the evening special for Tori, but they'd done it without conversing with Leona about anyone or anything. The only question now was whether the pain that hooded Leona's eyes was as a result of their behavior or her fractured hip.

"Can I get you something? A cookie? A piece of cake? Your pain medication? Anything?"

"I'm not hungry, dear, but perhaps you could hand me the crossword in today's paper? I could keep myself busy with that for a few moments while the rest of you snack." Leona lifted her hand to her forehead and kneaded the skin above her eyes. "And a glass of water. I feel a bit parched."

"I'll get the water," Charles said over Tori's shoulder. "You get the paper."

Tori crossed to the magazine holder beside the fireplace, plucked out the paper in the front, and held it up for Leona to see. "Is this the one?"

At Leona's nod, she crossed back to her friend's chair and laid the paper across the woman's lap. "Do you need a pencil?"

"I prefer a pen, but I have one right here." Leona scooted her paper plate to the side of the nearest end table and uncovered a pen in the process. "Doing a crossword puzzle with a pen shows confidence, dear."

Without thinking, Tori reached toward the paper in an effort to help smooth out a few wrinkles, but as she did, Leona gasped.

"Leona? Are you okay? Are you in pain?"

When her friend said nothing, she withdrew her hand and asked again. "Leona? Are you okay?"

Leona reached out, grabbed Tori's hand, and brought it back to the newspaper. "Flip your hand over, Victoria."

"Flip my hand over? Why?"

She heard the rest of the circle return to the room and gather around the chair to see what was happening.

"Just flip it over, dear."

She did as Leona asked, only to receive the same result as she had the first time.

"What's with the gasping, Leona?"

Leona bobbed her head left and right as she studied something pertaining to the newspaper and Tori's left hand.

"Leona? What's wrong?"

"Take off your engagement ring, dear," Leona finally said. "And let me see it for a moment."

"Um, why?"

Leona pinned her with a death stare. "Please, Victoria. Just let me see your ring."

"The ring thing is a game for a *baby* shower, Leona," Charles interjected as he set Leona's requested glass of water on the end table beside her chair. "Not a wedding shower."

Still, Tori did as she was told and handed her ring to Leona, who, in turn, took off one of her own. Holding them side by side, Leona breathed on both rings and then studied them closely. Within seconds, she handed Tori's back.

"Your diamond is a fake, Victoria."

This time, the gasp didn't come from Leona. Instead, it came from Tori's own mouth and was echoed by the eight now flanking her from both sides.

"You take that back, Twin!" Margaret Louise bellowed. "You take that back right now."

"I can't," Leona said. "Because it's true."

Georgina's finger shot its way through the gap between

Tori and Charles and stopped just short of Leona's chin. "Why must you always insist on stomping all over everyone's feelings?"

"What has Milo ever done to you to make you try to smear his reputation like this on today of all days?" Dixie placed her hands on her hips and added her long-groomed librarian death stare for good measure. "It's—it's *unconscionable*!"

Leona stomped her foot on the ground and then doubled over in pain.

"Don't you try to weasel out of this by playin' on our sympathy," Margaret Louise accused. "'Cause it ain't gonna work."

Inhaling sharply, Leona slowly lifted her head until her eyes were on no one else but Tori. "Do you think I want to be the one to tell you something like this? You know how important you are to me and how fond I am of Milo. I don't understand why he'd skimp on something so important, but maybe he just couldn't handle something real on an elementary school teacher's salary."

Tori looked down at the ring and recalled the moment he slipped it on her finger in front of her friends. No, Leona was wrong. Milo had scrimped and saved for her ring—her *real* ring. "I'm sorry, Leona, but you are mistaken. Milo has the papers on the ring in his safe, I've seen them with my own two eyes."

"Then they're a lie."

"Stop it, Leona," Rose hissed. "Stop it right now. I understand that weddings are difficult for you, but this is Victoria we're talking about. I can't and won't save you if you keep going down this road."

"There are several ways one can spot a fake diamond.

Victoria's diamond failed both tests." Leona slipped her own ring back on her finger and helped herself to a sip of her water. "The first test happened rather inadvertently when Victoria was trying to straighten the wrinkles out of my crossword page."

"What are you cacklin' 'bout, Twin?"

"When you put a real diamond—such as mine—over top of a newspaper, you can't read the print through the gem. But with a fake diamond, you can."

Gentle thumping to Tori's left broke through the white noise in her head and she turned in time to see Beatrice, Melissa, and Debbie quietly gathering her assorted presents into piles. Beyond them, Georgina and Dixie had extricated themselves from the spectacle that was Leona and were busying themselves with the task of collecting used plates, napkins, and cups.

"You know, I sort of remember reading something like that once," Charles whispered, bringing Tori's attention back to the always stylish woman seated in front of her.

"The second test is the one I just did with our rings side by side." Leona kneaded at the skin above her eyes once more, her voice reflecting none of the joy the other sewing circle members had accused her of having over her trumped-up revelation. "I breathed on each stone and watched to see how long it took for my breath to evaporate on each one. Genuine diamonds, such as mine, repel water vapor considerably faster than fake gemstones such as yours, Victoria."

Dixie slipped a protective arm around Tori and gently tugged her backward. "Let's go, Victoria. You deserve better than this on your special day. Melissa and Debbie are bringing your presents out to the car now and Margaret Louise will bring you home."

Slowly, Tori fell into step with the group as they made their way down the hallway and toward the door, her feet only slowing as Margaret Louise came to a stop. Turning back toward her sister, the normally happy-go-lucky grandmother of eight shook her finger in disgust. "Leona Elkin, I am ashamed to call you my sister."

Chapter 27

It didn't matter how busy she tried to keep herself around the library, Tori simply couldn't keep her mind from straying back to the exact moment Leona had pulled the rug out from under her feet.

In the grand scheme of things, she wasn't a materialistic person. She didn't need a mansion, an expensive car, name brand clothes, or designer purses to make her happy. As long as her life was rich with love and friendship, she was a lucky girl.

Yet even knowing that, she couldn't shake the overwhelming sadness that had settled around her heart the moment she'd walked out of Leona's house the previous night and headed toward Margaret Louise's car.

Yes, her friends had rallied around her, encouraging her to chalk Leona's assertions up to good old-fashioned jealousy. Yes, they'd successfully pointed out similar things Leona had done to all of them at one point or another. But none of it had been able to wipe away the woman's words or the genuine sincerity with which they'd been said.

Leona may have had a history of lashing out at people in successful relationships and creating issues to keep others from getting involved at all, but deep down inside, Tori knew that wasn't the case this time.

She could feel in it her bones—bones that had kept her awake for more than half the night, and tossing and turning throughout the rest.

It wasn't that she doubted Milo or his feelings for her, because she didn't. In fact, her bones were just as certain Milo didn't know the diamond was fake as they were that Leona was right.

The problem she was struggling with, though, was how and when to tell her fiancé he'd been swindled. Did she tell him before the wedding and risk ruining the anticipation he wore so endearingly well? Or did she wait until after the wedding and chance him being angry with her for keeping it a secret?

"I can see it in your eyes from all the way over here."

Tori dropped the book she was holding onto the counter and turned toward the front door to find Rose standing there, staring at her with a mix of disapproval and pity. "Oh, Rose. I didn't hear you come in."

"That's because you're still listening to Leona in your head." Rose shuffled over to the information desk and set her purse on top. "I figured you would be, so I asked my neighbor's son to drive me here so we could talk. Is Nina here to watch the floor?"

"No. Nina has the day off."

Rose shuffled to the end of the desk to afford a better view of the computer terminals and the line of shelves beyond. Then, doubling back to her starting point, she scanned the various reading chairs and worktables scattered around. "Doesn't anybody spend time in a library anymore?"

"An hour ago, I was inundated with toddlers. And in about two hours, I'll have the high school kids coming through with whatever project they're working on. But right now, I've got a lull." Tori stretched her arms above her head and then yawned. "I won't complain, though, because I'm a little tired after my shower last night."

"Did you have fun?"

She pushed Leona's voice from her head long enough to allow some of the other memories from the previous night a chance to shine. "Oh, Rose, not only was it a fun surprise all on its own, but getting to have Charles there for it, and playing all those fun games, just made it all the more special."

"I'm glad. I only wish Leona had kept her comments to herself for a little while." Rose let go of the counter and made a beeline for the closest table and chair combination. When she reached her destination, she slowly lowered herself onto one of the chairs and gestured toward the other for Tori. "Come. Sit."

She joined Rose at the table as the woman's words took root. "You're no longer saying Leona was being mean-spirited."

"Her timing left much to be desired, but I think she simply reacted in the moment." Rose leaned forward and covered Tori's hand with her own. "Anyone with two eyes knows Leona is quite fond of you."

Looking down at her free hand, she moved the underside of her ring with her thumb and tried not to let her sadness seep into her words. "So you think Leona is right? You think my diamond is fake?"

"If it failed both those tests Leona did last night, then yes, I do. But the only way you can be certain is to let Milo take it back to wherever he bought it."

She knew Rose was right. But she also knew how heartbroken Milo would be to learn the truth. He'd been so incredibly proud of his selection and so eager to slip it onto her finger the moment she accepted his proposal.

"Do you know where he bought it?" Rose asked.

Without taking her eyes off the ring, she shared what she knew. "Brady's Jewelry in town."

"That's good. Jim is a local boy and he'll make things right, I'm sure."

When Tori didn't reply, Rose squeezed her hand tightly. "What's wrong, Victoria? Surely you don't believe Milo intentionally tried to fool you . . ."

"No, of course not."

"Then what's the problem?"

"I don't know how, or even *when* to tell him it's fake," she whispered. "He's going to be crushed."

"And you're probably right. But I'm willing to bet he'd be even more crushed if you didn't tell him." Rose released her grip enough to give Tori a gentle pat before pulling her hand away completely. "The sooner you get it out in the open, the sooner it can be fixed."

"But our wedding is four days away, Rose. Is it really fair to drop this on him now?" She looked again at the ring and then left her chair in favor of a little good old-fashioned pacing. "And then there's Jim Brady to think of, too. I mean, a woman just fell to her death in his home a little over a week ago, and if that's not bad enough, I suspect a few of the people that were in his home at the time of the incident are about to be part of a murder investigation."

Rose's hand flew to her mouth as her eyes slipped closed behind her bifocals. "Another murder?"

Tori stopped pacing to return to the elderly woman's side. "Near as I can figure, Miss Gracie's hiring was seen as a threat to some of the other nannies. Beatrice is amazing, and her friend, Miss Gracie, was poised to be every bit as good. If even a few of the other nanny-utilizing families in town took notice, girls like Amanda Willey and Stacy Gardner might very well have been out of work."

"So they do something else," Rose groused. "They could wait tables at the diner, or deliver pizza at the pizza shop, or even polish antiques at Leona's place. Money is money and work is work."

"I know that, and you know that, but for some of these girls—Amanda and Cynthia in particular—being a nanny for families like the Whitehalls and the Bradys exposed them to a world and a way of living they've never seen or known before."

"That's not a reason to kill someone!"

"I'm not saying they have, Rose. I'm just saying there's a chance. A good chance unfortunately." By force of habit, Tori scanned all visible bookshelves in their immediate vicinity and noted three books that were out of place—one in self-help, one in mysteries, and one in general fiction. She crossed to the self-help aisle and returned the abandoned book to its correct location. Then, moving on to

general fiction, she plucked the misplaced title from its
precarious position on the edge of the shelf and carried it
to its proper spot at the end of the aisle, her thoughts rico-
cheting between her ring, telling Milo, and Miss Gracie.
"So needless to say, I'm a little wary about being the person who deals yet another blow to the Brady family."

"That's assuming Jim doesn't already know the ring
is fake."

Tori stopped halfway down the mystery aisle and
turned to face Rose. "You think Jim *knows* my diamond
is fake?"

Rose's frail shoulders hiked upward beneath her cotton
sweater. "He's a jeweler. It's his job to know what he's
buying and what he's selling."

She was aware of Charles moving around her office,
rearranging her stapler, Nina's pictures, and even the
sugar packets on the beverage cart, but every time she
decided to say something, a completely unrelated thought
would swoop in and take precedence.

It wasn't a bad thing necessarily, especially when those
unrelated-to-Charles thoughts were slowly proving themselves related in another way. She ran the tip of her pen
down the notepad and made a mental note of the people
on her list she most needed to talk to on her way home
from work.

Cynthia Marland.

Reenie Brady.

Amanda Willey.

How, exactly, she was going to find them and talk to
them, though, was the real question . . .

"Charles?"

He stopped fussing with the bowl of creamers and stirrers and turned, hands on hips. "Yes, Victoria?"

"It's time to step up the investigation. I want this figured out once and for all before I walk down that aisle on Saturday morning."

"Oooh, I love it when you talk dirty like that!" Charles sashayed his way over to Tori's desk and sat on the folding chair, legs crossed. "Tell me what to do."

She spun the notepad around and pushed it across the desk to Charles. "I want you to call Beatrice and ask her to find a way to get the Brady kids to the park sometime in the next hour."

"Okay," he said, looking from Tori to the list and back again, "but can I ask why?"

"Between the two older girls, we should be able to find out the name of every nanny that was in their house the night Miss Gracie was pushed." She pointed her pen at Charles. "You do have Beatrice's cell phone number, don't you?"

"Of course. Who do you think I call every time I read something about Kenny Rogers?" He stood, pulled his flip phone from the front pocket of his lavender-colored jeans, and sat back down, waving the antiquated contraption in the air as he did.

"After the park, we'll swing by Cynthia Marland's house."

"I thought she was off your radar."

"She is . . . sorta. But I can't shake the fact that I caught her sneaking out of the Bradys' home three days after Miss Gracie's accident. There had to be a reason she was there and didn't want anyone to know."

Charles pointed at the last name on the list. "And Amanda?"

She returned her pen to the wooden holder Charles had moved to the far side of her desk and then pulled her own cell phone from its holding spot inside her top drawer. "Amanda is last on the list because I think that's where we're going to end up when this is all said and done."

"End up?"

"With Sweet Briar Police Chief Robert Dallas in tow." She scrolled through her contact list until she got to the first name under *M*. "While you're calling Beatrice, I'm going to get in touch with Margaret Louise and fill her in on what we're doing and the order in which we're doing it. She'd be fit to be tied if we wrapped this thing up without her involvement."

Pausing his finger on the keypad of his phone, Charles leaned forward, looked around the empty after-hours office, and decreased his volume to a whisper. "Um, Victoria?"

"Yes?"

"Um, I'm all for playing detective with Margaret Louise but, um . . ."

She moved her pen in a rolling motion as she looked again at the clock. "Spit it out, Charles."

"Could *you* drive? *Please?*"

Chapter 28

Waving at the cloud of kicked-up dust that hovered in the space between them, Charles brought his lips to within centimeters of Tori's ear. "Thank you, thank you, thank you for insisting Margaret Louise meet us here instead of at the library."

She craned her neck around Charles to get a clear shot of her cohort in crime now making her way across the parking lot toward their bench. After returning Margaret Louise's wave, she reengaged her pal. "You live in New York City, Charles . . . Drivers like her are a dime a dozen. Only you pay to ride with them."

"Oh no, I'm a subway boy all the way. And on the extremely rare occasion I *take* a cab, I sit in the backseat . . . behind glass . . . with my eyes closed. Unless I'm in it with one of you. Then I act brave."

"Sorry it took me so long to get here, Victoria, but I

was sweepin' cookie crumbs up off my floor when Charles called and I had to finish the job." Margaret Louise dropped onto the park bench beside Tori and clapped her hands. "So when are Beatrice and the kids gettin' here?"

Tori turned to answer her friend, but got momentarily sidetracked by Charles's elbow in her rib cage and his breath in her ear. "It's only been eight minutes since I called! She lives a good twelve minutes away. And that's if she was sitting in a running car when she picked up the phone."

"Here they come!" Margaret Louise stood and started waving toward the sidewalk on the opposite side of the park, the smile on her face due as much to the presence of children as the prospect of investigating, no doubt. "Woo-hoo, Beatrice, we're over here!"

Tori looked from Margaret Louise to Charles and back again, the list of questions she wanted to ask the Brady children moving into the forefront of her thoughts. "Are you ready?"

"What do you need us to do?" Charles asked as he, too, stood and took a moment to smooth any visible wrinkles from his pants.

"She needs us to be her listenin' ears while she's askin' the questions. And while we're listenin', we're lookin', too."

"Looking? For what?"

"Hanky panky, that's what." Margaret Louise threw back her shoulders and tightened the drawstring on the waistband of her polyester warm-up suit. "And we've come across a lot of hanky panky in our investigatin' days, haven't we, Victoria?"

Tori stifled the laugh she felt building and turned it into a smile instead as Luke and the Brady children ran over. "Hi, guys, how are you?"

Luke thrust out his hand and opened it to reveal a paper plane. "I made this after school today and Miss Bea said I can climb to the top of the jungle gym and fly it from way up there."

"Sounds like fun, Luke." Tori gently tapped each of the Brady girls on the nose, making sure to address each one by name as she did. When she was done, she sent Sophie off to spot Luke's airplane and gestured Kellie and Reenie over to the swings. When each girl was on a swing with a designated pusher strategically placed within earshot, she posed her first question. "I was wondering if you two remember who was at your house the night Miss Gracie fell."

Kellie pumped her legs slowly at first as she got used to Charles's push. "Mom was in the kitchen with the other moms. Me and Sophie were in the TV room with Miss Gracie and some of the other kids and nannies. Except Miss Bea wasn't there. She was sewing one of her pretty things and Luke just came with his mom."

Reenie giggled as Margaret Louise included an occasional tickle with her push. "Luke and me played blocks."

"I know, I heard." Tori climbed onto the empty swing between the girls and used her long legs to get herself moving. When she was at a similar swinging cadence with the children, she continued. "Jeremiah and Jordan Whitehall were there, right?"

"Yup."

She smiled around the chains that separated her from Kellie. "And their nanny Miss Amanda, right?"

"Yup."

"And Miss Stacy and the kids she takes care of?"

Reenie giggled louder. "She takes care of Ronald."

"Were there any other kids there?"

"Maureen and Marcia were there in the beginning with their nanny, Miss Wendy, but they didn't stay very long. Marcia had a tummy ache." Kellie pumped her legs harder and harder until Charles finally stepped away and came around to the front of the swing set. "Anyone else?" he asked.

"Ra-Ra!" Reenie shouted.

Tori stopped moving her legs and rode out the built-up motion for as long as she could. "Are you wanting to be a cheerleader when you get older, Reenie?"

"Okay, everybody, watch this . . . I'm going to jump," Kellie warned. And then, just like that, Kellie was on the ground, smiling triumphantly over her perfect landing.

Charles grabbed hold of the now vacant swing while Tori's slowly drifted to a stop due to lack of leg power.

"Reenie doesn't want to be a cheerleader. Ra-Ra is our aunt, Tara. Reenie couldn't say her name very well when she was little so she just called her Ra-Ra. Now we all do it."

"So your aunt Tara was there that night, too?"

"For a little while. Until Miss Cindy finally left." Kellie wandered over to her sister and watched as the girl swung back and forth. "I'm glad she was there. Mommy would have been upset if she'd seen Miss Cindy."

"Yeah," Reenie agreed as she, too, stopped pumping her legs and drifted to a tickle-free stop in front of Margaret Louise. "I don't think Mommy could whisper yell like Ra-Ra did."

Tori stepped off the swing and squatted beside Reenie's. "So wait a minute. It was your aunt Tara you heard yelling at Cindy when you were in the closet with Luke?"

"Uh huh. She scared me a little. Luke, too!" Reenie's eyes widened just before they, too, turned to look at her friend as he readied his paper creation for flight. "You're not gonna tell Aunt Tara I was hiding in the closet with Luke, are you?"

"Would that upset her?"

"When Miss Cindy came into the TV room, Aunt Tara pulled her out and told us to watch TV." Reenie toed at a rock on the ground by her left foot and then played with the hem of her shirt. "But the TV was boring."

"I don't know your aunt, Reenie, so there would be no reason for me to tell. Besides, I don't think anyone would get upset with you for finding something quiet to play." She followed the girls' attention back to the jungle gym and then stole a peek at Charles and Margaret Louise over the top of Reenie's head. At their collective nod, she sent the little girls on their way.

When they were out of earshot, she sank onto her backside and plucked a small twig from the ground. She twirled it to the right and then the left as she replayed everything she'd learned.

"So the yelling Luke and Reenie heard was just a family member telling Cynthia to leave. Sounds pretty innocuous when you know the facts, doesn't it?"

Charles snapped two points of his imaginary triangle and then pulled out Tori's list. "So the kid was a dead end. We still have two more stops to make before we call in Sweet Briar's finest."

"You haven't met Chief Dallas, have you," she mumbled as she reached out to Charles for help in standing.

Tori turned left out of the parking lot and headed east toward a side of Sweet Briar she rarely drove through, let alone visited. For several blocks she said nothing to either of her companions, opting instead to focus on yet another set of questions she'd brewed in her head throughout the latter part of her work day—a set that was reserved for her once prime and only suspect.

"I bet it's nice to let someone else do the driving once in a while, isn't it, Margaret Louise?" Charles swiveled his upper body so as to be able to peer into the backseat of Tori's compact. "You get to enjoy the sights of Sweet Briar better this way, huh?"

"I look at all sorts of sights while I'm drivin'. Don't I, Victoria?" Margaret Louise scooted forward and rested her chin, puppy dog style, on the back of Charles's seat. "Why, just last month, I read an entire billboard— includin' the fine print—out on Route 100 on the way to the shoppin' mall, isn't that right, Victoria."

"And you're still alive?" Charles whispered to Tori.

"Of course she's still alive, Charles. I'm a grandmother of eight youngin's, I know how to multitask with the best of 'em."

Tori winked at her friend in the rearview mirror and then turned her full-wattage smile on Charles. "She can read, sing, and drive sixty-five in a thirty-five like no one's business."

"Now, Victoria, don't go tellin' tales. I was driving sixty-three. Not sixty-five."

Tori pulled her right hand from the steering wheel just long enough to gesture toward Charles. "I stand corrected. Margaret Louise can read, sing, and drive sixty-*three* in a thirty-five like no one's business."

"That's better." Margaret Louise tapped Tori's shoulder as they turned left at the stop sign and proceeded toward Cynthia's street. "And while you're standin' and correctin' anyway, I think it's only right I point out the fact that you *do* know Reenie and Kellie's aunt. Or if you don't know her, you're surely aware of who she is."

She slowed at the next four-way stop and then accelerated a bit as she got out onto the open road. "I don't know anyone named Tara. Not here, or in Chicago."

"Okay, so you don't *know* her know her. But you know *of* her."

"I do?"

"Sure. She's the one who gave all these girls their jobs in the first place."

"What girls? What jobs?"

Margaret Louise rolled her eyes at Charles. "It's like I told you. The most important thing we can do in this investigatin' is be her eyes and ears."

"Please, Margaret Louise, get to the point."

"Tara owns the Nanny Go Round Agency that employs Cynthia, Amanda, Stacy, and anyone else who works—"

Tori swerved onto the gravelly shoulder and quickly corrected with a decrease in speed. But it was too late; Charles was already white-knuckling the passenger door.

"Are you sure?" she asked the woman in her rearview mirror.

"That'd be like me askin' you if you're sure 'bout who wrote a certain book. You're a librarian, Victoria, you know books. I'm a gossip. Knowin' who's who is in my job description. If I don't know who's who, I might as well take down the fence in my backyard."

"So wait a minute," Charles mused as he tentatively released his hold on the door. "This Julie Brady fired a nanny who works for her sister and then totally dissed her sister even more by going to a different agency to find a replacement?"

She nodded along with Charles's recap but was saved from saying anything when he continued on.

"Sisters at each other's throats? I'm calling family tension in the Brady household right now."

"Tara isn't Julie's sister," Margaret Louise shared. "She's Jim's sister."

"Oooh, even better. Fighting between the in-laws is even more volatile." Charles turned, draped his hand across Margaret Louise's, and squeezed. "Tell me you saw last week's episode of *Explosive Secrets*."

Tori cleared her throat in an effort to nip the ensuing conversation in the bud, and when that didn't work, she simply pulled over to the shoulder and stopped.

"Now that I have your attention, ladies and gentleman, we need to consider this latest wrinkle."

Charles crinkled his nose. "I don't like wrinkles."

"Wrinkles are life's road map, young man. They tell a story 'bout where you've been."

"A story I don't intend to tell with my face." Charles turned back to Tori and waved for her to continue.

"Was Tara yelling at Cindy to leave because she knew the girl shouldn't be there? Or was she yelling at her for being a lousy employee—hence the suggestion she go wash cars instead?"

"Seems to me there's only one way to find them answers, Victoria."

Charles's front pocket began to ring, causing him to wiggle around in his seat until he was able to retrieve the device and check the Caller ID screen. "It's Leona."

"Ignore it," Margaret Louise groused as she threw her body against her own seat back.

Tori rolled her eyes and then nodded at Charles to take the call. "You need to make sure she's okay. She is, after all, home with Rachel."

"After what she did to you last night, Victoria, I can't believe you're wastin' one iota of your energy worryin' 'bout my twin . . ."

She considered telling Margaret Louise that Rose now suspected Leona was right about Tori's diamond, too, but she opted to stay silent as Charles took the call.

"Hi, Leona . . . Yes, gorgeous, I'm with Victoria . . ." He listened to whatever Leona was saying and then slid a sideways glance in Tori's direction. "I don't know, Leona . . . Is that really necessary right now? Don't you think you should lay low for a little—"

Reaching across the center console, Tori plucked the phone from Charles's hand and held it to her own ear. "I'm here, Leona. What's up?"

"I didn't say what I said last night to hurt you, dear. Please tell me you know that."

She pulled back onto Route 25 and continued on their journey, the investigation into Miss Gracie's fall a distraction she really didn't want to see end just yet. Still, she hated to hear Leona hurting more than she already was. "I know that, Leona."

"Then please know that I'm not trying to rub salt in your wounds by revisiting the subject now."

"What is there to revisit, Leona?"

"Milo wasn't the only one who was duped, dear."

She stopped, mid-sigh, and forced herself to absorb

what her friend was saying. "What are you talking about, Leona?"

"Debbie stopped by today."

"Oh?"

"And it wasn't to yell at me, either."

"Okay . . ."

"She wanted to talk about the tests I did with your ring last night."

A brief potpourri of sounds in her ear was quickly followed by a short-lived whisper. "If I were in the market for a new career, dear, I would open a caregiver agency. And I would actually make sure my employees like taking care of people." Then bringing her voice back to a more normal volume, Leona continued, "Turns out, the ring Debbie got from Colby for their fifteen-year anniversary over the summer is fake, too."

"Are you sure?" she asked as she recovered her breath. "Is Debbie upset?"

She could almost sense Margaret Louise's ears perking from the backseat, but her focus remained on Leona.

"She's angry. Or as angry as Debbie gets about anything. But I'm not calling to discuss her reaction, dear. I'm calling to inform you of the jewelry shop from which Colby purchased the ring."

Suddenly, Tori didn't need Leona to say another word. The reason her friend was calling was crystal clear. What the information meant in terms of the bigger picture, though, was still a bit fuzzy.

"Thanks for the call, Leona. I'll take it from here."

Chapter 29

She could feel Margaret Louise's frustration as she shifted the car into park outside the home Cynthia Marland shared with her parents. Sure, she knew her friend didn't handle being left out of things very well, but at that moment, Tori was on information overload. The realization that Brady's Jewelry was selling fake gems needed to sit on the back burner and simmer for a little while.

"You know, after livin' a lifetime bein' my sister's twin, I've got a keen sense when it comes to her motivations for sayin' and doin' things."

When Tori didn't take the bait, Margaret Louise addressed her speech to the occupant of the passenger seat. "Why, I remember a time not all that long ago when Leona was spoutin' 'bout somethin' she ate at the diner. Someone at the next table thought she was complainin' but she wasn't."

When Charles said nothing, Margaret Louise took it a step further. "I was able to do the decipherin' and make things right."

Tori shook off the troubling thoughts knocking around in her subconscious and tried her best to focus on the weathered shack-like structure on the other side of the road. It was hard to believe a street with such beaten-down homes fell inside Sweet Briar's town limits. Especially when families that were wealthy enough to employ nannies lived less than three miles away . . .

"Are we ready?" she asked as she took in the presence of a single light in the front left window of the house. "Let's get this over with."

She pushed open her car door and then met Margaret Louise and Charles for the trip across the road. As they approached the house, Charles stopped. "Why are we asking these questions?"

"I saw her sneaking around outside the Bradys' home a couple of days after Miss Gracie's fall, remember?"

"No, that's not what I mean. What are you going to say to explain why we're here, at her house, asking questions we have no business asking?"

"I'll figure something out. Just roll with it, okay?"

"Oh, I can roll with it, sweetheart." Charles ran to catch up with Tori and Margaret Louise as they stepped onto the rotting front porch.

"Of that, I have no doubt." She allowed herself the momentary reprieve the lighthearted exchange provided, then reached out and rapped the front door with her fist.

When there was no response, Margaret Louise knocked harder. "You gotta put some elbow grease on it, Victoria."

Sure enough, the door opened to reveal a close-up view of the young woman Tori had seen only twice before—once from across the park, and once from the front seat of her car as Cynthia snuck out of the Bradys' home and into her boyfriend's car.

Cynthia pushed open the door and eyed them curiously. "Yeah?"

"Cynthia, my name is Victoria Sinclair."

"She's the head librarian at the library in town," Margaret Louise added. "She's real smart with books. And I'm Margaret Louise Davis—my son Jake owns the garage in town that your friend's brother tried to rip off."

Tori glared at Margaret Louise as Charles stepped forward. "And I'm Charles. I'm visiting from New York City."

The faintest hint of a sparkle lit Cynthia's eyes as she shifted her attention completely in Charles's direction. "I've seen pictures of that place."

"The pictures don't do it justice," Charles gushed. "You really ought to come visit one day. You'd love it."

"That's what I was saving for before I blew it with that form for Reenie's school and she ended up having that seizure."

Bingo . . .

"People make mistakes, Cynthia. We all do."

Cynthia stepped all the way out onto the porch and let the door snap closed behind her. "That's what I tried to tell Mrs. Brady, but she was so mad."

"Did you like looking after those youngin's?"

Cynthia shrugged at Margaret Louise's question. "It was hard work, that's for sure. I mean, they were nice kids and all and it was fun living like that for a while, but the same kind of money to do nothing is way better."

"Did you apologize to Mrs. Brady?"

"A trillion times. But she didn't listen to me, or Tara, or Mr. Brady. She said she wasn't going to give me a second chance to kill her kid." Cynthia slumped against the wall of her house, shaking her head as she did. "I didn't try to hurt Reenie. I really didn't. I just didn't spend too much time filling out those forms I said I'd do."

"Mr. Brady and Tara wanted you to stay on?" Charles asked.

"D-uh. Of course. Family is supposed to look out for family, right?"

"So when you were fired, you had to pack your stuff and move out?" Tori sidestepped her way over to a rocking chair and perched on the edge while she waited for the girl's answer.

"That very day."

"Did you ever go back again?"

Two matching splashes of crimson appeared in Cynthia's cheeks as she stood tall. "Twice. I wanted Tara to give me another shot."

"You wanted *Tara* to give you another shot?"

"Of course. I figured I could just get back on the books again and keep saving for my ticket out, but she said I blew it. For everybody."

Charles clicked his tongue against the back of his teeth and rotated his head around his neck a few times. "Nuh-uh. One nanny does not an agency make."

"Well, in Tara's case, she had three of us with a brain in our head—Amanda, me, and Wendy. None of us really like kids, but we like money enough to put up with them. Jeanine, on the other hand, actually likes them, but she's kind of awkward and not exactly the face Tara wants to put out there for people to see. If I'd thought about it sooner, I should have played the dumb route. If I had, my Get-Out-of-Sweet-Briar fund would still be growing."

Tori gave a peek at both Charles and Margaret Louise to see if they were following everything Cynthia was saying, but the confusion she saw on their faces proved they were all in the same boat.

"And when you went back that first time to ask Tara to give you another shot, I take it she said no?"

Cynthia snorted. Loudly. "She *said* no. She *yelled* no. And she blamed me for ruining her life."

"Well, *that's* a little extreme." Charles crossed his arms in an almost over-the-top show of solidarity with the subject of Tori's questions. But for whatever reason, it worked, prompting Cynthia to return the gesture with a knowing nod.

"Isn't it, though? I mean, I made a mistake. If the other families go all psycho and start demanding better nannies simply because I messed up, that's saying something about *their* nannies, not me. And besides, you get what you pay for, you know?"

"Ain't that the truth, sister."

Tori avoided looking at Charles to keep from laughing and instead asked the question spawned by Cynthia's latest statement.

"The Bradys didn't pay well?"

"They paid pretty good, compared to the other families. But for the other actual placements, if you removed the chance to live in a fancy house, staying home and watching TV was a better bet. Virtually the same amount of money for a lot less headaches."

"So Tara was angry because she lost a commission on you?"

"Tara was angry she'd lose everything because of me." Cynthia's voice became more high-pitched, yet also whisper-like. " 'I'm telling you, Cynthia, if I lose everything to a car wash, I will make your life a living hell.' "

Tori toed the ground to stop the chair's subtle rocking motion. "So she wasn't telling *you* you'd have to wash cars?"

"Uh, no. Though if he ends up opening a car wash and I get a"—Cynthia hooked both her index fingers in the air to simulate air quotes—"*job* there, that would really tick her off, wouldn't it? Ha!"

Tori hated to admit it even to herself, but she was lost. She had absolutely no idea what the former Nanny Go Round employee was talking about. So instead of becoming even more confused, she moved on to the question that had led her to the girl's doorstep in the first place.

"You said you went back to the Bradys' house a second time after you were fired. Why was that?"

"Because I left the macaroni necklace Sophie made me in a drawer in my old room. I figured no one was sleeping in there on account of my replacement being dead, so my boyfriend drove me back there on a night the Bradys always go out to dinner. He waited in the car while I snuck back in, grabbed the necklace, and snuck back out."

"You went back for a macaroni necklace?"

Cynthia turned her head to the side but not before Tori

caught a hint of misting in the young woman's eyes. "Yeah. So what? No one ever made anything like that for me before."

They were almost at the park when Charles finally broke the silence, his normally confident voice sounding rather battered.

"That girl made my head hurt."

"You and me both," Tori mumbled as she pulled into the lot beside the park and rolled to a stop beside Margaret Louise's station wagon. "But I got what I wanted, I suppose."

"You still thinkin' 'bout callin' the chief and pointin' the finger at Amanda Willey?"

She tipped her head back against the seat rest and stared up at the ceiling of her car. "I think there's very good reason to suspect Miss Gracie was pushed. And Amanda seems a likely suspect. But somethin' doesn't seem right yet."

"Maybe Tara did it."

She let Charles's words loose in her thoughts and realized they matched with a feeling that had been building in her head ever since Cynthia started talking. All along she suspected Miss Gracie's murder was tied to the interest being shown toward British nannies in Julie Brady's kitchen that fateful evening. It was why she'd narrowed her focus on Amanda. But Amanda was young; she could find another job if the Whitehalls went elsewhere. Maybe that new job wouldn't come with car keys and a suite in an almost-mansion, but Amanda was one who would get where she was going in life one way or the other.

Tara, on the other hand, was an adult. The Nanny Go Round Agency was her livelihood in a way it wasn't for a young twenty-year-old who still had her parents to fall back on. Losing clients to an overseas agency stood to be a far bigger blow to the agency's owner than any of its employees.

"Before I get out of this car, are you goin' to tell me what my twin was callin' 'bout earlier?"

To continue resisting required an energy level Tori simply didn't have at that moment. Instead, she let her eyes drift closed while her mouth did the hard work.

"The diamond anniversary ring Colby gave Debbie over the summer appears to be fake, just like mine."

She heard Charles's gasp, even marveled at the way it harmonized almost perfectly with Margaret Louise's, but she had nothing else to say.

"Did he buy it at the same place?" Charles asked.

"He sure did."

"What on earth is Jim Brady doin' over at that shop? And who keeps pullin' the wool over his eyes?"

An odd sound from the other side of the car had her sitting up tall and waiting for Charles to explain himself.

"Mmm . . . hmmm . . . Maybe it's because I'm not from Sweet Briar and I don't know anyone here except my honorary sewing sisters, but I have to tell you I'm seeing this in a different way."

"Seeing what in a different way?"

"Now don't get me wrong," Charles said, waving his hands in almost surrender-like fashion. "This man might be positively lovely. But if you ask me, the only person I see pulling any wool is Mr. Brady himself."

Chapter 30

For as long as Tori could remember, the act of organizing her sewing box had always been a calming task. Something about seeing all of her colored threads lined up across a table alongside her collection of buttons, pin cushion, measuring tape, and scissors made her feel as if all would be well. It was almost as if by making sense of her sewing box, she was making sense of her thoughts and emotions.

At least that's the way it had always worked until that moment.

Now, no matter how many different ways she regrouped colors or rearranged the pins in her great-grandmother's pin cushion, the jumbled mess inside her head showed absolutely no sign of clearing.

"Think you'd feel better if you told me what's bothering you?"

She looked up from the various blue threads she'd accumulated over the past few years and did her best to feign surprise for the man she was set to marry in four days. "Bothering me? Nothing's bothering me."

"So you've switched royal blue with sky blue thirty times just for the heck of it? Come on, baby, I know something's up. Did something happen at work today? Or at your surprise shower last night?"

It was no use.

She could either keep staring at the contents of her sewing box in the hope they arranged themselves in a way that decoded her thoughts, or she could come clean with Milo about everything. Pushing her hand forward, she knocked four of the blue spools onto their side and watched as they rolled across the coffee table and onto the area rug that covered all but a one-foot section around the entire living room. "If I tell you something, will you promise not to let it ruin our wedding? Because there's not a *thing* on the face of this earth that's worth ruining that, right?"

He balanced the sports section on the arm of the plaid chair and moved onto the couch beside her instead. "Having trouble getting the vows just the way you want?"

Reaching out, she gathered the scissors, measuring tape, and pin cushion into her hands and transferred them to the same compartment in her sewing box they'd inhabited when she started. "No. They say everything I want them to say. The only catch will be whether I can say them without crying."

"Did something go wrong with the florist? Or the deejay?"

"Nope. They're all good to go. In fact, *everything* is set to go."

"Okay, leave the box alone." He leaned forward, took the handful of spools she'd managed to pick up, and deposited them back on the table. When that was done, he hooked a finger underneath her chin and turned her face until their eyes were focused on each other. "I've thought of little else except our wedding since the day you accepted my proposal. I'd be a fool to let anything ruin our day."

When she said nothing, he leaned forward, planted a gentle kiss on her lips, and then pulled her into the crook of his arm. "The only thing that can ruin our day is thinking you can't share things with me."

Milo was right.

She needed to come clean with what she knew.

Inhaling deeply, she gave herself a quick mental pep talk and then held her left hand out for his inspection. "The diamond is fake."

"Ha! Ha!" he joked. "Nice try."

"Milo, I'm not kidding."

This time his laugh was so deep, and so hearty, her head bobbed against his shoulder. "My bank account says otherwise."

"I'm sure it does. So does Colby's."

Her head stopped moving. "Colby? What does Colby have to do with this?"

She sat forward and then turned to look straight at her fiancé, the dimples she loved so much hovering in his cheeks, waiting for a punch line that wasn't going to come. "Last night, at my shower, Leona happened to notice that my diamond"—she turned her left hand and wiggled her fourth finger—"is a fake."

A flash of something that looked like anger erased

away his dimples and his smile. Raking his hand across his face, he released a frustrated sigh. "You know, I try to give that woman the benefit of the doubt most times, but this is over the top. What the heck is she trying to do?"

"Debbie went home and looked up the tests Leona did to determine the diamond is fake—"

"It's not fake," he protested.

She pressed her hand to his chest and pleaded with him to hear her out. When he quieted down, she continued. "So Debbie tried the test with her engagement ring and the diamond ring Colby gave her over the summer for their fifteenth wedding anniversary. The anniversary band failed."

"So these tests are crazy. I bought that ring at Brady's and I've got the papers to prove its authenticity in my safe at the bank."

"Colby bought Debbie's ring at Brady's, too. And he has the same papers."

"Then I don't understand. They can't be fake."

Oh, how she wished he was right.

But he wasn't.

"Debbie drove into Tom's Creek after Leona called me today and brought both of her rings into a jewelry store there. Sure enough, the jeweler confirmed her engagement ring is real, and the anniversary ring Colby bought at Brady's is not."

"But the papers . . ."

"When Debbie called me a little while ago, she said that the Tom's Creek guy looked at the ones for the fake ring and said they were doctored."

"But I paid for a real one!"

"Then someone made out like a bandit on that sale."

"Come on, Tori, a discrepancy like that—especially if it happened to more than just me—couldn't go unnoticed. Money like that adds up."

She sat up tall as bits and pieces of various conversations began arranging themselves inside her thoughts.

"Well, then maybe she can be a teacher on paper, too. After all, the money doesn't change much if you actually do it, so why bother."

And . . .

"But for the other actual placements, if you removed the chance to live in a fancy house, staying home and watching TV was a better bet. Virtually the same amount of money for a lot less headaches."

And . . .

"I figured I could just get back on the books again and keep saving for my ticket out, but she said I blew it."

"Unless it's hidden really well," she finally responded. "Like in another business . . ."

He stared at her, confusion pushing anger from his face momentarily. "You mean like money laundering?"

"I guess, yeah."

"But money launderers usually open up heavy cash businesses like Laundromat or car wash—"

They stared at each other as yet another piece of the puzzle drifted slowly into place. But even in position, it was hard to accept.

"But there *was* no car wash, no Laundromats," Milo said.

"True. But that didn't mean there wasn't a business . . ."

"Oh man, you're right. His sister, Tara, has a business in town . . ." Milo pushed off the couch and wandered around the room, his feet moving in no specific direction.

When he reached the dining room, he turned around, clearly torn. "I can't say I know Jim Brady terribly well, but we've crossed paths in town—at the school, volunteering, when I bought your ring, that sort of thing. Granted those encounters don't make me an expert on the guy, but I don't think he's all that tight with his sister. I mean, he's been a successful business owner in this town for years. Tara's really didn't get that way until about a year and a half ago. And looking back, whenever they're both at something, they're rarely hanging out together."

She glanced down at her ring and allowed herself a moment to remember Milo slipping it onto her finger for the first time. "You bought this ring within the past eighteen months . . ."

Bypassing the couch, Milo continued across the room to the window that overlooked the cottage next to Tori's. He stood there for several long moments, saying nothing. When he finally turned back to her, she saw only resignation in his eyes. "Assuming you're right with this, the fact that his own wife was passing out business cards for a British nanny agency had to send him over the edge."

"Or make him send *Miss Gracie* over the edge . . ."

She hadn't meant to say it, hadn't even realized she was thinking it. But now that it was out, it made perfect sense. "Milo," she half whispered, half gasped. "Do you think it's possible?"

Chapter 31

Adrenaline.

It was the only explanation for why Tori was still standing after a night of zero sleep and a full day of work.

From the moment she and Milo had finally called it quits for the night, she'd known she wasn't going to be able to close her eyes. Sure, she'd tried, even going so far as to warm up a little milk the way she remembered her great-grandmother doing on occasion. But nothing had worked.

Instead, she'd run through various scenarios involving Jim Brady and Tara Reed until she found one that made the most sense.

Now, roughly fourteen hours after her ah-ha moment, she was more than ready to tie all the strings together in a neat and tidy little bow for Chief Dallas. Milo, of course, had encouraged her to let the chief do the tying, but even he was aware of the lack of conviction behind his words.

No, she needed to see this through to the end—for Beatrice and Miss Gracie . . .

She looked up from the bench outside Brady's Jewelry and waved as her cohort in crime careened around the corner and into the empty parking spot in front of the store. Despite the exhaustion that burned her eyes, and the apprehension weighing on her heart, Tori couldn't help but smile as Margaret Louise lumbered out of her trusty station wagon and made a beeline in Tori's direction.

"Think we'll see some fireworks?"

It was a question she'd asked herself repeatedly throughout the day as Jim Brady's moment of reckoning drew closer. "I don't know, Margaret Louise. I honestly don't know."

"Well, don't you worry none, Victoria. I got some pepper spray in my bag and Chief Dallas's number on my speed dial."

She peeked inside her friend's bag and immediately spotted the spray can in question. "When did you get pepper spray?"

"This mornin', right after you called."

Stepping back, she shifted her focus toward the familiar door at the top of the stairs. "Are you ready to do this with me?"

"Ready and able," Margaret Louise said, patting her bag closed.

Tori took a quick, fortifying breath and then led the way up the stairs and into the shop, the jingle of the bells above the door barely noticeable over the roar in Tori's ears.

"Welcome to Brady's Jewelry." A man in his late thirties stepped out of a room behind the glass counter and immediately came to a stop, his lips stretching wide with a smile. "Margaret Louise, how are you?"

"I'm doin' just fine, Jim, thank you." Margaret Louise slid her arm across Tori's shoulders and guided them both forward. "You know my friend, Victoria, don't you?"

Jim held his hand across the counter and grasped Tori's firmly. "Yes, of course. Miss Sinclair. Ryan told me you stopped by last week and picked up your wedding bands. I'm sorry I wasn't here but, well, there was an accident in my home the previous evening and I was rather preoccupied. I hope you understand."

"Of course. Ryan took good care of me."

"I'm not surprised. He's been invaluable since I hired him. Quick learner, motivated, you name it. And judging by the comment cards people leave, I'd be a fool to ever let him go." He swept his hand across the top of the glass case and then looked from Tori to Margaret Louise and back again. "So what can I help you with this evening?"

Tori pulled her engagement ring from her finger and set it on the counter along with the paperwork Milo had gotten from the store. "I have reason to believe these papers were doctored."

"Doctored?"

"Yes. To say my diamond is something it's not."

She noted the shock in his face just before he grabbed the magnifier beside the register with one hand and Tori's ring with the other. "That's impossible."

Margaret Louise moved her hand to the outside of her tote bag and patted it knowingly.

Seconds turned to minutes as the jeweler turned Tori's ring this way and that, his face draining of color with each turn.

"It's fake, isn't it?" she finally asked as he pulled the ring from underneath the magnifier and stared down at it as if it were some sort of foreign object.

"Yes. But I don't understand."

"Oh, we think you do." Tori reached into her pants pocket and removed the ring Debbie had brought to the library earlier that day. Again, she put the ring on the counter and waited for the jeweler to take it. When he took Debbie's, Tori slipped her own back onto her finger. "And we think that because here's another ring, sold by you, that's every bit as fake despite paperwork and a price tag to the contrary."

Again, he held the ring under the magnifier, and again he turned it in multiple different directions. This time, though, he slumped against the counter as Tori's accusation came to pass. "I—I don't understand."

"How about I help clarify things," she said, her voice wooden. "You sold these two rings—along with countless others, I'm sure—for a hefty price tag knowing full well they weren't worth ten percent of that cost. And then, to hide the money, you funneled it through your sister's fledgling agency. Pretty soon, the Nanny Go Round Agency had lots of local girls on their books, even though many of them never left their own homes. A few legitimate clients such as the Whitehalls, the Downings, and even your own family kept things on the level—at least from afar. But when one of those horribly inadequate nannies almost killed your own child and your in-the-dark wife put her foot down, your little setup was threatened, wasn't it? You knew that if the Whitehalls and the other handful of legitimate clients went elsewhere, the jig would be up . . . so you pushed Miss Gracie to her death to drown out the talk, didn't you?"

Jim's jaw went slack just before Debbie's ring fell from his hand onto the floor. "I didn't kill Miss Gracie! She fell!"

"We believe she was pushed."

"Pushed?" he echoed in disbelief as Tori watched his gaze slip to the paperwork she'd lined up on the counter. Lurching forward, he looked from one paper to the next as his hands slowly tightened into fists atop the counter. "I didn't sign these . . ."

"It has your name. Your signature."

"But it wasn't signed with my pen . . ."

Holding up his finger, he disappeared into the same room from which he'd come when they arrived. Margaret Louise reached into her bag, pulled out the spray and her phone, and readied both for immediate use.

Less than twenty seconds later, Jim was back, a silver pen in his outstretched hand. "Julie gave me this pen when I opened the shop. It's the only one I use when I sign authentication papers."

"And you can tell, lookin' at these papers, that a different pen was used?" Margaret Louise asked.

"This pen"—he waved it in the air—"is black. Those papers have been signed in blue."

Tori spun Milo's set of paperwork around and looked at the signature line. "This isn't your signature?"

He crossed back to the counter and looked at Colby's papers, and then, Milo's. "I couldn't sign it better myself. But regardless of how dead-on it is, I didn't sign either of these papers."

"Then who did?"

She watched as he lifted Colby's papers off the counter, looked again at the signature in the bottom right corner, and then slowly moved his gaze up to the top. "This is dated July of this year. What's that one dated?"

"A year ago this past April."

"Okay, so it's been just Ryan and me since—"

And then she knew.

It wasn't Jim Brady who'd been laundering money from selling fake gems through the Nanny Go Round Agency. It was Ryan, the clean-cut employee who'd been so charming . . .

"Does Ryan know your sister?"

"He's a friend of Tara's son," Jim said, lowering the papers to the counter once again. "It's why I hired him."

"And he's here often?"

"All the time. Within the first six months of him being here, he was adept enough at the way I did things to be able to leave him on his own. It gave me more time to be with Julie and the kids, especially with Kellie getting involved in more and more sports." Jim cupped a hand over his mouth and exhaled as reality dawned amid disbelief and growing rage. "I trusted him explicitly when it came to this shop and my reputation. Heck, I even gave him a key to my house to bring by the day's earnings if I wasn't there when we closed up shop."

"A key to your house?" Tori and Margaret Louise echoed in unison.

"He was my right-hand man!" Jim marched to the back door of the shop and peered out over the parking lot that served all of the shops up and down Main Street. "He even dated our former nanny off and on, although I often wondered if he really liked her. And . . ."

Tori followed him to the back door and placed a calming hand on his upper arm. "And what?"

"Tara is my *sister.* Yeah, she's always been jealous of my success, but to strike back like *this*? It's . . . it's too much."

As much as she hated being the bearer of bad news, Tori couldn't help being glad it wasn't Jim who'd orchestrated everything. Somehow, knowing Chief Dallas's cuffs wouldn't be on the father of three quieted the ache that had settled over her heart during the night.

"I have to ask you one last question, Jim." She turned her thoughts to Beatrice and Miss Gracie and the bond the women had shared throughout Beatrice's life. It wouldn't be easy telling Beatrice her beloved governess had been killed out of greed, but at least she'd know the truth. "Was Ryan at your house the night of Miss Gracie's accident?"

"No, he—" Jim pounded his fist on the wall, releasing an angry groan as he did. "It was a Monday, so he closed up the shop for me at five and then dropped the day's earnings off on the desk in my home office just like I asked."

"So he *was* there that evening?"

Slowly but surely he began to nod, the horror in his eyes impossible to ignore. "Yes. He came in through the side entrance, put the money in the locked drawer beneath the mirror as he always does, and exited the same way."

"Side entrance?" Tori questioned.

"Yes. It's between the hearth room and the basement access . . ." His words trailed off as the reality that had been slowly assembling itself in his head came into complete focus. Tori stole a glance at Margaret Louise and knew the expression on the woman's face matched the conviction in Tori's heart. They had their man and they had a motive.

"He killed her, didn't he?" Jim whispered.

At Tori's nod, he groaned again. "How could I have been so incredibly *blind*? How could I not see him for what he was?"

"You saw what he wanted you to see," Tori whispered. "The only one worthy of blame in all of this is Ryan."

Jim reared back and gave the wall one last punch, the pain in his voice nothing short of heartbreaking. "Ryan and *my sister*."

Chapter 32

Over the course of her life to that point, Tori had witnessed many sunrises. Some were on vacations as a child, some were from her dorm room window when pulling an all-nighter for a college exam, and some had been on her great-grandmother's front porch as she waited for her parents to come for a visit.

Yet, as beautiful as so many of them had been, none had ever been as beautiful as the one that greeted her that morning.

From the moment Milo had popped the question, she'd eagerly looked forward to the day they would become husband and wife. And now, finally, it was there. In a little over six hours, she'd be standing next to the love of her life, each vowing to be true to the other throughout their remaining days on earth. It was a promise she couldn't wait to make, and a life's journey she couldn't wait to start.

A soft knock at her bedroom door widened her smile even more. "Come on in, I'm awake."

The door swung open and Rose Winters shuffled into the room carrying a teacup and a piece of toast on a small plate. "I figured you were already up."

Tori reached out, transferred the cup and plate from the elderly woman's trembling hands to the nightstand, and then patted the spot next to her on the bed. "Did you sleep well?"

"I did."

"Thank you for letting me stay with you last night. There's no one I wanted to share my last night as a single woman with more than you."

Rose wrapped her hand around Tori's and squeezed. "I know you wish your great-grandmother could have been here with you but—"

She quieted her friend's words with a gentle finger. "She *was* here, Rose. She always is. But I needed you, too."

"I'm glad." Slowly, Rose pulled her hand back just enough to reveal Tori's engagement ring. "I imagine Jim is going to make this right?"

"He already did. He gave Milo a full refund."

"But this looks like the same ring."

She extricated her hand from beneath Rose's and held it out for them both to see. "That's because it is. I don't want a new one. I want this one. It's the one Milo gave me when he asked me to marry him."

"But it's fake," Rose said.

"The sentiment with which Milo gave it to me, though, wasn't."

"And Milo is okay with that?"

Shifting her body to the side, she leaned against the

headboard and allowed herself a moment to digest the question. "He wasn't at first, but when I explained to him why I wanted to keep this one, he gave in."

"Leona would have a heart attack if she knew about this," Rose groused. "In fact, I think she'd consider having you committed."

"I already told her." Tori thought back to the conversation she'd had with her injured friend in the wake of Ryan's arrest and smiled at the memory. "And you know what? Leona actually told me I have something more precious than any diamond on the face of the earth."

"And what's that?"

"Milo."

Tori peeked around the vestibule's potted tree and watched, mesmerized, as Lulu Davis began her way down the aisle, her long dark hair, curled to perfection, cascading down the back of her goldenrod-colored dress.

"She's getting so big, isn't she?" she whispered to Rose, who stood nearby, dabbing at her eyes with a tissue. "When I moved here, she was still so little."

When Lulu reached the altar, she stepped to the left and smiled out at Tori and Milo's guests with such quiet confidence, Tori could hardly breathe.

Next went Melissa, her choice of Hushed Ginger stunning against her dark blonde hair. Tori's eyes immediately went to Jake Davis, the awe in his face as he watched his wife glide by, nothing short of touching.

Nina was next, her dark skin gorgeous against the Simply Sienna she'd selected to wear. When she passed

Lyndon on the way to her spot, the baby clapped, sending up a chorus of laughter throughout the church.

Debbie waited until Nina was positioned next to Melissa and then started her own walk down the aisle, her dark blonde hair glistening around the neckline of her Soft Russet gown. As Jake had been with Melissa, Colby couldn't keep his eyes off his wife.

The always-shy Beatrice, who blushed her way down the aisle in Quiet Barley, turned more than a few heads in her direction, a fact Tori vowed to share with the nanny in the very near future.

Georgina, decked out in Dusky Sunset, made short work of the white carpet thanks to her long legs and go-go-go personality.

Dixie, quietly elegant in Muted Pumpkin, helped slow things down a bit, clearly relishing her moment in the spotlight.

"I swear, Victoria, if my twin doesn't show for this, I will never speak to her again," Margaret Louise whispered as she moved into position, taking one last glance over her shoulder at the door as she did.

"She said she'd be here," Tori whispered back. "So that means she will be. Now go."

Margaret Louise set off in her Warm Cinnamon dress, the happy squeals the beloved grandmother received halfway down the aisle perfect on so many levels.

Tori tried to focus on her friends that were there, rather than the one that wasn't, but it was impossible not to when Rose was the only one left prior to the start of the wedding march.

A sudden burst of sunlight at her back made Tori turn

in time to see Charles wave and then push a wheelchair-bound Leona into the vestibule. "I'm here. I'm here. And so is Paris."

Leona snapped her fingers and in walked Sam, carrying Paris and the miniature satin pillow that would soon be tied around the animal's neck. "Who's going to carry her?" the EMT asked.

"No one. She's going to hop all on her own."

"Leona?" she gasped. "I—I didn't realize you'd have to be in a wheelchair . . ."

"I don't." Snapping her fingers softly in the air to alert Charles to her needs, their Big Apple friend opened the metal contraption previously tucked under his arm and set it in front of Leona.

Rose pointed but said nothing.

Leona, however, didn't have that problem. "Yes, you old goat, it's a walker, and it's mine. For now anyway." Reaching into a bag attached to the arm of her wheelchair, Leona removed a pair of shiny silver flats, which Charles promptly put on her feet. "Looks like it's up to you and me to make flats stylish again, wouldn't you say?"

It was fast and it was fleeting, but there was no denying the way Rose's lips twitched in response to Leona's suggestion, and Tori waited with bated breath to hear her response.

As Margaret Louise reached the end of the aisle, Sam set Paris on the white runner and gently nudged the rabbit on her way, to the delight of the crowd. When Paris and the wedding rings reached the edge of the altar, Rose stepped forward, helped Leona to her feet, and then looked back at Tori, waiting.

"I'm not supposed to be crying yet," Tori whispered.

Charles pulled a tissue from his pocket, pressed it into her hand, and then entered the church from a side door as Tori finally acknowledged Rose's unspoken question with a nod.

Rose smiled in return. "That's our cue, Leona. Let's go."

As two of her dearest friends set off down the aisle— Leona in Smoldering Blaze, and Rose in Harvest Wheat, Tori let her gaze skip ahead to the rest of their crew. Any surprise or momentary glee they may have felt at seeing Leona with a walker quickly disappeared behind pure joy.

For Tori.

Smoothing her hands down the sides of her dress one last time, Tori took her place at the top of the aisle and waited for the wedding march to begin. There wasn't a single, solitary thing she'd change about that moment.

Yes, it would have been wonderful if her great-grandmother could have been beaming from the front row as she became Mrs. Milo Wentworth. But if she'd learned anything since moving to Sweet Briar, it's that the people you held close to your heart were always there.

And because of that, her great-grandmother was in that church just as surely as her mom and dad, Lulu, Melissa, Nina, Debbie, Beatrice, Georgina, Dixie, Margaret Louise, Leona, Rose, and Charles.

She watched through tear-dappled lashes as her husband-to-be stepped onto the altar and turned to look at her with such love and devotion she could hardly breathe. And when he mouthed the words *I love you* as she made her way toward him, she knew, without a doubt, that she was the luckiest girl in the world.

Reader-Suggested Sewing Tips

From Cullum R.
via my Fan Page on Facebook:

- Glue a magnet to the end of a ruler for searching out the stray pins that end up on the floor.

- Freezer paper is perfect for cutting out small patterns. Just draw on the matte side, press the shiny side down (using a dry iron), and cut.

From Stephanie S.
via my Fan Page on Facebook:

- For simple gathering, use a wide zigzag stitch over a ⅛-inch ribbon or jean thread (don't stitch on it, just over it). Stitch one end of the ribbon down and pull the other end to gather up the fabric. This works for any fabric, but is especially handy when gathering heavy fabric!

🪡 When inserting a centered zipper, after basting your seam and pressing it open, instead of using pins, use a ¼-inch fusible webbing to fuse the zipper in place and then sew on as normal (just without bulky pins, and with a zipper that stays in place while stitching)!

From Shirley L.
via my Fan Page on Facebook:

🪡 Keep your pins and needles stuck in a bar of soap so they will go through the fabric easily.

From Michelle S.
via my Fan Page on Facebook:

🪡 I use an old bottle like from aspirin and keep it near my sewing machine. It's a perfect place to put bent pins or dull needles.

Sewing Pattern

Tori's Wedding Favors

(SHARED BY EILEEN E. PEARCE, MLS—ADULT SERVICES
LIBRARIAN AT WINDSOR LOCKS PUBLIC LIBRARY IN WINDSOR
LOCKS, CONNECTICUT)

Materials

tulle (white or ivory) on a 6-inch roll
ribbon to match, ⅜-inch wide (silky or sparkly)
Hershey Kisses
Hershey Hugs
business card stock in white or cream
tiny rubber bands
hole puncher

Cut the tulle into 6-by-8-inch rectangles and lay flat. Using 8 inches for the length gives a little extra fabric, but you can use a 6-inch square if you prefer the symmetry. Place 3 or 4 Kisses and 3 or 4 Hugs (an equal number of each) on the square and gather up so it forms a small bag. Fasten at the top with a rubber band.

Use a program such as Print Shop or Print Artist to create a business card with a picture of the bride and groom in their favorite pose or involved in their favorite activity. Put their names and wedding date under the photo. Leave enough space on the side for a hole. These can be printed in color, in sepia tones, or in black and white. Separate the cards and punch a hole in the middle of the left side of each one.

Cut 12-to-15-inch pieces of ribbon and tie around the rubber band at the top of the bag. Thread the ribbon through the hole in the business card and then complete tying a bow. The card should be in one of the loops of the bow.

You can add additional embellishments to the favors, such as a sprig of silk or dried flowers.